Tangled Knot

Tangled Knot

~~~

The Tale of
Eris of Suburbia

BB Clifford

A Zero Labels Book
~~~

Tangled Knot
The Tale of Eris of Suburbia

Print ISBN: 979-8-9851024-5-1   (Paperback)

Printed in the United States of America
First printing edition 2024
Published by Zero Labels LLC
143 E Ridgewood Ave, #1484, Ridgewood, NJ 07450

Cover design by Anabeth Bostrup
Images in cover photo used under license from Shutterstock.com

~~~

Life is messy, so a true depiction is going to make for difficult reading. *Tangled Knot* deals with some tough issues, including trauma, assault, and suicide, so it is important to include a content warning.

Should you have any questions about the material set out in this book, contact your clinician or doctor. If you are in crisis, seek immediate, professional help. Here are your options: Call 911 (if it is available in your area), take yourself to the emergency room of your nearest hospital, call a friend or family member, and ask them to take you to the nearest emergency room, call the National Suicide Helpline at 988 or https://988lifeline.org/

Trauma is hell on earth. Trauma resolved is a gift from the gods.
Peter A. Levine

~~~

For M,
Who accepts the tears,
And for L and W,
Who capture in joint imagery
Our greatest hopes and fears.

Chapter One

~~~

Retribution, and a suburban beast

I ce-white ash falls outside my window like tiny shards of glass. Then I see the smoke, dancing phantoms taunting me out of the kitchen and up the stairs to my daughter's bathroom. *Fire.*

The thick air hits my lungs hard, solid and clear, as forcefully as the point my child is trying to silently scream. Flames flicker from crumpled-up cloth that is in the sink, and my daughter Ania prods at it with her bare hands. She does not flinch.

"What are you playing at?" I shout above the screech of the smoke alarms, a chorus of frantic cheeping.

I notice that it isn't just any old cloth in the sink; it is an item of her clothing. I recognize the little panda pattern just before it darkens and disappears in the flames.

When I step closer to turn on the tap, I see the bruises around my daughter's wrists, dark purples and blues that I would have dismissed as paint or coloring pens if she hadn't just turned sixteen. Age has complicated the pleasure and pain that she derives from life, and I know that I need to keep a closer watch over her.

She flinches when I touch her skin. Finally a sign that she is still alive.

"What happened? Who did this to you?"

I no longer care about the smoke. The rush of cold water has dampened the flames, so we just stand there together, our eyes stinging.
~~~

"Leave me alone."

I wonder if her words are slurred or whether I have just not noticed age slowing that once- spritely enthusiasm for life.

"Not until you tell me what's going on."

"I said leave me alone," she shouts, shouldering me away from her.

"What's got into you?" I call after her as she runs out of the bathroom, the impotence of my voice infuriating me. "I can't help you unless you tell me what's happening."

But already she has slipped from view, down the stairs, and slamming her way out of the house.

I should have followed her.

Two years have passed, and still ice-white fragments fall like tiny shards of glass. I watch from the same kitchen window as they cover the gnarled branches of the apple trees, tiny crystals, each with their unique design, like fingerprints. It all melts away so quickly, as fleeting and illusory as the explanations from the school counselor, her therapist, and the police. As their explanations faded with time and closer scrutiny, showing the patchwork that was missing as much as the tenuous connections they made, I became an inconvenience to them. I could see it in the strain of their smiles. Then the pleasantries started to disappear altogether, and irritation hardened their features as I was reminded of vague concepts such as *best efforts, boundaries,* and *inappropriate behavior.* It was, after all, just their day job. They still went home to their loved ones; they did not really care.

Paris's face has started to harden with the same signs of irritation. He has grown tired of this guessing game. I have watched him linger for longer as he passes by each window, intrigued by the people of Mount Pelion Way. Is he lured outside by invisible forces, or is he repelled by something within this fortress that he longs to escape? I wonder how long I have before he tires of me altogether, leaving me tangled in this wreckage where we once created a family. That task hangs in the air, incomplete and stinging with regret.

There is no one left except Paris. I thought I could keep my family safe here in this fortress of latches and bolts and locks. But despite the cast iron and turrets of brick and stone, the dangers still invaded my home and gutted my family with bare hands.

Such a thing of nightmares, this kinesthetic connection between mother and child. It was once a source of such pleasure, the contented coos of the early years, the innocent joy of games, and the shared fits of passion for a movie, a song, or even a shade of color. We were tethered together, as if the umbilical cord still held fast. But now it chokes me like a noose around my neck, and as I twist and turn, it tightens.

It is the middle of the day, but the kitchen is getting dark as the snow intensifies. I can feel the weight accumulating on the boughs of the apple trees, and I wonder whether they will ever bear fruit again. I cannot stand to look at the gnarled, old, tangled branches; now they bear the weight of significance. Inescapable, as if my own feet were rooted in the frozen ground.

Paris will be angry with me because I didn't get the salt. He told me to this morning, and he even wrote it down on a Post-it note that he stuck to the fridge. He addressed it to *My Goddess*, harking back to a time when he was foolish and simple with me. I still don't know why he would call me this. Was it my auburn hair of glowing embers, my aquiline nose, or my eyes of shiny emeralds? Who knows, and, quite frankly, who cares. He was probably just turned on by women with excessive curves, and then he became trapped with me, to spend an eternity in my fortress.

In those early days, before we got married and he changed me from Eris Rose Gall to Eris Rose Brown, I believed that this was someone who was going to cleanse me. When he met me, I was earthy and strong, familiar with helping my father carry heavy loads around our home. But without a mother, I was unfamiliar with things that might have softened my edges or kept my fingernails clean. I knew my way around men, in conversation and in bed, but I hadn't appreciated that this scared some of them away. *Cowards*. But Paris was not scared. He was intrigued by a fire that burned within me, even though that made most others wary of me, when I would fight people over their inconsistencies and transform into my namesake, the mythical creature of discord and strife.

The last two years have only intensified my need to fight, but in this constant battle I fear that I will lose Paris. And that's the thing about a marriage knot. Stay still, stay the same, and it will not chafe. Earth-shattering movement like the death or disappearance of a child, and the knot only tightens, strangling what life or love there might have been.

I am still here.

I think I see a shadow on the stairs. She is playing with me. I sometimes catch a glimpse as Ania runs from the room like an afterthought.

I'm glad you're here, Ania. I don't know what I would do if you left me forever.

The phone starts to ring, but I ignore it. I have no one I need to speak to. Except Paris. I assumed he was still home, but we slip in and out of each other's lives like absent-minded ghosts, so he could have left for the day without telling me.

The salt. I know I must complete the task he has set me in case it is a test, in case failure would result in judgment, a choice that would lead to the end.

He has placed his reminder over the last school photo of our daughter. I remove the Post-it note, taking care to ensure that no sticky residue remains. Ania's shoulders slouch forward, awkwardly trying to hide the body that she was reluctant to inhabit. By the time the photograph was taken, she had returned from her first sleepaway camp and her arms and legs had grown long. I knew how much she wanted to cut her long, auburn hair. Now I look on that request as a plea to reduce herself, as if pruning a dying tree. I know some people might say that she was uprooted to clear space for new growth. I spend hours thinking of how I might tear these people apart and feast on their innards.

How about a plot twist where you killed them already, and you have their bodies stored in the attic?

I blame myself for my daughter's morbid and twisted sense of humor. And yet still, at sixteen, she sucked her thumb and cuddled her soft toy panda whenever she felt sleepy. Is this why I couldn't save her? I was distracted or confused by her contradictions, so I never saw the underworld that was opening up beneath her, ready to swallow her whole?

I still have her soft toy panda.

For Paris to cover our daughter's photograph shows how he and I are caught in a prism, divided by two years: I remain with Ania, retracing the final days of her life, and Paris has moved on, more preoccupied with a potential lawsuit from a mailman who might slip on our icy sidewalk.

But still, *the salt.*

I shuffle to the hallway, trying not to notice the heavy curves of my body. My breath comes in slower heaves these days, depressed under the weight of stagnation.

My hands flick at the latches and bolts and locks on the front door. These rituals run through my skin and bones, having watched my father follow the same patterns to keep us safe. He added the reinforcements when my mother died, fearing that the destructive forces that took my mother might come for me next. He made me promise never to show anyone on the outside where he kept the secret key that unlocked the door hidden behind a fake wall panel. I have never broken that promise, not even to tell Paris.

I stop before I open the door and I peep out through the venetian blind that covers a small window in the door. Paris would chastise me for being foolish and furtive, but I am glad I hesitated because a car pulls into my street and lurches into Athena Aegean's driveway. Out steps a meaty-faced seething mother who scans Mount Pelion Way; for what, I am not sure. I doubt this broad-shouldered lawyer has ever felt fear of anything. She might be looking for her next target, a form of entertainment who she can terrorize with a glare or the threat of a lawsuit.

After Athena's latest cease-and-desist, hand delivered to me by a petrified looking intern from her own law firm, I know better than to cross paths with Athena Aegean. She doesn't like the way I keep questioning her about my daughter's death.

As an experienced lawyer, Athena knows just what she can get away with, so she threatens to sue me each time I speak of her son, Cory Aegean, and his two friends, Smithson West and Aedean Marwood. After two years, Athena wants me to forget about that Halloween night when those boys met my daughter in the forest at the dead end of Mount Pelion Way.

Ania probably thought she was going to drink alcohol or set

fire to things—stupid kid stuff she had heard about in school. I can imagine that it scared her as much as excited her, walking into that dark forest alone. But she was invited by three popular boys in her grade, the ones who did well at lacrosse and football, the ones other girls wanted to kiss. Why would she squander this opportunity?

All I have left are suspicions and fleeting glances of the truth, so I gather these threads to try and form a coherent story. As surely as Frankenstein made his creature; I have a patchwork creation of what might have been. Words overheard, a gut instinct, dreams and nightmares alike. In hindsight, it is so easy to tell a different story; perspectives evolve as much as people do, as children grow old and eventually die.

Ania met these boys in the forest that Halloween night, and a matter of weeks later we found her dead. Ania isn't going to help me with these parts because she always goes quiet when I ask her what really happened. I hope it is not shame that silences her, and I hope she doesn't think I will reject her if I find out the truth. After all, what sixteen-year-old ever listened to their parents? Forever sixteen.

I hear laughter, and through the small window I see that Athena is air kissing and cooing over two more seething mothers of Mount Pelion Way, Freya Marwood and June West. Freya and June have also sent me cease-and-desist letters, delivered by the same petrified-looking intern from Athena's law firm. I still don't know who the aggressor was that Halloween night, and who was simply a bystander. Perhaps they took it in turns. No matter the truth, in my eyes I blame all three.

I like to think that these women are scared of me, that the *weirdness* they see in me carries an edge as sharp as a razor blade. I would like them to have nightmares of me waiting until the next time their husband or boyfriend is away on a business trip. I want them to know that I have been watching them, and I know how flimsy the lock is on their side door. I want them to anticipate me tiptoeing up the stairs, and I want to turn on the lights so they can watch in their full-length mirror as I slice them from ear to ear. As Paris and my father always told me, it is good to smile.

When it comes to vengeance, Ania remains silent. She might

be trying to protect me because she knows that revenge will involve a fight against the multi-headed suburban beast that some call *Community* and others call the *Wolf Pack*. These beasts haunt every town and village up and down the East Coast, and probably beyond. This horrific human centipede is a composite of seething mothers, brutish fathers, and their sociopathic counterparts in school administration, police stations, therapy practices, and religious institutions. These parents and their sociopathic counterparts live in close confines, so they know each other's secrets. Each could turn on the other, so they coexist in silent complicity, as efficient but lethal as an abusive family. And like all abusive families, the suburban beast only thrives so long as it is satiated with the occasional sacrificial scapegoat.

It wasn't that simple.

The sudden sound of Ania's voice makes me knock the venetian blinds against the glass of the window. This startles the three seething mothers and their necks twitch like zombies awoken from the dead. All three turn to stare at me, and I see that their eyes are reddening in the setting sun. How those hot coals burn for change; for too long I have been an ugly presence on Mount Pelion Way, catching and tearing their joy like barbed wire. They want me gone, no matter what it takes.

I slide down to crouch behind the door, a child again who was scared of the ghouls who haunted my doorstep each Halloween. I would hide here, illuminated by the red star that fires the winter sky, and I would cry until they disappeared. Every year they would foul up my letterbox with rotten eggs and spoiled vegetables, showing the hatred and fear for me that they hold in equal measure.

How I long for Paris to see how Mount Pelion Way is haunted by this suburban beast. Here is the twisted sentiment, there is the malcontent, and what nightmares continue to grow and coil around my brain. But he can never see it, unwilling to even listen to me, and he always demands proof. As if the death of our sixteen-year-old could not be evidence enough that this world is possessed of an evil that knows no bounds.

I have watched as his eyes narrow with suspicion, and I know that he suspects that the greatest dangers are within me, falling between the gaps of my broken mind.

I fear that his suspicions have been growing even before our daughter died. I was never liked by the people of Mount Pelion Way. I was clumsy in conversation, losing the thread and the point of it all, so I scared them away with awkward silences. Athena, Freya, June, and the seething mothers that came before them. I would hear them laughing about me when I walked away, hearing them refer to me as *weird* and *the gargoyle,* and eventually the name that stuck: the *Witch of Mount Pelion Way.*

Perhaps it is too much to ask for Paris to understand. Men are rarely considered to be witches because they are not expected to caretake, to fawn, to smile, all of which I have failed to do. I come from a long line of witches who failed to appease the suburban beast and who were isolated and scapegoated, tarred and feathered, condemned as temptresses and accused of being histrionic. If the people of Mount Pelion Way could weigh me against a stack of Bibles and drown, hang, or burn me at the stake, they would.

You're not a witch, you're my mom, and I love you.

And I love you too, Ania. I always have and I always will.

But then, what if I deserve this judgment? What if they were right all along and I deserve to be punished, to be exorcised from this world. I failed the most basic of duties: to protect my child. According to some, I became Saturn and devoured her myself.

I hear Freya squawking like a seagull, repeating, *amazing, so amazing* over and over again. And then there is the booming insistence of Athena, who proclaims something as *outrageous* and *unreasonable* and demands that someone uses their *best endeavors*. And there is also the simpering from June West, who beseeches everyone to *think of the community* and *the children* and *the need to feel safe*.

How safe was my daughter from their three sons?

This suburban beast remains strong because of a web of interdependence that binds them so tightly that they cannot wriggle free, even if they wanted to. Secrets and favors are bartered for and exchanged, as quid pro quo as basic capitalism, and it is the American Dream to be protected at all costs. They will not willingly tell me what happened, what their sons did, and whether it was one, two, or all three of them.

But I have my ways. If I survive this winter, spring will bring the first shoots of aconite. This bastard child of hollyhocks and amaranthine will create a chaotic display of purples and blues to decorate my yard. My beautiful wolfsbane, a curse on the wolf pack of Mount Pelion Way. How I will delight at crushing the root and flower to sprinkle into drinks or pies or even caramelized apples. I seek their bane in dreams of their hangdog expressions as their faces go numb, and I long to hear the irregular rhythms of their hearts, palpitations as chaotic as jungle drums. And at the point of collapse, they will beg for forgiveness, and then finally I will discover what happened to my daughter. I may not look like a bony old witch because I am soft and bulbous with thick auburn hair, but I will conjure up plenty of spells to plague their children with inexplicable illnesses that make their skin peel, their eyeballs pop, and their tongues wrap around their throats to choke the life out of them. *Quid pro quo.*

I hear the three seething mothers again. They are making plans for their children, plans that do not include Ania. *Amazing, so amazing* Freya repeats, a siren call to lure me out of this fortress. But I refuse to fall for the trap because they might catch me, these suburban witch-hunters. I have nightmares of them illuminated by a full moon, with their modern-day pitchforks of cell phones to record evidence of their preconceptions that are planted, propagated, and then confirmed by therapists and religious leaders alike. They winch me up to hang from one of their swing sets, the noose tightening around my throat as my legs thrash for life. How they will laugh and jeer and point, celebrating the exorcism of the Witch of Mount Pelion Way. How the neighbors will rejoice, and the street will be decorated with floral garlands of victory and brocades of joy woven into the finest gold and silver.

Silence now. I suspect the multiheaded beast has grown weary, dismembering as each seething mother slinks back to her own home.

I hear scuffling at my window, a branch perhaps, or fingers trying to pry open the locks. Looking up, I see a raven with something in its beak. It looks like a human fetus, all pink and white and moist. Eyes shut and writhing, it knows nothing of the world that is about to fall from its reach.

I stand up to take a closer look and I feel nothing. It is a long time since I lost any romantic notion about birdsong; it is usually a squawk of victory after the kill, or a cry for help as some other predator draws near.

I can see red veins on the thing in the raven's beak. I can see it pulsating. Beyond, I notice the lolloping of one of the three boys of Mount Pelion Way.

Smithson.

I don't want this.

The dead only whisper in riddles, so sometimes I wonder if Ania is purposefully trying to confuse me. You see, the dead are jealous that we are still alive, with all the scents and tastes and tingling touches to savor. And they also have an eternity stretched out before them, so they have time to dawdle and fabricate and weave.

We were in the forest together.

Ania could mean a multitude of things when she says this.

I always kept a close eye on Smithson West, June West's thuggish son, who was relentless when play wrestling with the other boys on this street. Even when their faces turned purple, with Smithson's arm around their neck, even when they croaked and begged for Smithson to stop, he would continue to laugh as he kicked and punched them into the dirt. If he was that savage with his own friends, just think what he did, given a quiet moment with no witnesses, to the daughter of the Witch of Mount Pelion Way.

There he goes to the woods again, and I am ready to give him a surprise. He thinks he is safe from me, that I am kept in check by social convention and the fear of public reprisals. He is too stupid to realize that I stopped fearing anything of the kind, and I am free-falling through the next stage of my life.

I open the door and reluctantly taste the ice-cold air. The ash-shaped snowflakes continue to fall like broken memories. Over there is where Ania bounced her basketball—and how it infuriated me when she would slam it against the house. Over here is where I tried to kiss Paris and bring him back to my bed after months of us barely touching each other. Ania had returned home from soccer practice early and caught us naked on the stairs, and she was mortified, although we all ended up laughing about it for a while. To think of kissing Paris now, in this fallout, fills my mouth with chalky flakes of ash. No moistness that characterized our kisses of two years ago—just dry, lifeless matter to fill our mouths and choke us.

"Smithson," I call, but he does not hear me. Or he pretends not to.

It was over there, where Smithson now walks, that Ania tripped and fell. It was just a week after her fourteenth birthday, and she refused to go to school for three days because of her swollen face. I know that at least one person on Mount Pelion Way sent child protective services to interrogate me inside my own home. And I heard the cruel words Freya hissed about my daughter's injured face. Ania heard it too.

"Why do they hate me?" she asked, tears streaming down her face. I wish I had given her a better lie than "Don't be silly, of course they don't."

I think I could have tolerated hurtful words from their children, but to hear it from the adults, with so much power to intimidate and attack my daughter on a daily basis. . . . Just because they could.

Over there is where the wolf pack chose to celebrate the joint sixteenth birthdays of Cory, Aedean, and Smithson instead of going to Ania's funeral.

Smithson's reaching the forest. He will be there in the dark again.

I am on fire again, burning with a desire to hunt out and exact my revenge.

He is probably going there to meet more girls.

I can barely hear Ania's voice above the beating of my heart that fills my ears. Is that wrath and vengeance or jealousy that I hear from my ghostly daughter? Fight or fear? It all sounds so distant, from two years ago. Buried by others, but I still hold onto her. I always will.

Smithson hears my footsteps and glances back, but he seems unaware of the threat that closes in. He has been spoiled by overindulgent parents, too protected to ever recognize the vicious odor of malice, that jaundiced resentment that can yellow the eyeballs. He thinks he is special, he thinks he is beyond the spite of a mourning mother, as pointed as a scalpel. He probably believes that he is immortal.

Gaining on him, I notice that he has a slight waddle to his gait; this is surprising given all the years of lacrosse and football coaching his parents paid for. Too spoiled to fend for himself, he seems ill-equipped to survive the realities of life, like a factory-caged hen that is overblown, fleshy, and bow-legged. I have thought about stealthily breaking into those factories and freeing those poor hens. The trouble is, they would probably perish in the wild. Far better to snuff them out, to end their suffering.

Smithson has been warned about this forest. His parents, all the parents of Mount Pelion Way, were concerned about the dangers of what might be in the oil cans and trash bags and unwanted refrigerators that were dumped there. Some of the parents tried to get the town officials to clean it up but no one cared enough to do anything. They never stopped to think that a witch might be living nearby, one who could scale any fence, and who spends all night pondering the cool smoothness of skin when it has been frozen by asphyxiation.

Smithson should have listened to his parents, but it is too late now. Too late also for my daughter, who he met here that Halloween night, tricking her into false hopes of love when all along he just wanted something to use.

I wonder if I should do it in broad daylight.

All the better to see him.

I'm doing this for you, Ania.

Don't.

Smithson plunges deep into the forest, forcing me to follow. My heart quickens with every pace.

Second thoughts are obscured by the fading light of the woods, and the darkened air is filled with imagined horrors of my daughter's face, distorted in pain. I wince when I imagine how he tore her. He had fun, probably for a second or two, and damaged her forever.

Stop.

Stepping into the woodland has caused all life to drift far from reach, as if my head has sunk beneath the surface of a lake.

Birdsong is muted, the leaves are still, and even the syncopated shuffle of the train is shut out from our world. We are truly alone together, Smithson and I, without anyone to stop me or serve as a witness.

"Smithson," I call, wishing my voice came with a growl rather than a girlish plea.

By now I am so close to him that I smell his vapor trail, the pungent male scent of leather and something else, something metallic and spicy.

"Smithson," I call again, this time using the deeper part of my throat, so it resembles a purr.

"Don't ignore me, Smithson."

He stops walking but still he will not turn to face me. With his thick neck, large hands, and overbearing height, he could fell me with one swipe. But his parents have taught him to keep his manners in check around his elders, so he is defenseless in my presence.

What happened to those manners when he was pinning my daughter down in this dirt? Was that also part of his parents' conditioning? Seize what he can from the young and helpless, and keep smiling afterwards, pretending to her grieving mother that he did nothing wrong?

"Don't you dare ignore me."

"What do you want?" he finally replies, turning back to meet my eyes. "Stop following me." Were these the bright blue eyes that had drawn Ania into these woods, in the mistaken belief that he might value her, might show her the sort of kindness that she had never experienced from any of the other children in her grade? Ania was never allowed to play with these boys, even as young as kindergarten. Their mothers treated her with contempt, as if she were a contagion they needed to guard against. They would never welcome the daughter of a witch, so she was cast out and left to play alone in the playground.

They did it with the other kids at the school, the ones who were not rich or white or Christian enough. The seething mothers cozied up to the school administrators so they could target these kids with false allegations of bullying or disruptive behavior, all with a view to cleanse this town of as many of these children as possible. Paris would make a joke about how vicious these mothers had proven to be, calling it the ethnic cleansing of suburbia. But the joke fell flat when our own daughter was eradicated, exorcised like a cumbersome blemish on the illusion of suburban perfection.

"What do you think I want, Smithson?" We are close enough to hear each other's breathing, so I snake my fingers over his cheeks. His skin is surprisingly soft. He just stands there as I finger his lips, and I wonder if he is going to smile, welcome my touch, and even kiss my palm.

"You silly boy," I purr, and I feel my whole body vibrate, waves rippling with every word. My hands slip down and around his throat, and I should throttle him here and now to even the score. But I want him to suffer a little longer.

"Did it thrill you to know that you made her bleed?" I hiss.

Listen to me.

"Did that make you want to do it again?"

Listen to me.

"Did you want your friends to have a go? Did you want them to watch?"

Listen to me, Mom. Listen to me, Smithson.

"Ania?" he gasps, staggering backwards and collapsing into the undergrowth. His foot must have caught on a tree root or fallen branch, and I wonder what I would do if the fall had split his head open. I imagine having to finish him off with a rock. I would have to drag his body into the thicker parts of the forest, up in the hills where there are no houses and prying eyes. I have buried other things up there, and no one has ever found any of it.

"Leave me alone."

Listen to me. Why won't anyone listen to me? Please, Mom, please. You have to listen to me before you make a horrible mistake.

Ania pushes her way back into our domain, through the dirt and the decaying things that are barely noticed underfoot. She squirms like a maggot, crackling into life with an aching, groaning sound that also smells of decayed flesh hanging loosely on the bone.

Smithson can smell it too. As he starts to tremble, he twists his mouth and nose as if he is going to cry.

"Aw, are you going to blub, little Smithson? And are you going to wet yourself? Do you need Mommy?" I sneer. I think of how my teeth have darkened over the last two years, and I take pleasure in showing them to him as I cackle.

"I mean it. Stay away from me." He sounds like a girl who is screaming for mercy.

I want to see Ania's dirty fingernails clawing her way through the undergrowth, tearing at his shoes and ankles until she penetrates him deep enough to touch bone.

"Oh come, now. I thought you liked to play in here, far from the watchful eye. What's the matter? Only like it when they're helpless? When they're held down by your buddies, perhaps?"

"Why are you doing this?"

"Am I doing this, or is it Ania?"

Still on the ground, he glances around, certain he has seen a ghost.

"What does it matter," I continue. "Ania is at the heart of this, without any heart of her own to beat because you ripped it from her chest."

I climb on top of him. I push my hand over his mouth because I am certain he is going to scream. I feel a distant panic, like the shriek of an approaching train far off in the distance, but I already know I have no escape. I don't know how this will end, any more than I can be certain who is controlling my movements. He probably feels like he has been dragged into the underworld, a dimension of unbounded pleasure and pain, where a woman can overpower a man, the opposite of what he has learned through his father's slap of his wife's behind, and a grab of the arm to steer her in the direction he wants. But none of this matters now; an older woman is silencing him, suffocating him, pinning him to the ground and doing what he should be doing instead.

"You all deserve so much more for what you did."

I want them all here right now, not just Smithson West. I want his stupid pimply friend Cory Aegean, of gawkish and lurching ways, and that chubby-headed, overindulged Aedean Marwood. In fact, I want their parents too, who created these whorish boys who think they can stick themselves into anything warm and moist.

I want to go home. Let me go, please.

The boy could have said this, but the sound is too translucent to be anything but the words of a ghost. Anything but Ania's words. She never liked violence, and she never liked the forest at the end of her street. She used to say it was haunted, and now, it seems, she was right all along. I created her, so it is so hard to distinguish her from me, it is so hard to know what she might have wanted of me, and what I would like to do to this boy right now, here in the woods. I bathed her for the first time, a body barely formed, so small and chubby and clumsy, and I bathed her for the last time, the shell that was missing her warmth, her smile, her wistful lean to one side when she tried to persuade me to let her have a puppy. (I never did, and I hate myself for that.)

I notice that the boy has slipped away from me. He scrambles to his feet, and I watch him race through the forest. Branches whip at his head but he doesn't appear to flinch.

I jump to my feet and run after him, his male scent still lingering about me. I don't know how I am running so fast, but I reach him just as the light explodes, and we are free of the forest. Back under the watchful eye of the inhabitants of Mount Pelion Way. Together again, eyes wide and panting in unison. So close we can feel each other's breath.

Chapter Two

~~~

Myths and legends

I could pull him back into the forest. With the strength I have discovered, Ania's strength, I could drag him to me to face his punishment. But there is a witness.

"Didn't you see me?" Pastor Pry calls after me, her voice distracting me so that I slow my pace.

She'll tell.

I need to shake her off. I want to run after Smithson to prevent him from reaching the safety of his home but the pastor won't leave me alone.

"You look well" she calls, trotting after me like a persistent street seller. She has always tried to push her drugs of hope and salvation onto me.

Leave.

"Great day for a walk."

The pastor dares to touch my shoulder and I smell her hand cream and soap. So sanitary and plain. I want to slap her or shock her with stories of my sex life, when Paris would choke me to intensify the thrill. I could tell her that his stranglehold always deadened my emotions so I was left as a dead-faced mannequin, and I could explain that nightmare images of my daughter left in a similar state justifies what I am doing to Smithson. I could ask her if she would do the same, or if she lets her husband choke her. Isn't this how the suburban beast is satiated; an exchange of personal information to create that web of interdependence? *Quid*
~~~

pro quo.

"You should join me at church one Sunday."
Pastor Pry is a raven that circles people, just waiting to feed on their grief and longing.

"Leave me alone" I snap, shrugging her hand off. "I'm not interested in anything you have to sell."
"I'm not selling anything" she says, squinting through bottle-thick glasses. "I just wanted to check in with you.'
I notice that one of her front teeth has discolored. I wonder how long it will take for it to blacken, loosen, and fall out in the middle of one of her sermons.

"Of course you're selling; the East Coast is always selling something. In return for the tithes, didn't you try to sell me the hope of her resurrection?"
"I don't know what you're talking about. I know things have been tough for you. Is there anything I can do to help? How *are* you doing with it all?"

I refuse to smile. If I give anything to her, I know it will quickly lead to more. She has a way of prying you open and she has already stolen enough from me, when I was at my most vulnerable.

"You never could tell me whether I would see my daughter again. Did you want to dangle that over me, so I would pay more?"
"You know I don't work like that," the pastor says as she shakes her head.
"I don't know that. I don't know that at all."
"How *are* you?" she repeats. She is an automaton with a glitch. "We really should catch up."
It takes an iron-clad will to resist the edict of a Presbyterian preacher. I managed to once, when I had nothing left to lose. I wish I had slapped her in the face with full force that day, when she hovered over my grief. That was the only time I would have got away with it, while Ania was still lying in the morgue.

"We haven't seen you for a while. We've missed you."

I try to draw a circumference around *we,* but it ends up a tangled mess in my head. Is *we* a reference to the pastor and her god, the god who left my daughter to suffer in that forest, and the god who watched as the people of Mount Pelion Way celebrated the sixteenth birthday of those three boys while my daughter lay frozen by death? I burn with spite and jealousy when I think of how the pastor's faith can transform my daughter's death into a temporary loss, as if she is on a trip to Disneyland and will soon return. I cannot ignore the inconsistencies and contradictions, no matter how much my husband wants me to.

How the pastor circled me two years ago, waiting for any signs that I was going to break. Anointed with significance during those days after Ania's death, that hungry raven clung to me so she could feast on my grief. The pandemic had reduced church attendance to critical levels, so she needed this tragedy to remind people of her relevance. Daily, she circled Mount Pelion Way, and I would hear her croaking call for more to join her congregation; carrion to keep her insulated against the cold winter that loomed on the horizon.

When I asked her if I would see Ania again, when I begged her to tell me, she watched how I twisted my fingers together, tangled in the tissue she had given me, and then she took my hands and squeezed them. Hers were surprisingly warm.

"In these early days, you need to look after yourself," she had told me.

"That isn't an answer."

I feared she was going to tell me that my daughter had gone to hell. I feared she would confirm that we would forever be separated, and for that, I wanted to slap her.

"You are getting yourself worked up" she had told me. "Is Paris around? Maybe we could ask him to sit with you for a while."

"Why are you talking in circles? Why won't you just answer the fucking question? Where is she?"

The pastor slipped out her cell phone and started to dial a number. I snatched the phone from her and hurled it against the wall so hard that I heard the screen smash.

"Answer me."

I stared at her long, pointy nose and watery, distant eyes. I was desperate to find some kind of answer, a fragment of hope, but I found nothing.

And today, two years later, still the pastor offers nothing but those same watery, distant eyes.

By now, Smithson has disappeared into his house, and the pastor and I have reached my car, which is sitting in the driveway. Through the window I see the garish colors of wrappers from Ania's after-school snacks. Two years later and I still refuse to clear them out. They will forever serve as a memorial to my failed bid to be a parent. A flag in the moon, frozen in the ice-cold climate of a memory. I hate myself for complaining about the mess she would make, always assuming she was careless or forgetful. Now I wonder whether she was preoccupied with her attempts to avoid the dangers that ultimately consumed her. My gut twists to think about the times Paris told me to *Go easy on her.*

Ania Brown, my shape-shifting daughter. So quickly she transformed from girl to woman, only to disappear again, to hide in the opacity of my dreams. And I am left here, painfully aware of the real world.

"I am here if you need me, Eris. How is Paris?"
This pastor, this quick-witted raven, always spots the vulnerability. She thinks my husband is a chink in my armor, that if you want information or compassion or forgiveness, just look to the simplicity of Paris Brown.

I ignore her and climb into the car, slamming the door so the pastor's words become muffled. I think of returning to this scene tonight, when I can peel the skin from my fingers and watch the blood pool around my nails. The pain will be useful, to remind me that I am still human and not a witch or some mythical beast.

Watching Pry, my breath comes in shorter and faster gasps. I am starting to cloud up the windows of my car, so I use my forefinger to draw a face with no mouth. It is silent, unexpressive, shut down; it is a face of desolation. Through the opaque haze of my windscreen, I can see that Pry has started to retreat. She'll be back, I am sure, and next time she might bring reinforcements. Another member of the clergy, perhaps, or a police officer who will bundle me off to hospital where a nurse can forcibly medicate me. They are all the same, this multitude of heads that comprise the suburban beast. They prefer it when I am passive, when I am a limp recipient of the bullshit they want me to swallow.

I fire up the engine and I feel a tremor of excitement when I see how frightened she looks. I quickly reverse without checking

in my rearview mirror, and I wonder if Paris would forgive me if
the pastor had been behind the car. I doubt he would share my
pleasure if I'd heard the crack of each bone, conscious that the
tires were squeezing the life out of her. I doubt his blood would
stir with a thrill, heart pulsing faster as he watched her limbs
twitching with the final signs of life.

It is these moments when I feel the most alone, and that
isolation scares me. If he were to disappear from my life, who
would keep me from enacting these fantasies?

Mount Pelion Way is in Rotherwell, a town like so many others
in the northeastern corner of the United States. Although I am the
one they call a witch, it is the Realtor who casts a spell in each of
these towns. Up and down the East Coast, Realtors trick seething
mothers and overblown fathers into paying ridiculous amounts for
a home simply because of the myth that the schools are the best in
the country. They fall for this trickery because these desperate
parents grew up in pageant shows and lacrosse tournaments, cast
under the spell that they were special, yes, but also *better* than
anyone else. And so, they dare not stop to question the claims
about the schools, claims that are whispered from head-to-head on
this suburban beast. Because if they do, it might shatter the illusion
that they are better than anyone else. Myths and legends are left
unchallenged.

They relegated my daughter to the dark corners of a myth.
They might even claim that she never existed in the first place. To
allow a witch such human emotions as grief and despair might
weaken their resolve to expunge me from their town. But I still
see her as I drive through Rotherwell. She flashes by my window
as I pass the place where she first got her ears pierced. And I see
her outside her favorite café, where we used to get ice cream.

This battleground, this endless war. So determined to get their
greedy hands on *that* house in *that* town with *that* school. They
forget there are countless other entitled and greedy parents, all
who have grown up in the same competitive pageant shows and
lacrosse tournaments. What better conditions to create a war,
where families in each suburban town fight for every last
opportunity.

Caught in the crossfire. That's how I view Ania's death.

Another casualty of war, lost in the gap where basic humanity was lost. Is it any wonder that I burn with rage when I hear these mothers and fathers claim that the community, this suburban beast, exists for the sake of the children. No one will admit that they are only talking about the welfare of their own child, who they will allow to seize whatever they wish in a darkened forest. Just because they can.

In this daily fight, I have one small corner of comfort. A tiny space to breathe. It keeps me going to know that I sit in a fortress high up on a hill while the seething mothers and overblown fathers live in the lower parts of Mount Pelion Way. Their homes are slowly sinking back into the swampland on which they were built, and it makes me smile to see their frantic attempts to bail out their basements every time there is a sudden downpour. I know this makes the mothers seethe more and the fathers balloon, working out their frustrations and disappointment in a sweaty, greasy gym. I am certain they spend each day working out a way to get rid of me once and for all, but a childish voice squeals inside of me: *I was here first.* My fortress once sat alone on that hill, before my grandfather got greedy and sold as much land as he once owned.

With each parcel of land sold to a house builder, my grandfather encroached on his own freedom. In turn, he condemned me to the well-manicured lawns of suburgatory and the resentment that burns through the people who live in the smaller houses. Most nights I am woken by the sound of frolicking and fighting; like foxes howling at the moon, they scavenge amongst each other and leave a trail of trash and disease.

By now I have driven far from Mount Pelion Way, and so my grip loosens on the steering wheel. I cross the railway tracks with a bump, and on the side of the road I see a young fox caught in a twist of barbed wire. Either the creature is dead or in shock because it is frozen, its eyes and head trained upwards as if someone has told it to *sit*. I have driven past it too quickly to see if it was alone, but my imagination takes me on a strange and winding journey to the fox's parents pacing somewhere nearby, searching for their infant. I know of the powerlessness, I know of the longing for an answer, even if it is bad, just to fill that dark hole of uncertainty. I can feel how deeply the metal noose will cut the young fox's neck, and every movement it makes to struggle free will only tighten the trap.

It was the same when those three boys on Mount Pelion Way found a fox tangled in the net of a goal post. They prodded the fox with sticks and threw stones at it until it died. I think one threw paint into the creature's eyes. Just because they could.

I think of grief as a tightening knot, inescapable and deadly, and I push down hard on the accelerator, longing to escape. I could keep driving, faster and faster, and I could slam into the car in front of me. I imagine hearing the dying gasps of breath as parts of their body fall like chunks of meat being sliced from a rotisserie. Already I can smell the blood and gasoline and urine of human life and machinery, spliced together like a hastily made noxious pie.

Stop all this. Please.

She, I, *we* ease the pedal of the accelerator, and a safer distance is created between my car and the car in front. The passenger in the back, a hunched blond woman with AirPods in her ears, glances back at me with a mixture of relief and fury.

You live to fight another day.

Chapter Three

~~~

Afterlife?

You think I am foolish to believe that Ania can talk to me. But think of her in that darkness. She is sixteen, no age to be left all alone for eternity. Think of the maggots and the dermestid beetles, think of the putrefaction and decay. She is beautiful; she wasn't old and withered, tired of life and ready to die. She is inside of me, she started life inside of me, every strand of her was my creation, and now she will forever be a part of me.

How could I not return to those woods repeatedly, to seek out the truth, to reenact what might have happened and somehow try to complete it. This is what trauma is made of. It doesn't make sense but sometimes it makes certain things feel right: To empower the powerless, to reenact, and to complete the incomplete. To fight back when you've been trapped for so long.

Let Smithson run home to his mommy. His daddy too, although Max would only care that his sporting-hero son let an old hag like me get the better of him. He won't let that one slide. Flesh on flesh I am no match for the mighty Max, so I hope that the phantasmic will conjure up some sort of intervention, some pentacle of protection around me so I can survive long enough to right what went wrong on that cold day, just two years ago.

And after that? Will Ania help me to wage a war across the toxic East Coast and beyond? There are so many entitled young lads who stick their smelly protrusions into girls, whether they want it or not. If caught, they run home to mommy and daddy and
~~~

ask them to pay for an expensive lawyer to expunge their record. This is the sort of contamination that needs to be cleaned up in industrial America.

Too much is feared about hauntings and spirits. Even my forefathers went to great lengths of superstition and ritual to prevent any spirit from piercing through an opening in their house or church. But I take comfort in Ania's haunting. Godlike, she guides me, but her words are fleeting and often without context. She sometimes hints that there were others in the forest, people who meant her harm. I think she is saying that there were others beyond Smithson, Cory, and Aedean. How many ways can a story be told? And when the story involves trauma, it distorts things, making a victim become a perpetrator, or the perpetrator a victim, and you end up stuck in a perpetual loop of different potential perspectives. Trauma knows no bounds, and the ripples of it are unconstrained by space and time, and in a perverse way this gives me hope to know that Ania's presence might be felt for an eternity.

Full of disappointment and dread, I pull into the overcrowded parking lot outside the hardware store. Mothers pull their children close to them when I emerge from the car. They didn't seem bothered when I was *driving* close to their offspring because cars are viewed as a necessary evil. I, on the other hand, with my unruly hair, unwashed shirt, and threadbare jeans, am considered just to be evil.

I need to find the salt Paris wanted me to get, but I also need knife sharpeners, rat poison, and jute twine. I browse the aisles, painfully aware that people are coming too close to me. I want to scream at them or bite them, but I know I'll make too much trouble for myself.

I imagine what it would be like if Pastor Pry followed me here. Would she question me about the items I was buying? I could make up some story that she probably wouldn't believe, or I could just cut straight to the action and follow her to her car, binding her hands and legs together with the rope. Would I then use the sharpened knives or rat poison? Or perhaps I could bind her to the steering wheel and crash her car.

Come on, that's not very nice.

I know. I'm sorry. I wasn't sure you'd stuck around.

Where else do I have to go? You've got me here for as long as you want.

Good. I don't ever want to lose you.

"Just these things?" the shop clerk asks me. I have seen him here before, but I cannot remember his name. He isn't wearing a name tag, and because of his age, I assume he owns the store. People on the East Coast remain vigilant for details like this because they are always looking for favors or an informal business arrangement. No one cares beyond what they can get out of a person, and so there will be an exchange of small talk and Christmas cards, and even a box of sprinkle cookies thrown in for good measure. To survive this quid pro quo community these small gestures are essential, especially if you need someone to keep your son out of jail for drunk driving, drug dealing, or rape. As long as you've given enough, you'll get the benefit of the doubt as the police shrug their shoulders with an excusatory *Boys will be boys* and *He comes from a good family.*

"Haven't seen Dylan for a while."

Dylan.

How easy it is to forget that there was once another child, a brother to Ania. Best forget all that now, or he might end up defeating me. The only one who had such power.

"He doin' okay?"

Whoever this person is, store clerk or owner, he knows enough not to ask about Ania. He peers at me from the items he is ringing up. He is waiting for a reply. In this quid pro quo community, I have nothing to offer, and I want nothing of anyone except the truth. I don't want the benefit of the doubt or excuses. In my silent refusal to barter small talk, I am a misfit that poses a threat. And this threat is so terrifying for them because they cannot put their finger on the precise nature of the dangers I represent.

"How is Dylan?" he tries again, placing the items in a bag as he stares at me. If Pastor Pry had been here, she would've filled the space with nervous chatter and laughter to make my skin pop with goosebumps. Freya, June, and Athena would compliment the store owner on his wares or lie that a visit to this store is the highlight of their day. Instead, I just ask "Will this take long?" with a stone-flattened tone. I know this is out of cadence, a sudden jolt to him that disrupts the natural rhythms. You'd think I stabbed a baby while it was rocked by its mother. A small part of me enjoys seeing the panic in his eyes, knowing I am not giving him what he expects of me, not kneeling before him and unzipping him just because he is a man.

"Not long," he mutters, finally.
He still stares at me, expecting some sort of softening from me—a surrender of a smile or a laugh to make him believe that he is attractive or funny. He is probably used to a wife or elderly mother who smoothes down his hair and tells him that everything is going to be all right. *Who's a big boy?* I imagine him in a big diaper suckling at a milk bottle; I hear that some men are into that sort of thing.

"Strange" he says, shaking his head, a double chin wobbling like luncheon meat.
"What is strange?" I ask, but instantly regret taking the bait.
"Strange that I haven't seen Dylan for so long."
I want to ask him whether he thinks I have his body buried in my backyard. Do they think that I have my own private slaughterhouse in the far reaches of my attic? I should burn that fortress down, along with every other house on Mount Pelion Way. Isn't that the way some people cleanse things or make room for new growth? Isn't that the way they pillage and conquer lands, so they can build their own empires of column-fronted mansions on acres of land, just so they don't have to hear their neighbors passing wind every time they step out to dispose of the trash? Most nights I dream of locking everyone in as I pour gasoline through their letterboxes. I would do it under the cover of night when they are the most defenseless. I might like to see them shrunken in their nightwear and careless under the influence of Ambien or too much wine. To burn is to punish and eradicate. I would hear them beg for forgiveness as I light the match, as I anticipate the hiss and pop of burning flesh. They would try to bargain with me, offering to sacrifice their own lives if I would spare their children. *"But the children are the best part!"* I would scream at them. *Quid pro quo.*

I want to verbalize some of my fantasies. And then I want to ask this prying nobody what he really thinks of all this, what's really going through his mind. I need a bit of honesty for once, no matter how graphic or disturbing. But then I see a little girl standing to the left of me. I should smile so she isn't afraid of me. Father used to tell me that a smile eases things, and Paris encourages me to do the same. I always assumed they meant that it made things easier for the other person, but maybe if I smile, this store clerk will leave me alone and finish checking out the items in silence.

The little girl breaks free of her mother's hand. She stumbles, perhaps accidentally, and steadies herself against my waist. Fine strands of nerves are awakened by her, and I wonder if they can see the shock of red that must be pulsating beneath the skin of my cheeks. For a moment, she becomes my daughter, and I allow myself to believe that I am holding Ania again.

"You seem sad," the little girl says with a pout. It is accusatory, the same tone she would use if she said that I'd stolen her toy. From the corner of my eye I can see that her mother looks appropriately embarrassed, so I soften towards her a little. I dare not say anything, knowing that whatever words I choose will be wrong. I want to believe that the little girl resembles my own daughter, with the same soft, rosy cheeks that she inherited from her father. I want to imagine this girl has the same lack of social grace, so she doesn't smile unless she really feels happy, and she doesn't look people in the eye or say please and thank you when she speaks to them.

Until the store clerk slowed me down, I managed to block out any other patrons in the store. But now I can see them all, clustering around me like a clotting artery. I notice I am breathing faster but shallower, so my head feels light. I hear them murmuring around me, and I think I hear one of them say *Ania.*

If they wanted to, they could block my escape. They could tie me up and rip out any information they want from me. I was foolish to even smile.

My father once told me that people only want our money, but I can now see how woefully incomplete an explanation that was. People want to see the thin trickle of sweat that creeps down your forehead, they want to see the shake of your hands, and they want to see you run for your life.

I see a police officer. He isn't one I recognize, and he won't stop staring at me. I think of how Smithson or his parents might have called the police. There might be evidence from a dog walker or one of Smithson's friends, loitering behind the trees with a cell phone to record it all. I could survive prison, but I cannot afford to lose what remains of my life inside that fortress. I will not let them take that from me.

Keeping his eyes trained on me, the police officer says something inaudible into the radio that is clipped to his shirt, and he starts to walk in my direction.

"When am I going to see Dylan again? Such a great lad."

It occurs to me that the clerk is deliberately trying to provoke me. He might want to see the blunt instrument of my sudden rage and regret, and he could have plotted this with the police officer. They are, after all, both part of the suburban beast.

"I mean, it just seems strange for him to be here one day and gone the next. Without any word to anyone before he left. That's kind of strange to me."

I turn back to face the aged clerk. I want to scream at him to shut up.

"He's doing just fine, thank you."

The man looks relieved. The simpleton.

"Oh. Oh, well then that's great. Tell him that Mark said hi, and that if he needs to earn some more cash, let me know. We can always do with another pair of hands."

The police officer has almost reached the counter, so I gather the items into my arms.

"Listen, I need to get going, so can we just finish up here?"

The store is suddenly silent, and the police officer still stares at me. I wonder if I shouted this, and I'm afraid of what else I might do without realizing it.

Lost time.

I lost the most time after Ania died. Paris describes it as a war zone when I hurled words of judgment and persecution through the air like arrows over the parapet. I had boundless energy, and I was ready to wreak havoc on everyone. My husband feared who might get hurt, so he convinced me to take the pills that the therapist had prescribed. I took them once, and my edges were so blurred that I became passive, spaced out like aquatic life floating across the sea. So I flushed them down the toilet and regained the energy that burns vengeance through my every vein.

"You've got quite the handful there."

"I'm fine."

"Let me at least have one of the boys help you to your car."

"I said I'm fine," I snap.

If I were one of the overblown men who is waddling around this store, or if I had been Dylan, the clerk would have backed off after the first answer. Dylan would tell the clerk to *Relax, dude,* with his jaw thrust forward in defiance. On the East Coast and beyond, women are talked over, dismissed, and expected to let men run the show—provided those men are rich and white and Christian. Power held by the few and used to subjugate the masses; the hallmarks of a dictatorship that this land of the free claims not to be. Look away, look instead at the dark corners of this globe, not at this gleaming white land of hypocrisy. Paris tells me I should just ignore these inconsistencies and play the game, but isn't the game set up to make people like us fail? We have the absence of our daughter as proof of that.

I pay, grab the bags, and race out of the store. As the door swings shut behind me, I think of what the store clerk and police officer might conspire to do next. Would I eventually hear sirens in hot pursuit behind me? But for what—forgetting my manners? Or will they find in the trunk of my car bloodied duct tape, ropes, or razor wire? Within the last two years, I have learned that anything is possible.

Chapter four

~~~

Malevolent fairy

I glance back to see if the police officer has followed me, half expecting to see him with Max and Smithson. The street is empty, but I do see the post office, a place that calls to me, drawing me back more and more frequently. There is a woman who works behind the counter, and she smiles at me when no one else will. She first showed me kindness when I brought a pile of letters there, when I had to attend to the formalities around Ania's death. Paris couldn't bring himself to do it, and this was the first sign that I couldn't rely on him.

Over the last two years, I have come to crave Mary Anne's kindness, even though I never knew I had a taste for it. She makes me curious for a life beyond my fortress of latches and bolts and locks, a prospect that terrifies and excites me all at once. But isn't that the hallmark of true freedom? It carries so much hope that it intensifies the perceived risks.

Ever since I met her, I crave more of Mary Anne's smile and the sound of her laugh. But I must tread carefully. It is so easy to get carried away and confuse love and kindness with longing and grief. Faced with the dry, stone-cold reality of death, I could be forgiven for craving the opposite. But I know nothing about this woman at the post office, and whether I can trust that her kindness is real.

"Back again so soon!" Mary Anne said with a smile on my second visit, just three days after Ania's death. I didn't expect her
~~~

to remember me, let alone greet me, but she beckoned me over to the counter as soon as I was through the heavy door.

"What is all this? You have so many envelopes."
I told her about my daughter. I didn't hold anything back, and I did not soften my tone. In hindsight, I feel a twinge of guilt because I made her cry.

"I'm sorry," I said. "I shouldn't have said so much. My husband always tells me off for my brutal honesty."
"*No, no, no*," Mary Anne sobbed, shaking her head. She retrieved a tissue from her pocket and removed her glasses to dab at her thickly mascaraed eyes. "You shouldn't be saying sorry to me. I am so, so sorry for your loss. I really am."
It was the first moment in a long time that I realized I was not perceived as a witch. Or if she did view me in this way, she wasn't afraid nor disgusted.

Mary Anne slipped from behind the counter and disappeared for a second. I thought she had run off, but then a side door clicked open. She threw her arms around me and squeezed me to her body. As her scent surrounded me, every one of my fibers came alive with the hope of something real. It felt foolish to even use the word, but was this what people referred to as *friendship*?

Today I approach the post office and I catch my reflection in the glass front. I think of my mother's old dresses hanging at the back of my closet. I never even considered them to be mine, yet now I wonder what it would be like to slip one on and try on a pair of her high heels. Just to see if they fit. In broad daylight, far from the confines of my fortress, it seems so easy. But whenever I return home, I remember how my father would howl whenever he saw me going near my mother's belongings. And when he had drunk too much, things would get broken around my head.

There is a sound of metal scraping against something hard, and I flinch. From the other side of the street, I see a family walking by, and I realize one of their children must have kicked a can into the road. They have a teenage daughter with long, auburn hair and brown, polished shoes. If I screw my eyes up, I can believe that it is Ania. She has chosen to live with another family where she can be a sullen teenager and kick cans into the street. I could accept this if it meant that Ania was still alive. The family also have a younger daughter, no more than six or seven years old. If I screw up my eyes again, I can believe that this little girl is me, when my mother disappeared and left me alone with a wailing, raging father. I rarely have the comfort of faith in normality, reason or logic, so that means anything is possible. Even if that suggests that the people who pass me in the street are apparitions from another time, sent to keep watch over me.

The mother of this family walks along the street with the same elegance I remember of my own mother. I watch as this mother tells her younger daughter something, and I can almost feel the warmth of my own mother's breath on my ear as she would urge me to be kinder to other people. "Try a little harder to forgive," she would say, but she didn't live long enough to explain the multiple dimensions of this.

As the mother of the can-kicker catches sight of me, she reaches for her necklace, patting it to reassure herself that it is still there. She probably thinks I will rob her, given half a chance. My own mother was protective over her own jewelry, and I remember how careful she was to lock up her diamonds and jade and sapphires in the vaults in the attic. As a child, those vaults terrified me. I was sure that one day I would find myself trapped in there. When my mother disappeared, that left only my father and I with the knowledge that the vaults were accessed via a hidden door. When he once caught me searching for my mother in the vaults, he seemed thrilled when he told me that no one would ever find me in there.

There is a problem with terror that remains hidden in the further reaches of your mind. It distorts in those hidden depths, becoming misshapen under the weight of time. Like the malevolent fairy that they paint me to be, I let a wicked smirk smudge my face when I think of Dylan locked up in one of those vaults. During those moments when I have lost time, have I let slip about the hidden parts of my fortress? They could say that the loss of my daughter has made me hang on to my remaining child so tightly that I have trapped Dylan as I might a butterfly under a drinking glass. Do they think I feed him scraps as I watch him flutter and flap within captivity, letting time tick by as the air runs out? Perhaps the hardware clerk is telling the police officer this story right this minute, and I have only moments left of freedom.

If only they knew how much I wanted Dylan and Ania to live free of that fortress, so they did not suffer the same fate as I. That might have been my story, a lifetime locked up out of fear of the world, but I never wanted them to be prisoners with me.

I wave to the family that is walking on the other side of the street. The father scans me from head to toe, and he recoils. It might be my unruly hair, or I might have stains on my clothes, I am not sure, but he snakes an arm around each daughter and draws them in tightly to his side. He is fat and balding, and I wonder whether he would pop if I punctured him with a knife.

As they walk further away, the two girls not even noticing me, I hear the younger child start to sing something silly about a *quacking, wiggling, waggling duck.* It is a distant echo of Ania, or me, or both of us, singing this song together, and it makes me feel like I am slowly collapsing in on myself—reality, air, all leaking from every part of me.

For all these patchwork memories of Ania, for all these representations through the bodies of other girls, the malevolent fairy in me delights at the prospect of becoming a Victor Frankenstein who stitches together these patchworks and recreates my daughter anew.

Would never be as good as the original.

I could turn back and grab that little girl and run. With this newfound energy, I would make it to the car before anyone caught me, and once on Route 80, I could be in Pennsylvania in about an hour. Many children have disappeared this way.

You know you won't really do it. You're all talk.

"Just try me," I spit, frustrated by Ania's constant doubts. After all, it is her kindness, the benefit of her doubt, that left her so vulnerable, so ill-equipped for this world of suburban beasts.

I must have spoken out loud because the family stop to stare at me until I disappear inside the post office. As the door swings shut, I hear the little girl ask her mother if I am okay.

The green-tiled walls echo with the stirrings of people going about their day. The security camera across from the door stares at me with the shine of its one menacing red-light eye. The echoes of the high ceilings give this place the feel of a swimming pool.

How I hated the times my mother would try and coax me out of the house and to those changing rooms, where big-thighed and bushy-groined women would stand and stare.

Mary Anne is serving behind the counter again. Her hair is tied back, but a few strands have fallen free, so she looks tired. Her eyes twinkle when she smiles, and it awakens something in me that I thought was extinguished when Ania died. She has a dainty head that twitches with alertness to the demands of her customers, but this seems out of proportion with her wrists and neck which are so large they look swollen. Less kind people would call her matronly, but I prefer to say that she seems nurturing and attentive. I wish I knew more about her, about her age and whether she has children or a partner. I would guess she is of similar age to me, in her forties, or even early fifties. Despite her kindness, I can't imagine asking her for anything more than a box of stamps. Around her, I feel stunted and underdeveloped, and this ignites a tiny fire of hatred for what my father did to me.

Someone at the counter is taking a long time with his order, so a line of impatient customers is starting to form behind him. He keeps gesturing over to the wall of postal boxes and waving a key in Mary Anne's face. His voice has reached a crescendo and it echoes around the tiled ceiling. I know I should not intervene because if I do, I might lose time again, and that increases the risk of losing Mary Anne's friendship.

Blood pulsating behind my ears, I tap my thighs as I count the postal boxes. As I do, I promise myself that if I stay present in this green-tiled hall, I will reward myself by renting a postal box and writing to people using a new identity. I could become a man and tell stupid people to *Relax, dude.* Paris has never been interested in role playing, inside or outside the bedroom, and so I hoard these fantasies for furtive moments, safe within the confines of my mind.

". . . isn't my fucking problem."
I hear the voice, and then sudden laughter, like a ghastly choir that has burst into a church halfway through a funeral service.
"Fuck knows."
I know that voice.
"Why should I give a shit? Why bother, right?"

Again, more laughter, and I recognize the big sunglasses perched on top of a mountain of hair. Today it is a jet black of polished marble, but it has been an array of different colors in the past. Freya Marwood, one of the three seething mothers of Mount Pelion Way, seems restless with her looks, a source of greater preoccupation than any of her children. I wish she had paid more attention to her son Aedean that Halloween night. She might have noticed how he had slithered down to the forest to meet my daughter. But then, Freya might have seen Aedean and not even cared, as long as he got away with it.

She's just a few feet away from me, and I try to stand as still as I can, so she cannot see that I am shaking.

"You shouldn't either. It isn't fair," she squawks. Usually she doesn't stop talking and talking and talking, but for one brief moment, as she recognizes me, the air freezes in silence.

Caught in her snare, I imagine chewing at her fingers. I would probably not like the taste, but I could bite them clean off if I bit hard enough. My father always told me I had a strong and confident jaw.

"Anyway . . ." she continues, breaking the brief silence, ". . . you have to see it; it really is amazing. They are selling out fast, so I'll get the details to you." This time she has a quieter voice because she doesn't want me to know about the opportunities she has discovered. She thinks I care.

As the line of people shuffles forward, Freya steps closer to me. Still we do not acknowledge each other. I can now see that she is standing with a woman who has a large wart on the bridge of her nose, and I am surprised that, in this part of the East Coast, she hasn't had it removed. I don't recognize her, but she is staring at me. I can imagine Freya has whispered all sorts of ghoulish horror stories about me.

Suddenly they both burst into squawks of laughter like a flurry of caged parrots that have escaped. I wonder what happens when those vibrant creatures get old and lose their color. Do they get a burial like a beloved family pet, or are they thrown out into the trash, compressed and dumped into a landfill somewhere, with other unwanted remnants of suburbia? I wonder what will happen to the vibrant and brightly painted Freya Marwood when the last of her children graduates high school. It makes me smile to think of her bony body dumped in some landfill, the seagulls pecking at her tattered hair and skin. It is a full, cheek-aching smile, and I turn my head to face Freya, full on. Still she will not look at me, but her friend seems afraid, because she stops laughing.

I reach the front of the line, but my trip here is now futile. If I show any signs of interest in Mary Anne then Freya will see, and she will twist this to her advantage. Freya will probably wait until I've left the post office and tell Mary Anne any number of lies about me. This is what wolves do; they neutralize by isolating any potential threat.

"A book of ten stamps," I say with the flattest tone I can muster. I refuse to meet Mary Anne's eyes as she replies with a cheery "Great to see you again, old friend."
I wish she would realize that I am trying to protect her with my silence.

Her smile falters.

"Are you okay?" she asks.
Still, I offer no warmth or kindness.
"I was getting worried about you," she continues. "Haven't seen you for a while."
"Yes, well . . ."

"How are you doing?" She leans forward, urging me to reply. Another burst of squawking laughter and another flurry of caged parrots escape. There are hundreds of them flapping about the green-tiled hall, and I wonder if my ears are starting to bleed. I need to leave.

"Just the stamps, thank you."
I snatch the book of stamps from Mary Anne so rapidly that it slices my forefinger clean open. I'm not sure if she notices, or if she is offended by my sudden change in nature, but her eyes look deep with sorrow. I promise myself that I will make it up to her. I could write her a letter and apologize, and I could explain the pressure I am under, living on Mount Pelion Way. I know that she will not understand. She probably thinks that I view myself as a princess in a fortress, waiting for someone to save me from the dragons that circle outside. She might say that if everyone on Mount Pelion Way has a problem with me, then I am probably the

cause of it all. She might be right. But knowing this illuminates no paths to freedom, any more than it can lead my daughter back to my arms.

I will never leave. Not now.

As I race out of the post office, the heavy door swinging shut, I hear Freya hiss *"What the fuck."* Paris would tell me that she could've been saying that about anything or anyone. He was always too naïve for his own good.

Chapter Five

~~~

Witch bitch

The snow has stopped falling, and so the memories of ash melt away. But the fury still burns. Dylan hated me for my indignant rages at the seething mothers. Every time we drove along Mount Pelion Way I would hiss and spit about them, and eventually he turned to me and screamed "For fuck sake, Mom, knock it off". He was around twelve or thirteen at the time, so I chalked it up to hormones. But it was the first explosion from him, and there were many more to come.

"You're all talk," he would shout. "You let these people treat you like shit, and all you do is bitch and moan to me. No good telling me any of it, I can't help you."

"I'm not asking you for help," I would say, my voice reed-thin and wheedling.

"Good. So tell it to someone else."

He filled the car with his solidity. There was nothing I could say or do in response, and he was the only person who could make me feel so powerless. This alone might have been the reason I found it easier to let him go. I could never have done that with Ania.

Given time, you might have. With age, I might have grown cranky.

Never. Not you. Beautiful inside and out, until the end.

There is no end.

I pull into Mount Pelion Way, make the short drive down past the smaller houses, and then turn in to park on my driveway.
~~~

Before I get out of the car, I check my surroundings. I wonder if Smithson has told his parents anything about the forest. How would he put that into words? Weirdness? Creepiness?

Assault?

I let out a bitter, chalky laugh.

He's a hypocrite.

I thought Ania would have chimed in with this, but she has fallen silent. There seems no rhyme or reason as to what makes her come and go. I wonder if she visits Paris in a similar way, or if she is flitting between places and settling old scores, as only ghosts can do. I only hope that when she returns to me, she will stay forever.

I open the trunk of the car and I congratulate myself on a successful task. Despite the distractions, I still managed to get the salt and the knife sharpeners and rat poison and twine.

When I slam the trunk shut I see in the distance Max, Smithson's father, walking from the forest. Fear and hatred crackles in the pit of my stomach as I calculate how quickly he will reach me, and how soon I can get into my house.

Just like the other husbands of Mount Pelion Way, Max is clench-jawed and overblown, but unlike the other husbands, Max is uniquely cruel. He is known for getting away with things, having made millions with various tax-avoidance schemes. His biggest success was during the pandemic, when he skewed the price of protective clothing and equipment used by healthcare workers. I would hear him talking to the other overblown fathers on the street, rubbing his hands with glee as the mortality rate spiked. The latest allegations are sharp employment practices from which people have died because they have been deprived of salaries due or healthcare benefits. Yet each day I see him grinning in a gleaming white collar shirt, his skin as tanned and soft as a teenager's. Paris says that he has a haunted painting in his attic, but I suspect he is drinking the blood of the young.

"Eris" Max calls. "Do you have a minute?" His voice sounds calm, so maybe shame silenced his son. Regardless, I choose to play it safe, and I ignore him. Turning sharply on my heel, I head towards my front door, only to slide on the icy footpath.

The salt.

I land awkwardly on my back and pain screams through my coccyx. I feel queasy, and I am afraid I have chipped or shattered something, causing permanent damage.

"Perfect opportunity for a chat."

Already Max is standing over me with his big boots so close to me that I imagine how easy it would be to stamp on my skull.

"What did you do to my son?"

I notice he has the same bright blue eyes as Smithson, and I wonder how many young girls Max has taken to the woods or to his bedroom when his wife has been out of town. There are rumors that there is a club, in an abandoned warehouse near Newark airport, where they take turns with underage girls, boys, anyone they can get their hands on. Something to do with a dark web, payments with bitcoin.

It's true. It's all true.

Hearing (remembering?) Ania's voice charges fire through my veins.

"Keep away from me, you animal" I hiss, struggling to get to my feet. I don't manage to because the pain screams through me and freezes me in position.

"Animal? That isn't very neighborly." When he grins, he flashes the glare of expensive white teeth. "I want to help you" he continues. "Didn't you help my son earlier today? That's what neighbors do, help each other." His singsong tone, dancing round kindness and aggression, makes my eyes go blurry.

"I'm going to ask you again. What happened with Smithson?" He leans down and his face is so close that I think he might kiss me. Instead, he snatches at my skinny wrist and squeezes it. I have seen him do the same to his wife and daughter. Never his son, though. Coward.

"He was fucked up when he came home" he hisses.

I turn my face so I can gaze at the snow. I wonder what it would be like to just go to sleep like this and never wake up.

"I have never seen him cry like that" he continues. "He said you followed him into the woods."

"He's a liar."

I wonder how much the pastor saw and whether she betrayed me.

"What's the matter, not getting enough at home? Paris can't get it up, so you thought you'd follow my son into the woods and try it on with him? You're disgusting."
I start to shake my head.
"I've seen you watching him come home from practice" he said.
"That might be what is known as projection" I reply. "Anyway, you do know that your son is a rapist. Did he ever tell you that?"
Still, I will not look at him.
"You leave my kids alone. You hear?" He squeezes my wrist so hard that I fear I'll hear it snap.
"Why didn't your son leave my daughter alone? At least Smithson is still alive."
"You need help."
Unless.
"Where were you that day?" I ask him.
"What?"
Like father, like son. It could have been Max. I always assumed it was Smithson or one of the other boys, or all three. But what if *he* had been the one?

I need to get myself up. My hands feel around in the snow for a rock. I could slam it into his skull like breaking the top of a boiled egg. I might even drink his blood.

I try to push against the ground, but the pain tears through my back and down my left leg. Regardless, I push again, my hands slipping and sliding in the snow until they work their way down to the rough surface of the path. My palms start to scratch and burn as I try over and over again to get myself upright. I wonder whether my hands have started to bleed. How beautiful the crimson might appear against the lily-white snow.

He seizes the lapels of my jacket and tries to haul me up, the pain searing through my spine and down my left leg like raging hot coals. How comfortable must he feel, using his strength to attack a woman. Far less disturbing than the thought of his mighty son being overpowered by me. That flips the world upside down so we are in the underworld, and someone has left open the gates to hell.

I smell the pungent male scent of leather and something metallic and spicy.

"Fuck you" I gasp. Still on the ground, I manage to grab hold of him between his legs and I squeeze the softness. I wonder if they will explode like kumquats and if the stickiness will be sweet or sour.

He winces and drops me as if I have become a live electric cable.

"Bitch," he seethes.

"Indeed. Would you like some more?"

His face hardens, and he swings his hand back.

Careful! He could kill you. Scream "fire." That's what you always taught us. You said no one will care if you shout "Help!" so scream "fire" instead. Please.

"Fire!" I scream. "Fire!"

Get your hands off her, you fucking animal! Get off! Get off! Get off!

"Fire!" I scream again. "Get off me, you fucking animal! Get off! Get off! Get off!"

Max finally backs away from me. The last thing he wants is to be associated with the weirdness that twists me into this ugly mess.

"What the fuck" he hisses. "Freak show. What the fuck is your problem?"

After all that hard work hanging out with the other fathers of Mount Pelion Way, laughing at their inane jokes and slapping their backs at barbeques and trips to the shore . . . all that effort could lead to nothing if he becomes just another *freak* like me.

"Don't you ever touch me again," I scream at him, still on the ground in the snow. I hear my voice rippling through the street and reverberating off the flimsy facades of the little houses that surround my fortress.

I watch him run away and then there is a slam of his front door, punctuating the point that he is more of a coward than I realized.

For a moment, I feel peace. I wonder whether Ania felt this way at the end.

I hear a car approaching. Through the pain, I lift my head and I see Freya pulling into her driveway. She comes to a sudden, clumsy stop. My path and her driveway are right next to each other, so she could easily have run me over and claimed that she didn't see me. My guess is that she really didn't see me this time.

I watch her swing her car door open, then one of the rear doors, and she shouts at her children to get out. As she unstraps the youngest from the car seat, she turns and finally notices me, freezing for a moment as she inspects me on the ground. Her eyes narrow as she considers her next move.

"What is she doing?" one of the children asks. There are four of them, including Aedean. No matter their age, they all have the same golden ringlets on a chubby head with cheeks as rosy as polished red apples. I imagine climbing to my feet and racing over to take a bite out of each of them, just to hear the squeal of those overindulged cherubs.

Slamming the car doors, Freya leads her children up the driveway to her own front door, trudging through the snow a little more carefully than usual.

"What is she doing, Mommy?" one of the children asks again.
"Ignore her. Stupid old witch," she hisses.
"Yeah, the Witch Bitch rather than the Rich Bitch."
"*Aedean!*" she shouts at him. She sounds like she is going to laugh.

With the slam of Freya's front door, the street is silent again. A raven soars in the sky, higher than the houses and oldest trees.

I use every last ounce of strength to pull myself upright. A fingernail breaks as I thrust my hands against the ground, but I manage to get myself to my feet.

"What the fuck is your problem?"
I keep hearing Max's words. It was something Dylan used to say to me. Day by day, as he grew, he saw what kind of a mother he had, and he was disgusted.

"What the fuck is your problem?" Dylan would scream when I used to hurry inside the house, avoiding the other neighbors. *"No one does this,"* he would shout, pointing at my mannerisms, my clothes, my hair, and how I spent my time each day. He hated the latches and bolts and locks that I would turn and turn again each night, locking my family in upon the count of four even turns. He didn't like how orderly I would keep things, with coasters under cups and little trays under food, so I didn't have to deal with spills. He didn't like the books and artifacts all lined up in size order, and

he didn't like the fact that no one came to visit our house.

"Losers," he would call us. *"Fucking losers."* He blamed us for the fact that he was never picked in the soccer tryouts, even though he claimed that some of the other boys had less skill than him. *"No one is like you,"* he would scream at me. *"Can't you see it?"*

He blamed us when there was a birthday party he wasn't invited to, or skiing trips and weekends at the shore that he found out about at school on the Monday morning after they had already had fun without him. He blamed us for not having a best friend that he could hang out with in town, and he blamed us for having to sit in the library alone and pretend that he preferred to study during lunch breaks. Worst of all, he blamed us for what happened to Ania. *"You did this to her,"* he screamed, and screamed, and screamed. "You kept her locked up in here and then suddenly sent her away to sleepaway camp, expecting her to just know how to survive that. You saw how much she changed when she came back, yet all you cared about was keeping yourself safe in this place. Why didn't you care?"

Maybe Dylan hoped that I didn't see all of this, and that once he pointed it out to me, once he screamed at me all the things I was doing wrong, that I could change. High hopes.

There was a time when I was also fooled by this delusion. When I first met Paris, I thought that I could finally discover what it meant to be the kind of human that others seemed to want to have around. Blinded by lust, I believed that it was just circumstances that kept me trapped in this fortress, with latches and bolts and locks on every door and window. I believed that it was my father who held me prisoner like this.

But when my father died, I remained in this fortress out of choice, because I found it comforting and safer that way. The more I saw of the outside world, the more Athenas and Freyas and Junes and Maxs, the more I wanted to lock myself up in this fortress.

"What the fuck is your problem?" The same words from my son and Max, as if they crafted this together, carefully curating each word as each thread gathers to form a rope to loop a noose around my neck. Why did Max linger around my son, offering suggestions about his baseball swing and the way he would shoot a hoop?

"What the fuck is your problem?" This was something Ania would never have said to me. Trailing two years behind her brother, she never got the chance to fill the home with her own vitriol. Dylan used up all that space, leaving her on the sidelines to play with the much-neglected toys of sadness, defeat, and hopelessness.

Ania never flinched as her brother punched his way around the house. She was always following him around and trying to coax him into a different mood. No matter what he did, she adored him.

How quickly she circled this world, and then, as each day shrank that spiral, she went further into herself. And then, eventually, she disappeared altogether. Very true to form, just silently no longer here, leaving no trace, no mess, no trail of destruction.

If there ever came a day when Dylan was no longer on this earth, I would imagine that he would explode outwards, taking with him as many people as possible.

You should get inside. You'll get cold.

The pain throbs through my back and leg. I see that the chipmunks have removed the wire-mesh covers I wrapped around the end of each drainpipe. I didn't want to poison them, but I can see that I have no choice. I have heard that rat poison works well if you leave enough to cause the convulsions and bleeding and organ failure that culminate in paralysis and coma. Paris never wanted me to leave poison around the house when the children were young, and then, when they became teenagers, I feared they might use it on themselves or someone else. We never spoke of these dangers but now, with hindsight, it is glaringly obvious.

"Coming in?"

I hadn't even noticed that Paris had opened the front door.

"Welcome back," he says. He is turning fifty-one next year, but already he is starting to look old; the skin around his eyes is creasing tightly, like clothes caught on brambles.

Chapter Six

~~~

Marriage knot

I wonder how long Paris has been standing there and what he witnessed of my interactions with Max. Did he not hear me scream? If he did, and he let Max violate me like that, then the marriage knot has finally come loose. That terrifies me, to think of such a freefall into oblivion. Before Paris I always had my father to protect me from a world that breaks bonds between parents and children and unleashes all manner of chaos and disorder. If Paris leaves, I don't know how I could survive in this fortress, having to fight the suburban beast alone.

But you'll always have me.

It's not the same.

"Let's get in," Paris says with a dour tone. "It's cold."

I let him walk me inside and close the door behind us. I drop on the floor of the hallway the salt, knife sharpeners, rat poison, and twine. Having freed my hands, I can turn the latches and bolts and locks four times each way with equal force, and after miscounting one round, I repeat the process.

"I think it's locked, don't you?" he says. For all the years he has watched me go through my rituals, he has never challenged me about it. Until tonight.

"Leave it and come through," he orders. Before I can object, he points to my leg.

"Why are you limping?" he asks. Now he has reminded me of it, I can feel tiny fingernails of pain scratching and crawling inside
~~~

my nerve endings, making me want to howl.

"I'm fine," I lie. "Just twisted my back a little."

From the look on his face, I can tell that he doesn't believe me.

I long to ask if he can see Ania as I do, in the spaces between each tick of the carriage clock that sits on the mantlepiece. Then I wouldn't have to feel so lonely. We could watch for her as she flits in and out, between each heartbeat and tick of the clock; a face of wonder, then a face of pain, and back to wonder again. On and off, on and off she would play, light switching so that she was here one moment and gone the next.

But I have already shared enough with Paris. These last two years of raw pain, it has been too much for one person to handle, and I am afraid it has damaged our ability to love each other. Like blunted nerve endings, some of it might never grow back. Others who have experienced grief might have shared the burden with friends to lessen the load on their loved one, but without friends, I piled it all onto my husband. He has seen how the pain has filled my throat, leaving me unable to eat or drink, and he has seen me slip through reality in a perpetual state of light-headedness. He has heard the bolts of misplaced laughter that would pulsate throughout our day, leaving him unsettled—frightened even. Yet no matter how much I knew it was affecting him, I could not control it.

"You need to look after yourself a little bit more," Paris declares. "I've told you to see a doctor about your back."

"I'm fine."

"You don't look fine. I really want you to take this seriously. I can't end up carrying you around for the rest of your life."

I hear how much of a burden I am to him, and then malice twists in me and I wonder whether he has just been playing the role of concerned husband for the last twenty-one years. I see myself on the ground, under the sheer weight of Max's six feet, and I see my diminutive five-and-a-half-foot husband, hiding inside as he watches. Is this why I haven't yet talked to him about what happened with Max? I'm too afraid to listen to my husband lie.

I limp through to the living room where I pull at the curtains to close the gaps, preventing any potential peepholes. Through the sudden darkness, I try to translate Paris's expression. It could be the beginnings of despair as much as it could be fear, suspicion, or just plain exhaustion. I realize now that I am no longer attracted to him—neither his body nor his spirit. He was once fresh and new, and during those early days, as I drank in his bright-blue eyes and firm body, we were blind to everything but our voracious lust for one another. But now we have softened, and we have both seen too much to derive excitement from each other.

"How was it today?" he asks.
I pause before I reply. I wonder if he notices that I am blushing.
Don't tell him.
I can keep from him a secret portion of the house we share—vaults behind a hidden door and a secret key—yet I struggle when it comes to the secret of a potential friendship with Mary Anne.

"Do we have to talk about it?" I sigh.
"I'm just showing an interest in your day. You know, it's what couples do."
"Couples do a lot of things that we no longer do."
"Okay." He shrugs. "I can tell you're in a bad mood. I'll leave you be."

Don't make him angry. Please.

To think of those days, more than two decades ago, when I had just turned nineteen and I did not fear the outside world . . . I would visit my father at his office on Sixty-Eighth and Broadway, and it was during one of those visits that he asked me to take notes at one of his long and tedious meetings. For some unknown reason, my father had fired his secretary, and the replacement had been delayed, so I agreed to fill the gap. Paris was working with my father at the time, and I remember how blown away I was that someone could speak so forcefully and yet so softly. It was a sharp contrast to my explosive father, who would frequently lose his voice because he thought he had to intimidate everyone to get his way.

I remember how Paris guided everyone through the meeting with such grace that I started to call him the shepherd. In my naivety, I wondered whether this shepherd might one day guide me to a gentler and safer passage so I would not wear myself thin fighting every inconsistency. High hopes. I try not to believe that

Paris failed me. Maybe without my shepherd I would have been in a lot more trouble, burned by my own fury of discord and strife.

"Okay, that was mean of me," I sigh. "You don't have to go anywhere. I just don't feel the need to give you a blow-by-blow account every time I step outside of this house."
"I just wondered how your trip was. There was a time when we enjoyed sharing our innermost thoughts with each other."
"Fine. It was fine. What do you want to know about it?"
"There you go again, with that impatient tone. You don't have to be so unkind."

To think that there was once a time when I agonized over every word I said to Paris, running my hands over fresh sprouts of meaning and plucking only the finest, the most delicate that could season our love. Before Paris came along, I had enough self-awareness to realize I had a brutish, clumsy manner, and that my words often fell short of the full embrace that human interaction required. But until I met my shepherd, I didn't care. It was only when he showed me that I could rest for a little in his presence, that life was not only about vigilance and overpowering, that I knew I wanted him to stick around. So I kept Paris satiated by sprinkling our conversations with the finest words. I told him that he was *beautiful, fascinating, my soulmate* and *the one.* I even let him think that he was a monster in bed. I should have known that all of this was unsustainable.

"It was the usual. You know, just the usual. Too many people, not enough air to breathe. Everyone staring at me like I'm a circus act."
"I'm sure people don't think that."
"Really?"
"Did you see anyone we know?"
"Her next door. Freya Aphrodite."
"Oh. Were you polite?"
"Why do you always ask that? Why don't you inquire how she was with me?"
"I was getting to that."
"Well, I gave as good as I got."
"So you ignored each other."
"Yes. But I'm sure she was whispering about me as soon as I left."

"How can you be sure?"

After all these years I still don't know whether Paris is too naïve or ignorant to know about the twists in a person's soul. No matter who he meets, he dazzles them with that smile of his. It once shone like a beacon in my darkened world, and I viewed it as a ray of hope or a fiery torch to ward off the suburban beast. But now I wonder if he just wants to blind me to the truth.

"I just know her. Freya cannot resist an attack on someone's character."

"Much like you are doing right now."

"Stop. You're supposed to be on my side. In sickness and in health, 'til death do us part, and forsaking all others."

"I am on your side, and I always have been."

To my surprise, he takes my hand and squeezes it. I notice that the skin on his palm is rougher than usual.

They advise against signing legal contracts and driving cars under the influence of drugs or alcohol, but they never tell you about the dangers of signing a marriage contract under the influence of lust. I would have done anything to keep those half-day marathons when we became dehydrated and dirty, experimenting with parts of our body that had until then remained uncharted. I always wondered how Paris reconciled a return to work each day with my father after he had done so many sordid things with his daughter. It was that blatant duplicity that left me with one eye on my gentle-mannered husband, always acknowledging the possibility that another version of him could exist. And in this alternate version of Paris Brown, he could be propagating the perception up and down Mount Pelion Way that I am his captor, and it was because of me alone that our lives are so tightly knitted together. Even worse, he blames me for the loss of both of our children.

"You could be a little kinder when you see Freya," he says, his tone suddenly hardening again.

I drop his hand.

"I hear her husband just lost his job, so they are going to face some pretty tough times from now on."

This is not the first time he has taken the side of the people on Mount Pelion Way. I don't want to be here with him right now, but I have nowhere else to go.

"Where did you see Freya?" he asks.

"The post office. I needed stamps," I lie.

"Thank you for getting the salt."

"No problem," I sigh. I choose not to chastise him for placing the Post-it reminder over the picture of our daughter. "The man at the hardware store kept asking about Dylan."

"Oh. I think Dylan helped the guy out a few times, and he earned himself some extra bucks."

"Why? We always gave him what he needed."

"I guess he wanted a little independence."

"Yes, well, he got that in the end, didn't he?"

Paris flinches, and I know I should be more careful. If my husband does eventually leave, I wonder if it will be in the light of day or stealthily, under the cover of night. I hope he is not afraid of what I might do in response; I saw how wide his eyes were when I unpacked the knife sharpeners, rat poison, and twine. He should know that I could never hurt him.

Love and hatred, such close bedfellows.

My father told me I was too young to marry and that we should wait a few years, but I could only last eleven months before I defied him. Despite the strength associated with the Gall name, I chose to lose it in favor of the paper-bag simplicity of the Brown family name. What could be safer and simpler than the unadventurous Browns, who never thought to explore further than their little village in western Massachusetts, and who only named their son Paris because he was conceived in a bedroom that was decorated with a watercolor of the Eiffel Tower? The Browns of paper-bag simplicity—I never stopped to think that when a paper bag is wrapped around something damp and dirty, something as dark and toxic as me, it ends up just as contaminated and disposable.

My back and leg are starting to throb, so I finally allow myself to sit. With all this change and chaos, it helps to feel a sense of safety and order in this living room. Here are my blank-faced terracotta warriors lined up in perfect symmetry. Over there are my books in ascending size order. In this stillness, with a sense of perfect alignment, time finally stops, and I can make space for

Ania to return.

I was here all along.

There you are, reflected off the smooth surface of the vases that my father brought back from China. I hear the clink of the lid as your clumsy child-sized hands felt inside, searching for jewels or fairies or even just the sweet hope of candy. You must have been about six or seven at the time.

I never found any.

No, you didn't. By your teenage years I guess you were looking for cash or cigarettes or secrets.

Remember how I used to play with those brass geese that your father brought back from Laos?

Yes. I would tell you about faraway places that my father would visit as he accumulated more wealth. I promised you I would take you to every one of those countries.

And then I got older and realized he was plundering resources simply to make a rich family richer.

It meant that you could live in a big house like this.

Whitewash.

I can't change what has already happened.

I notice there is a chip out of the back of one of the terracotta warriors. I glance around the room, half-expecting to find the culprit hiding behind the long, thick curtains.

"What happened?" I ask Paris.

"Come again?"

"There's a chip in one of the warriors."

"Oh really? Never noticed."

Paris looks tired. She was his daughter too, after all, and I need to keep reminding myself of this. He never used to look this weary of me, and my questions, and my constant vigilance for the slightest details around our home.

How excited he looked in the days leading up to our wedding. Just two months previously, we thought the world might end, so many people were in a rush to do this sort of thing. We secured November 2, 2001 as the next available date at the registrar, and we hoped that we might embark on something spectacular. But when the day finally came, when we sat in the wood-paneled office and exchanged our rings, I felt no excitement. The registrar raced through the ceremony so quickly that I was married without the chance to change my mind.

I still remember how that office smelled of mothballs, and how I cried in the bathroom afterwards.

Twenty-one years later, and I am waving a terracotta warrior at my husband. "Who did this?" I ask him. I feel petty, and I don't even care about it, but I have nothing else to discuss with him. It is this or retire to bed.

"My goddess," he says with a laugh, "that could've happened any time over the last decade or two."

"Oh come on. I would've noticed."

"Would you? A lot has been going on in the last couple of years." Why does he remain so calm when he says that? Clearly we both know what pain the *last couple of years* have caused.

"I just wish you would care a little more" I sigh.

"About a statue?"

"About anything."

"Let me take a closer look," he says. When he leans over my shoulder, I smell garlic on him, and it makes me feel nauseous.

"That?" he asks, pointing to the chip that is the size of a dime. "That's nothing. No one is going to notice."

"But I notice."

"Okay, I'll fix it for you tomorrow."

"Why not today?"

"I have a few things to straighten out today."

"Like what?"

Paris starts to fuss about the room, attempting to straighten cushions on the sofa but only making them more untidy.

After our wedding ceremony, we returned to the home that I had been sharing with my father, and this fortress became Paris's home too. I now see that my father was right when he said that we were too young to get married; neither of us had explored the distant corners of our own minds, let alone each other's. And we certainly had not appreciated the dangers posed by dark corners of the world that surrounded us. Before Paris, I had been so reckless and naïve, waking up in strangers' beds without remembering much of what had happened. How could I possibly protect myself, let alone the fragility of a new relationship, if I did not see how twisted life could be? Too quickly, after just two months of marriage, I was pregnant.

How strange to think of our fibers, our hair and skin and eye color, even the pallor of our skin, twisting together to multilayer our genes and make a child. The first composite of Paris and I would be Dylan, our son. Newly in love and newly pregnant, I wanted to create someone as far removed from me as possible. I wanted no hint of myths or legends, and I tried to encourage his spirit, his genetics, the curve of his chin, to follow the shepherd towards Paris's side of the family. My husband had Welsh heritage from more than a century ago, when his ancestors sailed across the Atlantic from Aberystwyth on a trading ship loaded with lead and tanning bark and coal. I thought of Dylan Thomas, I thought of pastures and rolling hills far away from the smog-filled clouds of New Jersey. So it felt like a safer option to lead my newborn son to these pastures and rolling hills. Better that than the discord and strife of my own genetic chaos.

But still, Dylan found a way back to the fire and vengeance that defines the genetic makeup of the Gall family. I should have known. There were omens all around me, even from the first hour of his life, when the nurse explained that there is a dragon on the Welsh flag. How could I have missed that? I tried to laugh it off, and that worked until my battle-lustful son discovered his tongue and he unleashed his first weapon: His words of fire.

Two years later came our daughter. By then I thought it pointless trying to search for a name that might take me away from myths or legends, so Paris and I chose Ania because we liked the sound of it. Pure and simple, as she was the moment she opened her eyes to me. It was only later that I discovered the name had associations with trouble, but by then I'd realized she needed all the help she could get to stand up to Dylan and the rest of the world. I urged her to have a little fight to stir up trouble and not let Dylan or the world swallow her whole. I was foolish to ever believe that I could bestow such power on her by simply giving her a name.

After twenty-one years of marriage, we are back where we started, with only the two of us. Only this time we are filled with frustrations rather than lust.

"What is with you?" I ask him. "Why are you so fidgety?"
"Nothing. I'm fine."
"Oh come on, what is it?"
He starts to bite a loose flap of skin that hangs from the small finger on his left hand.
"I'm fine."
"You've said that. Look, either spit it out or leave me in peace."
By now he is dancing on the spot like a five-year-old who is about to wet himself.
"Okay, okay. Cassandra is coming."
"What? When?"
"Tomorrow. I forgot to tell you."
He races to the kitchen, and I hear him rattling each drawer.
"What are you doing in there?"
"Finding the tablecloths," he replies. "The ones with the lilac flowers stitched around the edges. Do you know where they are?"
"No."

Chapter Seven

~~~

Insanity and the stranglehold of grief

There is another reason I don't tell Paris that Ania is back in my life.

He would never understand.

That's true, my love. He would probably get straight on the phone to Marigold Meeches, Licensed Clinical Social Worker. She would say that I'm suffering from psychosis, and if I don't drop the act, she will admit me to a psychiatric ward.

I remember Ms. Meeches. Before the pandemic she covered our school counselor when she was off having a baby.

She did? Meeches never told me that. I'm sure that's a conflict of interest, but then nothing surprises me about that woman.

Do you remember her old rust bucket of a car?

I do. And after the pandemic she replaced it with a shiny new blue sports car. She made quite a profit off all those stressed-out people who were losing their jobs, losing their homes, and losing their loved ones.

I can't see you going to a therapist.

Neither can I. Your father made me go, a few weeks after . . .

I know. You don't have to say it.

Does it hurt for me to talk about it?

Not now. Nothing hurts any more.

I don't know whether to feel sad or relieved about that.

Maybe ask Ms. Meeches how you should feel.

Funny. She has a habit of doing that.
~~~

I once said to her, outright, "You should tell me how I should feel because everything so far seems to be wrong".

You spoke to her at school?

Yes.

About what?

Silence.

Ania? Why did you need to talk to a therapist?

I don't want to talk about it, Mom.

No. We don't have to. I'm sorry.

It's okay.

Do you know I challenged Meeches about her new sports car?

What did she say?

She just fluttered her eyes as she always did when I unearthed a truth that was a little too inconvenient.

Do you remember her long, painted nails and her hair extensions?

I do. I also remember the sweat that soaked through the back of her clothes. At the end of each session, when she got up to walk me to the door, a pungent odor of ripe flesh followed her through the room.

Stop it, you are being mean again. I bet you didn't let it drop about the new car.

I didn't. I asked her straight out, "How can you afford that when therapists are known for surviving on a dime and a prayer?"

"I am more interested in how you are feeling today," she replied, looking distinctly satisfied with her answer. I noticed she had a slither of spinach stuck between her two front teeth.

"Sure," I snapped back at her, "and we have plenty of time for that, but why won't you answer the question?"

She told me this wasn't relevant to our work. She liked to use that strategy to control the dialogue. She was there to help me, but only if I played her game. To do that, she expected me to dumb down with the medication I flushed down the toilet. She expected me to ignore every inconsistency and every injustice.

"I heard you increased your fees twice since the pandemic started."

I hadn't heard this, but I wanted to trap her in her own inconsistencies. Paris would say that I was taunting her. During the first year after . . . well, during that difficult time. . . .

You can say it, you know. After my death. . . .

. . . he was only brave enough to point out my cruelty when he had the therapist present to support him. She seemed to agree with anything he had to say, smiling and willing him on as she threw around vague concepts like *healthy relationships, assertiveness,* and *secure attachment* as if she were using them to sage the room.

Marigold stared at the clock, no doubt willing it to run out the therapeutic hour. When she failed at such black magic, she switched tactics and attempted to shut up shop on me.

"I am beginning to wonder whether you want to be here today," she said. "It is important that you buy into this and trust the process. If you are not willing to be here and do the work then perhaps you would like to reschedule."

"If we do, will I be charged for today?"

I see her as a vulture who feeds on the carcasses of the stressed, depressed, and lonely.

"We have discussed my reschedule and cancellation policies. If you would like another copy, I would be happy to provide it."

She was no better than an automated telephone service. *Press 1 for empathy, press 2 for a reminder of the boundaries of a therapeutic relationship, and press 3 to terminate this endeavor.*

"Do you remember the first time I was here, just forty-eight hours after my daughter died, and you wanted to swipe my credit card before you even knew my daughter's name?"

"I think we need to draw things to a close today."

"Her name was Ania, in case you have forgotten."

"What I suggest is that you write this down in a journal, and perhaps we could explore it more when we meet next week."

"Oh, don't worry, I write it all down anyway. I keep a careful log of everything that happens, just in case I need it in the future."

"For what?"

I could see her hand hovering over the shiny red buttons she had earned with her master's in clinical social work. One was to call the police for suicidal intent, and the other was to call the police for homicidal intent.

"I was referring to a reflective journal to explore your emotions, but your tone suggests there may be an ulterior motive. What sort of recordkeeping were you referring to?"

There was also the termination button that she seemed all too eager to use, especially if she was threatened with legal action.

"My goodness, Marigold, you seem jumpy. I thought this was your job, to keep your cool and contain my freneticism. If I can't unleash it in here, where can I?"

"There is a limit that even I have to set."

"Oh yes, boundaries. Those elusive things that are supposed to be clear yet flexible, consistently inconsistent, right? Flexible when it benefits you and rigid when it applies to me."

At that point, my head started to spin. I could remember all our inconsistent conversations, when Meeches would talk me in circles. She would speak of *appropriate grief* and *inappropriate grief, prosocial behavior* and *authenticity, individuality* and *following the herd,* and any attempt I made to clarify anything was met with a smile, a nod, and a *Yes and no and both* before she laughed. *Confusing, I know!*

Like someone who is willing to tolerate abuse for the sake of the kids (even though their blackened eyes prevent them from seeing that the kids have long since left), I continued to show up for my sessions with Marigold Meeches. Each week I would arrive on time, pay, and tolerate the inconsistencies, the thinly veiled self-interest, and the imbalance of power that was misused on a weekly basis. Besides, I had nowhere else to go.

I was never honest with Meeches, any more than I was honest with Paris. If I had been, I can imagine how Meeches would sweat with glee as she signed the paperwork to get me out of her office and into a secure unit. And this would have destroyed Paris. He would finally have to give up his delusion that everything can be okay if you just smile and ignore it for long enough. Paris the watchful one, the alert shepherd of his familial flock. Always attentive to our children and always alert to the wanderings of my mind. He was a comfort, and he was calm, but that meant he had a tendency to take naps, and when he woke up, both of our children were gone. Not so watchful after all.

When I returned home from challenging Marigold about her new sports car, Paris held my shoulders and glowered at me. I knew I was in trouble for being so combative.

"She is only trying to help," he told me. "You have to stop

this."

He did not call me his *goddess,* his *love*, or anything else softened and endearing. In fact, in recent times, our fights have made me think that Paris views me as a proprietary interest, an asset to maneuver. What makes things worse is that Meeches, a woman herself, appears to support this patriarchal bullshit. She implies this in the way she judges my behavior, and I am sure that if I don't shape up soon, she will happily diagnose me *pathologically obstructive*, if there is such a thing, or *antisocial*, or even good, old-fashioned *deranged*.

"The only thing she's doing is helping herself to a shiny new sports car," I told my husband that day. "Just wait—by next year, it'll be a red one. I hear those go faster than the blue ones."
"Come on. Just stop."

He must be weary after two decades of defending my poor behavior and protecting himself from my explosions of anger and withdrawals. I am not surprised that he has lost his devout faith in love, no matter how many of the pastor's sermons try to convince him otherwise.

Why are you so afraid of ending up alone? You always told us that it was good to have time on your own.
You're right, and I'm surprised you remember that.
"Stand alone in the playground," you would tell me when no one would play with me.
It still hurts to remember that, to imagine how you had to suffer the bullies at school.
I didn't mind after you said it was okay to be alone. So why does it frighten you so much?

Being alone leaves you vulnerable to the distortions that come at night.

And I leave it at that. I choose not to tell her about my father, her grandfather, who would howl at the moon when he could not find his wife. He still lingers in this fortress, throwing aside the occasional chair and leaving the scent of his bourbon. On the nights that he drinks, he loses his wife again, only to sober up and reunite with her once more, a perpetual loop of anguish and relief.

This fortress is ripe for haunting, and not just in the welcome kind that brings my beautiful Ania back to me. There are worse things that happened if we go further back. This land is still stained by the blood of the Lenni Lenape people who were raped and decapitated by my forefathers, just so the Galls could seize this land and make their millions. The land, the soil, the roots and the tree branches, they never forget.

Meeches tried to talk to me about trauma, but I didn't want to hear it from someone like her. Later that night, however, when I returned home to my fortress, I slowly unpacked each word, holding it up to the light to see if I could make it fit.

Trauma, casting ripples down the line of generations. Trauma, through the process of epigenesis, altering the regulation of gene expression, changing the molecules of our chromosomes. Distorting me. My father, grief-stricken after the sudden, early death of his wife, took to beating me when he had drunk too much of the bourbon that he loved so much. He would howl at the moon, becoming Frankenstein who ultimately made me his creature, this bitter, twisted and fearful flincher.

"Freak." They would call me that school. "Why do you flinch so much? Why are your dresses so dirty? Why don't you have a mom to clean them for you? Did you scare her away? Did you hit her over the head and chop her up into tiny pieces? Did you eat her?"

Trauma bonded me to this fortress. When Paris came along, I thought that he might free me, but without realizing it, we trapped ourselves here along with my father.

Even after he died, my father still haunted us. At night, I could hear him scrabbling around behind the fake wall panel that hides a door that leads to a secret room that I was forbidden to tell Paris about. Was that another way my father kept me his creature? The secrets, the collusion, as interdependent and ugly as inbreeding.

I am sure it is only when my father is sober, when he is reunited with my mother, that he sees, with horror, what creature he has created in me. For years I feared that he was haunting the attic because he was waiting to destroy me, to extinguish his shame for creating me that way. Don't all parents fear that they have made so many mistakes they wish they could reverse time and start again? To clear up the mess they created.

Is that what really destroyed Ania? My father wanted an

auburn-haired girl dead, and he mistook his granddaughter for me?

Meeches would say that I am now trauma bonded to Paris, and we are trapped together in this fortress. She would call this home of ours a tomb, and she would be right. I will never let anyone invade this sacred place.

But Aunty Cassie is arriving soon.

My heart freezes at the prospect of her intrusion. I swear that whenever I turn my back, my sister-in-law is trying to find clues of the insanity she suspects of me. I can just picture the chaos as she blusters in, arriving later than the time she agreed with Paris and walking in a trail of dirt. One time she walked in dog feces, and she just sat on the sofa while Paris and I tried to clean up the mess.

Cassandra Brown was Cassandra Ford until she discovered all the affairs that her husband had indulged in. Salt was rubbed into the wound when he took everything, because she had been so blissfully in love that *dear Cassie* failed to read the prenuptial agreement he snuck into bed with them the week before their wedding.

Now she is forty-two, working as a receptionist in a local dental practice ten miles from here and is renting a small apartment in Fort Lee. There she drinks into the night as she sobs over the social media updates of her ex-best friend, the new Mrs. Ford.

Once inside, Cassandra will stare at the latches and bolts and locks, and say *Gee, are you expecting to be robbed tonight?* She says this every time, as if she is seeing the place for the first time. I don't know if she means to do this, but she has a way of making me feel like Paris and I are a strange and unsightly speck on her horizon. For Paris, his sister is everything, but I suspect that her obsession with an ex-husband and ex-best friend leaves little room for concerns about a brother, let alone her sister-in-law. Even if that brother and sister-in-law had their family gutted in one twisted night.

Paris is still racing around the house, straightening things that were not out of place.

"It will be good to see her," he says. "I realize I should have told you sooner."

I wonder whether my husband kept this from me until the last moment so I couldn't object, so I couldn't try to change his mind. I know the threat Cassandra poses now that Ania and Dylan have gone. She will try and make Paris see that there is nothing left here for him. And I wouldn't be so scared if I did not believe it myself.

Chapter Eight

~~~

Invasion

Paris watches me carefully over the rim of his wine glass. He is ready to jump in if I swing sideways and launch an attack on his sister. He has seen it all before.

A solitary dust mote parachutes down through the air between us, and I catch it between each heartbeat. I smile at my husband, but he does not offer one in reply.

I will play nicely with Cassandra. I would concede too much ground too soon if I leapt on every little arrow she fires over the parapet. When she arrives late, for example, I will not react when she blames the layout of our town. I will not snap back when she offers her commentary on the number of shops that are now boarded up, plastered with FOR RENT signs that scream of desperate landlords. I know that this is groundwork to prepare for the speech that she will deliver with her back to me, urging Paris to pack up his bags and move into her apartment building in Fort Lee.

I should not squander my time anticipating petty squabbles with my sister-in-law when I could recreate images of my daughter. As I wait for Cassandra, stillness descends and the living room goes dark like a movie theatre, and I can see her once again, dazzling with white light projected onto the wall with all the awe of cinematic beauty. I hear my voice from behind an imaginary camera, urging her to smile as I remind her to put her shoulders back a little more—so much primping and preening when what I
~~~

already had before me was perfect. Why did I have to spoil it?

"Do you see her?" I ask my husband.

"Hmm?" He is distracted by something, and he jumps up and races across the room.

"I am trying to tell you something about our daughter," I say, but he has already run up the stairs, muttering something about the embroidered tablecloth that Cassandra admired the last time she was here.

"You already tried to find that" I call up to him.

Then the doorbell rings.

"She's here."

I really don't want to be the one to answer it. Neither Cassandra nor I want to be left together without Paris to mediate.

"Just answer it," he shouts down to me.

I wait for a minute, hoping he will dash down the stairs, but then I give in, hissing "Fuck sake" before I open the door.

Cassandra offers me no embrace, walking in snow-dampened leaves that are plastered to her high heels. She stands in the hallway, waiting for me to take her coat as she offers me an air kiss. I can see that she is scanning the hallway for her brother, and the beginnings of panic start to break out across her face.

"He's upstairs," I say. "Looking for a tablecloth."

She inspects my knotted hair and wash-faded skin, noting the lackluster clothes that hang off my softening curves, and as she returns her eyes to mine, she appears horrified.

"Oh, fun, amazing" she says with a grimace, her upper lip sticking to the dryness of her teeth.

"Great." I shove my hands deep inside my pockets, uncertain what else to do or say.

"Gee, are you expecting to be robbed tonight?" She gestures to the latches and bolts and locks. "I heard crime levels were on the increase in Rotherwell."

"The crime levels are not rising, at least not in this town. On the other hand, we are being overrun by poky, small-minded parochials who try to squeeze their way into my life. Now *that* is a danger I need to keep locked out."

"You always talk in riddles," she says with a laugh, waving her hand at me as if she is dismissing the hired help. She chooses not to understand, she refuses to make space in her mind for me. If I were Freya, June, or Athena, Cassandra would agree with every damned thing I said because they all have the same big, blown-out hair and the same sunglasses perched on top of their heads. They have been taught that birds of a similar plumage should flock together, because there is *safety in numbers*. I do not look like them, so they have no reason to listen to me, but if they did, I would tell them how lethal it seemed to exist inside one of those flocks. I have seen the vicious competitiveness over the slightest flutter, each stabbing at the other with a razor-sharp beak. I have also seen how their close confines spread diseases and viruses. How quickly they have forgotten how unsafe it was in these numbers, and how quickly these flocks spread the Covid virus, overpowering and weakening each host before it moved on to the next.

And the germs are just a small part of the potential for invasion. These birds of a feather allow each other into their thoughts and hopes and dreams. They seem unaffected by the prospect of whole battalions of these invading forces rifling through the private corners of their mind as they lay a flag to seize each new friend as their own possession. I could not bear that, to become someone else's so my deeds and thoughts are dictated by others: A protectorate, a subject of someone else's empire.

When I tried to explain this to Marigold Meeches, she held up her hand and requested my silence. She said "Freya, Athena, and June are friends. That is a good thing."
I shook my head in reply. "It isn't good when those friends try to become your conquerors," I explained.
She never gave me a straight reply to that, never offered a clear demarcation between compromise and capitulation, or love and abuse. So I thought it safer to live within the confines of my fortress, and this worked out, except for the occasional invasion by Paris's sister.

Be nice to Aunty Cassie.

I know I have lost time again because Cassandra is now sitting on the sofa. How did she get there?

"*Oh, fun,*" she says, blinking like a dazzled deer.
"What?"

"Great," she coos, realizing we have lost the thread of our social exchange.

I wonder if I called her Freya without even realizing it.

"Cassie!" Paris calls, running down the stairs. His feet thunder like a locomotive, and I flinch at how this house is starting to sag under the weight of time.

He joins her on the sofa. Their arms thread around each other, fastening their bodies together in a tight embrace.

"Have you been working out?" she coos. "You've got muscles again."

"Oh, come now," Paris says, laughing. "Just all the heavy lifting to keep this place in order."

I feel like I have seen this scene in a movie, where the woman wants a promotion, so she gushes compliments to her boss. Or, in a horror movie, where she tries to distract the villain so he does not stab her.

"You are so beautiful" he says, smiling.

"Thank you, my love. Lies, but I'll take them anyway. And can I just say this—and it is because I love you—but you need to get out of dodge and quick. I can see the signs all over the place. Rotherwell is not what it used to be."

I can hear the ticking of the carriage clock, and it pops goosebumps up and down my arms. It is the flicking of nails right next to my ears, it is the wail of a dying fox, it is the creak and sway of a rope in the breeze.

"This used to be a great commuter town for New York," she adds, "but who's commuting to that rathole these days? Since the pandemic, it's become a ghost town."

Paris looks nervously at me.

"This is a dignified place but it's miserable as the gallows," Cassandra continues. "You would make a killing if you sold now, but if you wait, you might end up having to give it away."

She is trying to alchemize the death of my daughter and create good fortune for herself. One person's curse is another person's fortune, so now that her husband has abandoned her, why not plug that gap with a brother who will go fetch anything you throw for him?

"I mean, gee, Cassie, that is a big ask for someone who grew up in this home. You might have forgotten, but Eris was raised here. Her father, and her father's father, the whole Gall family have owned this land for eternity. The place has memories for her."

He chose not to say *good* memories.

"Memories for you too," I add. "There were memories here for you with me and Dylan and Ania."

Why won't he look at me?

"I should bring out the photo albums," I say. "Perhaps you just need to be reminded."

"I haven't forgotten. That isn't what I was saying." He glances at his sister with that *What the hell is she talking about?* smirk.

"Let me fetch you a drink," he says, turning to his sister. "Wine? Vodka?"

"Nothing, thanks. I'm fine."

I catch Paris's eye, and he seems equally surprised. Cassandra notices our reaction.

"I'm cutting back," she says, smiling.

I want to ask her if she has stopped drinking because her husband left her. I want to ask whether her drinking drove him away because she was too clumsy and sweaty and smelly for anyone to want to share her home. I want to ask her if she is here now out of spite, because if she cannot have a husband, then she doesn't want me to; her spite is a noxious substance that she is going to use to keep my husband away from me, in the same way her noxious alcohol, which oozed from her every pore, repelled her own husband.

Be nice to her.

"I am being nice," I say, a little too loudly.

"What?"

Cassandra looks a little scared.

I should explain myself, but I don't know what to say. I could tell her that I hear my daughter even though I know she has gone, and I could say that I also see Ania when I am calm enough to allow her in. None of this would be received well, by Cassandra or Paris. So, I remain silent, making my sister-in-law even more uncomfortable.

"How is Dylan keeping?" she asks, looking to her brother for reassurance. Her eyes are wide, and I am certain that she is about to scream at him for not doing more to end her discomfort around me. She has raged at Paris many times before, and the worst of it was during her divorce. Throughout all of that, he never wavered. It makes me sad to see that he has grown up with volatility, only to marry it.

"I haven't heard from him for a while," she adds as she stares at me.

"No, I imagine you haven't," I reply. This time, I offer a smile that seems to unsettle her because she breaks her gaze and glances around the room.

"Is he okay?" she asks.

"Yes. He says that he is doing well," I lie.

"Tell him to call his aunt once in a while. I can't remember the last time I heard his voice."

"I will."

"Look," Cassandra sighs. "I need to free you of this place. I know a good Realtor who can help you. She is a good friend, so she won't screw you around." Already she has her handbag open and she retrieves a shiny gold business card, thrusting it into Paris's hand. "I'll make sure she handles it properly, and she could have you out of here in a few months."

"Why are you doing this?" I snap.

Be nice.

"For you." Her eyes are so wide that she looks like she has just seen something horrific. I look behind me, hoping to find Ania instead of Dylan, or worse, my father.

"I want you both to live a little," she continues, "while you still can. Don't you want to see the world? If you sold up and bought an apartment, you could stop stagnating in this place. You have slowed your life down so much that this place is growing around you, like vines around a dead tree."

"I am fine. We are both fine."

She thinks I sit here all day and do nothing. She does not see how frantic I get when I race from latch to bolt and lock, checking each one four times and searching for signs of an intrusion. She does not know that I have discovered small changes within this fortress: The cup that I drink from and put in the sink that mysteriously reappears on the kitchen table. The lamp I turn off when I leave the room then find shining brightly with renewed vigor. I hear the scuttling of feet in the roof voids and attic above my head, and I smell them, that yeasty, sickly sweet curdle of spoiled life. They leave sticky patches from their footsteps, even moments after I have mopped the floor clean.

I wish it were Ania playing games with me, but I know it is a malevolent force. Something that wants to destroy me.

Has Cassandra forgotten how I once spoke to her about all of this? I shouldn't have said so much, but it was just a matter of weeks after Ania's death, and I didn't know what I was saying. I told her about the shaken door handles that I heard at night. I suspected the people on Mount Pelion Way; the suburban beast was closing in because it knew I was finally vulnerable. Cassandra let me hold her hand as I spoke of more. I couldn't catch my breath as I tried to keep up with telling her it all, and my palms were so sweaty that I made hers damp. I was afraid that my voice would slip out through the gaps around the doors and the windows, to the ears of the suburban beast, so I leaned in and whispered into her ear.

"Do you know what they think?" I asked her. I must have tickled her skin with my breath because I saw her shudder.
She shook her head in reply.
"They think I had something to do with it. They think that I killed her."
I whispered quietly that they were gaining momentum, and could easily overpower me. I thought she would believe me and want to help fortify this place. I felt a rush of hope charge through every vein that I might no longer be alone with this.

Instead, she flinched. She broke free of my sweaty hand and called for her brother. She told him that I needed professional help, and that is when he took me for my first appointment with that vulture Marigold Meeches.

I was foolish to think she would understand. How could she, when she had never felt someone growing inside her, day by day adjusting their shape and size to fit her, stretching into her crevices like an inquisitive explorer. How could she understand, when she had never watched that fascinating explorer push out into the world, still holding on with one hand, but with the other outstretched to discover the world. How could she understand, when she had never felt that explorer's recoil when things were too hot, and that flinch when things came at them too quickly. And when they explored further, when there were brambles and sharp things, how could Cassandra understand any of this when she had never experienced catastrophic failure, when that explorer slipped away so suddenly, forever out of reach?

The doorbell rings.

Dylan?

Is it really him?

"That's my surprise!" Cassandra squeals as she jumps from the sofa and races to the door.

She returns to the living room with a tall man that she is squeezing into her side.

"Meet Larry, a true friend who has been supporting me through these recent dark days. We met at a Peloton class and have been firm friends ever since. Larry, this is my brother, Paris, and his wife, Eris."

"Great to meet you both."

Larry grins too much and his hair is ice white in sharp contrast to his tanned skin. He is long and foppish, and his eyes scan the room as he waits for a reply. I want to ask him what he makes of the darkness, with curtains covering every window, and I would like to know what he makes of the books arranged in ascending-size order, and the blank-faced terracotta warriors lined up in perfect symmetry. Such order and such a contrast to my knotted hair and stained shirt, and the smell that must be emanating after three days of not washing. Does he notice that I have been itching so much that my fingernails are crusted with blood?

"Won't you join us for a drink?" my husband offers in his outdoors voice that makes him sound stronger and more confident than he really is.

"That would be wonderful, thank you," Larry replies.

"We have wine and vodka, or if you want to join Cassandra with her health cleanse, she is having nothing whatsoever."

Paris is trying too hard, and his face is blushing a little too brightly. I wonder what a heart attack would look like. I have heard how people jump to action in response, but I would not know where to begin. I am afraid I would just go up to bed and sleep until it was over.

We sit in silence while Paris gets the drinks.

When he returns, he realizes that no one has been speaking, and he gives me a hardened look.

"So how long have you known my sister, Larry?" he asks, still staring at me.

"We've been hanging out for about a year now."

I watch as Larry gives my sister-in-law's knee a playful squeeze. She straightens her body as a flower would come into bloom, and I wonder if she is remembering what it was like to receive male attention. This could tip the balance, filling her with the joy of hope, or crushing her with despair for all that she has lost. Ania would tell me off for sitting back and waiting for the drama to unfold. "That's unkind," she would say. "You should want the best for her."

"We haven't been *hanging out* as a couple," Cassandra giggles. "He's so gay—gay as gay can be. All the better-looking ones are."

"Aww, Cassie, come on," Larry smirks.

"Are you staying long?" I ask.

"Oh, Jesus, Eris," Cassandra hisses. "Way to make a guy feel welcome."

"I didn't expect company."

"You knew I was coming," Cassandra sighs as she rolls her eyes.

"I didn't expect strangers."

"Larry isn't a stranger; he's my friend."

"He's a stranger to me."

"Why does she have to do this?" Cassandra is shaking her head and looks at her brother. "Why can't your wife just be nice and welcoming?" she continues. "Lord knows she needs people in her life."

"I don't need anyone," I hiss.

"Oh, you do. But you've scared everyone away."

"Cassie."

"I'm sorry, Paris, but I had to say it." She turns back to me. "You may think you have everything under control, but your husband sees things differently. You are losing it, Eris."

"I didn't say *that*."

"When we spoke on the phone, you told me how worried you are."

"Worried, yes," Paris replies, nodding his head. "I didn't say anything about *losing it*. Come on, Cassie."

"I know you've been through a lot," Cassandra says as she squeezes out a smile, "but it's been two years now. You have to move on at some point. You shouldn't feel ashamed to go out, to live your life again. Everyone deserves a bit of happiness every now and then. There's no shame in that."

"Shame?" I snap. "Why should I feel ashamed? I'm fucking angry, I'm fucking livid, I want to tear . . ."

I can feel my father's rage squeezing my fists tightly. If he were here, he would smite them with his red lightning to crack open their skulls. I once saw him punch a man so hard that blood came out of his ear. It was some official from the town who had been sent to inspect something— maybe a fence or structure we were adding to the house. My father hadn't even raised his voice when the man waggled a finger in his face. I knew it was a bad idea for him to do this because my father started to massage his stubble ever so slowly, as a carpenter might sand some wood, and he only did this when he was about to let his rage take over.

At first I thought the man was dead, and I think my father did too. He told me to go inside and not look, but I hovered at the doorway, more out of curiosity about what he would do next. Would he dig a hole in the backyard and bury the body? And if I did not follow his rules, would he do the same to me next? I heard the splash of the hose when I realized my father was spraying the man, and after a cough and splutter, the town official was back on his feet and out of our yard.

I always wonder why my father didn't end up in prison for that. It probably had something to do with his wealth and how easily the police could be paid off if the price was right. For all that the Galls were lacking in subtlety and social grace, they had plenty of money to pay off any official who needed to be silenced. I came to learn about the power of our wealth when the child protection officers, like puppets on a string, never returned after that one visit. How foolish they looked on my doorstep that day, with their fixed stares and round blushes painted on their cheeks. I knew the dumpy looking one would be the most incensed when she found out that her boss had been paid off by me. She probably still cannot sleep when she thinks of the injustice of it all.

I feel someone grabbing my wrist, and I expect to see my father when I turn my head. But it is Paris.

"You should go rest for a while." It was an instruction not a suggestion. "I'll handle dinner."

We have been entwined together in this tangled knot of grief, and now Paris wants to cut himself free. I can see that now.

I choose not to fight back this time and retreat up the stairs.

Alone in the attic, I hear the laughter of my husband, his sister, and her friend. I would once feel excluded from the laughter that echoed outside my home, from the people of Mount Pelion Way. But now the weapon of exclusion is being wielded inside my fortress. The dangers have got in, no matter how many latches and bolts and locks.

In this isolation, I run my hands over the fake wall panel. Gently, I pop it open to reveal the hidden door. Retrieving the secret key from underneath a floorboard, I unlock the door and let myself into my private sanctuary.

There I run my hands over the remnants of my daughter's life. I have her schoolwork and report cards and birthday and Christmas cards. I also have her clothes and cell phone and charger, along with her artwork and books and photographs. And of course, I have her soft toy panda.

I wonder if I sensed that I might someday lose her during the final years of her life, because I consciously started to package up her belongings as she grew out of them. Even the morning of her death, I sneaked upstairs and slipped her nightgown from beneath her pillow, bagging it like I was in forensics and gathering evidence of a crime yet to be committed. How could I have possibly known why I was doing this, unless I sensed something, an echo of a nightmare to come, and I was too afraid to acknowledge it?

I hold that nightdress against my face, and I can still smell her, the creamy and metallic concoction that keeps us bound forever. Sometimes her smell is of comfort, and sometimes it makes me want to hurt people.

All of this should not be locked away up here, any more than I should be hiding in my own home.

I make my way down the stairs and the laughter grows louder. I stand at the doorway to the living room, uncertain whether to join them again, and I feel foolish when I realize I am waiting for their permission. I can tell that the wine has warmed up my husband and Larry. They are both louder than before, accentuating each word as if they are speaking to someone who barely understands English.

"I'm getting hungry," I say.

"Ah, that's perfect timing. The chili is almost ready."

I feel like they view me as a petulant child who has got a tantrum out of her system.

"Join us," Paris says, smiling. "I was just telling Larry that the Gall family created Rotherwell. Mount Pelion Way only exists because Eris's father and grandfather put it on the map, and all those houses that you see up and down this road were built because her family granted permission."

He is showing off about an ancestry that is not his, and I want to call him out for being mediocre and foolish and weak.

"I am sorry about your daughter."

Paris whips his head in Larry's direction, a little too late to silence him.

"What did you say?" There is a good chance I misheard him, and I long for this explanation, because I have no energy left to fight.

"Oh come now, Eris," Paris tuts.

"I am sorry about Ania," Larry continues. "I heard what happened to her."

"Why are you even talking about her? Don't even say her name. I don't even know you. Who the fuck are you?"

"I'm sorry. It really is tragic."

I see a slither of perspiration snake down his temple.

"Why don't you just leave?" I spit. "I don't even…"

"*No*," Paris shouts, cutting me off quickly. "He is a guest. He is Cassie's friend, and he should stay. If you feel uncomfortable, you can always leave."

There he goes again, choosing others over me. *Chop chop chop.* Paris is really going to town cutting away those threads that have bound us for all these years. In the small clearings he makes, I can see parts of him I had forgotten about, and maybe even parts he has chosen to keep hidden from me.

Larry swallows hard and catches Cassandra's eye. He is sending a distress signal that she doesn't know what to do with.

"I don't want to cause any trouble," he says, his words scratchy and dry.

"It happened here in the backyard," I say with a thickened tongue. "Did you know that?"

Larry shakes his head.

"There was a lot of speculation, but it was here. I see the spot every time I wash the dishes. She was born into this home, and she loved the orchard we have in the back, so I suppose it is fitting that she departed from there. I wonder, Larry, what rumors are circulating these days? Do they say that I killed her? They would never say that it was my gentle-natured husband, but then, you never know, right? Always the quiet ones."

I glance over at Paris who is shaking his head as he stares at his shoes. Shame hangs heavily on his slumped shoulders.

"I wonder if some people suspect my son, Dylan. Has anyone spoken about him? Quite the fighter, and he always has been. There's a term for people like him: An *incel.* Insane with jealousy and resentment for never getting picked, never attracting anything beyond derision, and so his sort end up shooting people in schools, becoming a neo-Nazi, or pouring acid on homeless people. I am sure he did any number of hateful and illegal things on that computer in his bedroom throughout his teenage years. Lord knows I tried to monitor it, but when you are that determined, well . . ."

"I am so sorry," Larry mutters.

"You don't have to keep saying that. You know, even if it was Dylan, the people out there on Mount Pelion Way, the people in Rotherwell who scour their social media accounts for the latest updates on my daughter's death, they would still find a way to point the finger at me. A mother never escapes any culpability. The father ejaculates once, and that is that, but the mother, well, she is in closer contact with those children, and for longer. What spells did she cast as she baked them for nine months? It feels a little like a game of *tag, you're it*. Grow them in your belly and any malformations or personality quirks are down to you, so you deserve to be witch-hunted and burned at the stake."

"Okay, that's enough." Cassandra struggles to her feet and pulls at Larry's arm.

"I think you should go. It's getting late."

"You don't have to, Larry," I say, but Cassandra has already started walking him out.

A moment later I hear them arguing on the doorstep like two teenage lovers.

". . . .needs someone to talk to," I hear Larry say, and then the door slams shut.

"You need to step it up with that therapist," Cassandra hisses as she returns to join Paris and me. "Or switch the medication. Does everything have to be a fight? Don't you get tired?"

"I feel fine, actually," I reply.

"Well, I don't. You humiliated me in front of a good friend tonight, and I need him. I really need all the friends I can get right now."

She begins to cry, and Paris walks over to hold her.

"You can stay here tonight," he says as he squeezes her into him.

"Why?" I ask. "She has her apartment."

"She needs time with us."

"I wasn't expecting overnight guests."

"You aren't listening. She is staying. She needs us right now, so the least we can do is let her crash in one of our many rooms."

Just say it. Just say that the rooms are now empty.

"Not one of the kids' rooms."

"She can have Dylan's room."

Even he knew it was too much to offer Ania's.

"I'll go and make her bed," Paris sighs.

Hours later, Paris slips into bed next to me.

"I love you," I whisper into the darkness. I don't know why I say it, because we haven't used those words for a long time.

His body tightens when I touch it, a little afraid, perhaps, of who is really talking.

"Sure," he huffs. "You too."

We lie in the darkness for the rest of the night, neither of us able to fall asleep until the sun starts to rise.

Chapter Nine

~~~

Inescapable purgatory

That night I dream of hooded people standing around my bed. They are still, as if they are asleep, and they smell of oil and hemp and apples and bark. I can also smell their urine and sweat and death that lingers beneath the dirty dark-brown sacks that hang over them like ancient body bags.

Something awakens them and they start to shuffle and murmur; impatiently they await my torture.

I have seen them in other dreams, but they have never done anything to me, just shuffled and murmured and reminded me that I am owed bad things.

Bad things happen to bad people, Dylan would tell me, even when he was very young. He probably heard it from a teacher who was having a bad day, or another child in his grade, but he thickened it with repetition, stirring dread into my blood.

I want to know who these hooded people are, and when I reach out to pull a hood off one of them, they all twitch to life, making me snatch my hand away. And then they start to wail.

I try to wake up. I tell myself that it is a dream, but the wailing only gets louder. They rend their garments and lurch this way and that, driven to lunacy by their longing and need for the bad things to finally happen.

I know who one of these figures is. I know the shape of the head and the length of the neck and the curve of the shoulders.

I try again to wake up, but they jostle and moan until one of
~~~

them steps forward. He is taller than the rest, and he is encouraged by the gestures of the others to climb the frame of my bed to sit over me.

He obeys and takes his position, balancing with his dirty feet wrapped round the head of my bed frame as he peers at my sleeping face. He smells of dirt and rotting meat, and I somehow know that he is here to sit in judgment over me. He will forever watch me sleep, and if I make a move or tell a soul, he will crush me with his bare hands.

I plead with him. Through sleep-filled silent screams, I beg him for one last chance. The murmuring of the other hooded people grows louder; I have stirred up dissent. Perhaps the one who sits in judgment over me is the one person who can save me from this. If I could try harder to break my silence and give voice to the kindness, the softness that I know he wants to hear, he might set me free.

I try to speak but still my words are silent, so I try to reach him through a meeting of our eyes. I can just about see the glint of life through the eyehole of his hood, but then he turns from me and starts to speak. His words grow slowly and thick, snaking their way into my ears and up around my brain. The words are roots of a tree, so we are joined together, and he pulls me close. I then know that he is saying that I have one final chance. Before I can ask him what he means, he drops me, and the fall wakes me with a gasp.

I have tried to keep him out, but no matter the latches and bolts and locks, memories of my son start to flood back. I didn't want to remember Dylan, not least because his overwhelming presence squeezes out any space that my daughter might occupy. But his clumsy aunt has contaminated my fortress, walking Dylan in with careless conversations about him.

It isn't her fault. She never knew how much things deteriorated within this household. Shame silenced me, and Paris.

Part of this shame is because I feel responsible for creating Dylan. In the early days, I did little to quell his anger, and there were times when it felt all too familiar, like the wrath of his violent grandfather.

Take, for example, the time he heard laughter rippling down Mount Pelion Way. He must have been just nine or ten years old, but the force of his fist slammed into the kitchen wall seemed ancient, an accumulation of wrath and vengeance for generations before him. The ripples of trauma.

"Why weren't you invited?" he shouted at me, when he realized the laughter was coming from a block party.

"Keep your voice down," I snapped back at him. "You'll make it worse if they hear you. They'll love it if they know that they've got to me."

"So, you hide inside and listen to them enjoying the party?"

"What other choice do I have?"

"You don't talk to any of them, the other mothers on the street. Are you angry at them?"

"No."

"So why don't you talk to them?"

"I don't want to."

I was starting to feel like a petulant child being interrogated by a parent. "Let's drop it."

Just a few years later, with a deeper voice, he was referring to them as *bitches* and *whores* as we drove along Mount Pelion Way. I am ashamed that I never told him to stop. Maybe I was afraid of him, especially when I thought of the greater freedoms that would come with his ever-increasing age. Soon he would be wandering the streets without my supervision, and soon he would be driving a car. Just one of a whole arsenal of deadly weapons that would be at his disposal.

I wonder if the parents of school shooters look back on those early years with the same regret, longing to have done more to change the course of history. And how could I admit to anyone that the biggest source of Dylan's rage were my own inadequacies? *Where's Dad?* he would say whenever I collected him from school. As we walked home, I would run my throat dry trying different variations of *How was your day at school?* and never get a reply. It was only when Paris returned home that he suddenly brightened, as quickly as the flick of a light switch, his face shining with an enthusiasm for his father that left me alone in the dark. I might have tried harder to work on this if I hadn't agreed with my son. After all, I would have chosen Paris over me, too.

But then there was Ania. Whether she was just being kind or really cared for me, she never stopped throwing her arms around me and squeezing me tight. When she would hear her brother's criticisms of me, she would say *Don't worry, I love you Mommy*. This was when she was young and foolish enough not to realize that to disagree with Dylan Brown was a dangerous strategy.

An early indication of this danger, perhaps, although I will never know for sure, was a late fall afternoon, when I collected Ania from school. She was in fifth grade and starting to show reluctance about me walking her home. But that day she held me tightly as I greeted her. Usually the teacher barely noticed me, too exhausted from sidestepping angry parents who refused to take any responsibility for their own children. But that afternoon, she stayed to watch me walk away with Ania. After a moment, she called me back, perhaps having second thoughts about her liability as a mandatory reporter of child abuse.

"Is everything okay with Ania?" she asked.
"Fine. Why?"
I was ready to turn back towards home, but I didn't want to make it seem like I was running away.
"I just . . . I just wanted to check. Is there anything we should be aware of? Anything going on at home?"
"Such as?"
Paris always told me off for being obstructive and combative, but sometimes it was hard to remain polite to people who dance around an issue.
"Whatever you want to say, just say it," I blurted. Paris would not be happy.
"I . . . well . . ." The pockmarked skin on Mrs. Kibble's cheeks ignited with embarrassment.
"I just wanted to check on Ania." She turned to my daughter. "Ania, if anything ever troubles you, just come and speak to me. Okay?"
My daughter nodded. She would have agreed with anything the teacher said, she was just that kind of child.

None of this made sense until we returned home and Ania

flinched when she removed her coat.

"What's the matter?" I asked, dreading her reply.

"Nothing. I'm fine. What's for dinner?"

"Why are you moving like that. Are you hurt?"

"No. It's fine."

"It's fine? What's fine?

I put a hand on her shoulder, and she flinched.

"Let me see. Have you hurt your shoulder?"

"No."

"Then let me see it."

"I said no."

"Okay, I'll do it myself."

I gently opened the top two buttons of her shirt and pulled it down to reveal an angry, red mark on her shoulder.

"What happened?"

She shrugged.

"Come on, Ania, you can tell me."

"Nothing happened. I guess I just fell. I don't know."

"So why didn't you tell me that in the first place? Did someone do this to you?"

It could have been one of the children in her class. For all the school knew, she could have been attacked when no one else saw, in the bathroom or a quiet corner of the school playground. Or it might have been one of the boys on Mount Pelion Way. But for some reason, I knew the threat was closer to home.

That evening, I felt sick as my eyes kept falling on my own son. I watched him pick the skin from a scab on the back of his arm and then flick it at his sister's hair. Even if she had noticed, she probably would have made an excuse for him.

"Knock it off," I said. He turned and sneered at me, popping the bits of the scab into his mouth instead and chewing on it with his mouth open. "How did you get that cut?" I asked him. I already asked him the day before, but sometimes his stories changed, so I wanted to see if I could catch him out. He had just turned thirteen and his biceps and forearms were getting muscular. Other mothers would be proud of how their sons were shaping up, but the thought of Dylan gaining more strength filled me with dread.

"Oh, Mother, you're slipping. You asked me that yesterday.

Maybe we need to get you checked out."

He walked over to me, so close that I could smell his salty sweat. I realized that he had grown so tall that my eyes were now in line with his Adam's apple.

"I wonder whether it's dementia or Alzheimer's." He widened his eyes as he used to when he was trying to scare his sister with a horror story. "I never know the difference between the two. Does one make you drown on your own spit when you forget how to swallow? Or does that happen in both cases?"

I pushed past him and sat with my daughter. I watched the silly cartoon that was hypnotizing her in the hope that she might mutter the truth about her injury. But while her brother lingered behind us, I feared that she was keeping silent to protect him.

I wonder if I will ever know the truth.

The last time I heard from my son he wrote me a long, rambling diatribe about the harm I had inflicted on him. I wondered whether he'd had help constructing it, because it lurched from unconstrained meanderings to polished, eloquent sentences. It felt like the voice of at least two different people. I regretted ever telling him that he could use his skill as a writer or a lawyer, because it helped him realize he had another tool for manipulation. Another weapon at his disposal.

Snips and snails and puppy dog tails.

Dylan left the letter beneath my pillow, of all places, as I slept the final night before he disappeared. True to form, his parting shot was to act like a cat burglar, sneaking through the dark and leaving me uneasy with the thought that he had stood over me as I slept. He left the letter for me, not Paris, and I am grateful for this. I could not bear to see the pain split across my husband's face if he ever learned what his son was really made of.

Before he left, he stole my car and about ten thousand dollars in rolled-up notes. I still don't know how he got into the small safe in my bedroom, not after I had changed the code a number of times. I am just grateful he never discovered the vaults. When I am up here, I still look over my shoulder to see if he is floating in the air like an evil spirit that is waiting for my downfall.

I still have the letter; I don't know why I kept it. Evidence, perhaps, of some crime that he is yet to commit. Or a defense for when he comes after me, so I can show that the insanity was his, not mine. Really, I should have burned it along with the rest of his belongings, but I kept it underneath a loosened floorboard in my bedroom. I didn't want it to pollute my sanctuary, my hidden room in the attic.

I could not read it all the first time I found it. Instead, I returned to it repeatedly over the days and weeks, reading line after line as if it were a cancerous growth slowly blossoming before my eyes.

Eris,

I cannot even call you Mother because you do not deserve this title. You disgust me, you vile, vile creature. They were right that you are a witch, and I wish they had burned you at the stake. What you have done to this family, your self-centeredness, your inability to be a parent, and your failures at even the most basic standards of a human being, are deplorable.

I hope that you will read this and perhaps learn from it. If for no one else, do it for Dad, who has done nothing but love us and try his best. You should try to learn that life is not just about feeling safe and secure locked up in a fortress, any more than it is just about smoothing the tangles in your mind. There are other people to think of, people who need help, who stay awake at night scared of what is going to happen, and who deserve your support.

You left us alone. For years you locked yourself away from us. When Dad was away for work, you left us to fend for ourselves. Why? If you were not willing to care for us, why did you have us in the first place? Have you forgotten about the time Athena found me in the woods and brought me home? I was eight years old. It was dark and cold, and I was scared. Why didn't you care? It was Athena who wrapped her sweatshirt around me and took me home. You were more concerned about your reputation than what had happened to me that day.

Why didn't you notice when Ania would cry in her room? Where were you then? You left her alone to cry herself to sleep. How dare you. You knew what was happening to her, and you did nothing. All you did was watch from your fortress, making daily commentary on the comings and goings of your neighbors. And for what? To store up more petty jealousy? To ignite a greater rage in you that they could live a life that you could never achieve? You're pathetic.

I know there are other parts to this house that you have not told us about. In time, I will find them, and I will discover what you have been hiding from us. Dad deserves to know everything about you, even if it hurts him. Besides, he has played a part in all of this by failing to divorce you. He should have done that a long time ago and saved us all of this anguish. Maybe if he had, Ania would be alive today.

You disgust me, and you do not deserve to have a family.

When the time is right, I will return and take what is left of yours.

Dylan

Inescapable purgatory. If Dylan is right, I am a bad mother. But if he is wrong, and he is abusing a grieving mother, I am still bad because I created him. The apple never falls far from the tree. There was never a chapter on this in the books on grief, the books Marigold Meeches suggested I read. And Pastor Pry never covered this in any of her sermons.

Beyond hope and faith, beyond sanity, and beyond comprehension.

I know of the time he is referring to, when Athena found him. Before he ran to the woods, we had argued about tidying up his room. When he refused, I threatened to take away his favorite toy truck, the one with a fox on the side of it. When I reached for it, he snatched it from me and swung it at my face. In the blink of shock, I thought he hadn't hurt me, but then a throb of pain started to swell, like a rapidly blooming flower.

I told him to stay in his room as I applied an ice pack to my face. An angry scarlet smear was emerging beneath my right eye, and I knew the blues and purples would surface a day or two later. By the time I came out of the bathroom, he had left the house, and that must have been when Athena found him in the woods.

By the time Paris returned home from work, I had found Dylan, so Paris never got to hear about his son's disappearing act. He didn't flinch when he saw my wounded face. He seemed more concerned that Dylan would feel badly, even though there were no signs of this. He took the children out for ice cream that evening, telling them that *Mommy needs a break*, and as I heard the door close, he told them calmly about mistakes and how we can learn and grow from them. In Paris's eyes, his children would always be The Fairest, that much was to be expected. I just feared there would come a day when Paris had to choose between his two children. After all, if he tolerated his son's violence with me, would he tolerate it around Ania?

Chapter Ten

~~~

Judgment

Light awakens me. Limbs heavy, like tombstones to drag, I reluctantly leave the safety of my bed. I sit for a moment, mouth hanging open and dry-lipped.

It is barely six in the morning, and Paris is snoring, so I slip on my dressing gown and tiptoe down the stairs.

The air is thickened by the stench of boiled eggs. I see a handful of them all lined up in little cups next to the stove. I watch the garish yolk spill from one of them, and I want to clear it up, but my sister-in-law is blocking my way. The pan looks heavy as it hangs in her hand, and I wonder if she has ever cooked breakfast before. With her spare hand, she picks something out of her teeth, and I try not to think about where she has been putting the detritus.

"Did I wake you?" she asks, knowing full well that she did. With her hair flattened by sleep, she looks so much smaller than last night.
"No," I lie.

I know how tenuous the bonds are that bind me to my husband, so they will not withstand the weight of any further conflict with his sister. I have no choice but to try again to play nicely with Cassandra Brown then Ford then Brown again.

"I'm usually an early riser anyway."
I fix a small smile, and it seems to unsettle her because she coos "*Oh, fun*" as she fusses with her hair.

I decide to be the one to offer an embrace, and our arms collide
~~~

in an awkward mess as she tries to place the pan back on the stove.
I think how terrible it would be if I knocked the boiling water onto
her feet and Paris found us like this. I think of the assumptions he
would make.

"I couldn't sleep," Cassandra sighs.
"After your late night I'm surprised you didn't sleep until noon."
"Blame your husband."
Like a mouse cornered in a cat's kingdom, her movements are
quick, bright-eyed, and edgy.

"He drank a little too much," I say, trying not to make this
sound like an accusation.
"He doesn't usually. Perhaps he has something on his mind,"
Cassandra mutters.
"Does he?"
I want to ask her where I stand with Paris. After I left the two of
them together, and the wine continued to flow, did he tell his sister
how much he wanted to cut himself free? Is it going to happen
soon? If it is, I just want to know so I can brace myself.

I watch her reach for a glass and pour some orange juice into
it.
"You should put something beneath that," I say without thinking.
"What?"
"The glass. It will leave a sticky mess."
"I see."
"And that cloth is really for wiping hands, not counters. There is
a separate cloth for the counters. And another separate one for the
dishes."

I bite my lip when I imagine her reporting all this to Paris. I
see her taking the form of an old-fashioned housewife and wiping
the corners of his mouth after she has cooked him a breakfast of
delicious eggs. Her bright smile will cast me in the shadows,
highlighting my dirt and filth to show how twisted, dark, and
miserly I am. And she will recreate these verbal hand slaps, baking
in doubts and suspicion as she kneads his shoulders. The doubts
will swell to fill this house, loosening the latches and bolts and
locks and squeezing and pushing me up into the attic and through
the roof, so I fly away with the smoke that climbs from our
chimney. Up into the sky like the witch they always said I was.

She hounds me, she will cry. *She wants to intimidate and haunt me, so I run from this house, so you never see me again. You will lose me, your only sister, just as you lost your daughter.*

I know she would stoop this low with such cunning because I would do the same in her position.

"I thought some food might help me to sleep, but my stomach is no longer my friend," Cassandra says. "Not since I abused it with medication."

"What medication?"

"So he didn't tell you?"

"About what? What medication?"

"I think we need to talk about something."

Panic rises in my chest like bile. Whatever she is going to bring into my life is another form of contamination, and I need to clean it up before it spreads further.

"Look, I need to get on," I snap, desperate to leave the kitchen. "I have a few things to sort out before Paris wakes up."

"Can't it wait?"

"No."

She grabs my elbow, and my breath catches on something. It feels like I am ensnared on barbed wire, and I know that if I struggle, I might start to feel the pain.

"Why won't you ask me how I am?" She leans so close I can smell the toothpaste on her breath.

"What?"

"Since I arrived, you haven't asked me how I am feeling. You never do."

"I'm not your therapist," I reply.

"No, but you are family."

I've never really considered her to be family.

"Okay, I will start, and hopefully you can follow my lead," she says. "How are you?"

"I don't want to play a game."

"This isn't a game. How are you?"

"I am fine."

"Now you ask how I am doing."

She has a matronly tone, and it takes all my energy not to slap her.

"Okay," I say, "I'll play along. How are you?"

"Did Paris really not bring you up to speed?"

I shake my head and she releases her grip on me.

"You asked about medication," she says. "The truth is, what medication have I *not* been on?"

"You really should watch that juice doesn't spill. It's full to the brim." I point at the glass, even though it is obvious what I am talking about. I just want her to stop staring at me.

Instead of turning to the glass, she cocks her head and scans me up and down, as if I am a book she isn't interested in reading. "I don't know why I am even bothering to tell you."

"Tell me what?"

"I'm tired. I might try and go back to bed for a little. But I also wanted to say that last night, when I was talking about you selling this place, I didn't want us to get into a fight. I do, however, stick by my words when it comes to living a little. You really need to make the most of life while you can. After all, you still have Dylan."

"Not anymore, and that is a good thing."

"What are you saying?"

"Dylan is no longer welcome here."

"But last night you said…"

"Yes, well I lied. I haven't heard from him in more than a year."

"Are you kidding me?"

"Dylan is a monster, and I'm glad he has gone."

"Why are you saying this? He's your son."

"Not anymore."

"Paris never said anything."

"No. He promised me he wouldn't. I don't want him back here."

"He's your son."

"You've already said that."

"Aren't you afraid of what might happen to him . . . ? What might have already happened to him?"

"I am more afraid of the harm he could inflict on other people. He would never come to any harm himself; he's too smart."

"You two should have woken me," Paris says, yawning as he stretches in the kitchen doorway. His throat sounds thickened by sleep and alcohol. "Is the coffee fresh?"

"I guess so," I say as I watch the two siblings thread their arms together with a tighter embrace than last night's. I feel foolish when I get the urge to squeeze in between them and ruffle Paris's hair before she does.

"You barely mentioned Dylan last night," Cassandra says as she lifts the glass of juice to her lips.

He shrugs.

"Nothing much to say."

"He's your son."

Paris eyes me warily.

"Yes. But he has a bit of growing up to do."

"He's only twenty, and his sixteen-year-old sister died when he was just eighteen. That's kind of a lot to deal with."

"A lot for all of us," I interject. "He chose to leave."

"Okay, fine, but . . . You know what, I've gone off the idea of breakfast," Cassandra snaps. "The two of you can have it."

She slams down the glass of juice, and we all watch the splashes of orange decorate the counter and wall.

"I can't keep fighting you on every last thing," she says.

I take a sponge, wet it under the tap, and slowly wipe up the spillage as she stomps up the stairs.

"You and Cassie should talk," Paris sighs.

"About what?"

"Stuff."

"She knows about Dylan."

"Okay. But you and her should talk about more than that."

"Why does everyone keep talking me in circles?" I snap. "Like what? What does she want to talk to me about?"

"I'll let her tell you."

"Of course you will. Why make it easy for me? Is this how you Browns create entertainment; dropping little hints and watching the rest of us follow your breadcrumb trail?"

"She might have been trying to tell you, but you do tend to get focused on other things."

"Other things like what?"

"Like the cleanliness of the kitchen. And it's hard for her; it isn't something that she can just spit out. Maybe you could help her."

"I don't know what that means. Help her in what way?"

"Maybe go to her, offer to sit with her, and try and listen."

"Fine."

I find Cassandra in Dylan's old bedroom. She is crouched, the contents of her handbag strewn all over the floor. She seems to be looking for something, and she reminds me of a street seller who is begging for patronage.

Even though there are scrunched up used tissues thrown on the floor, just out of reach of the wastepaper basket, I choose not to comment on her slovenliness. Her nephew was never much better, and when I tried to guide him in the right direction, he would lash out at whatever was nearby. Most of the time it was these bedroom walls, and if I didn't retreat quickly enough, I was sure my face would get caught in the line of fire.

"Paris said you might want to talk to me."
Soften your tone, Paris would say. *Do it for me.*
"Do you need any help with that?"
Cassandra stares up at me.
"I was just looking for my pill bottle. I didn't bring any more, and I need to keep to the regime."
I point to a pill bottle that has rolled into the corner of the room.
"Oh. Right. Thanks."

On three separate occasions, Paris patiently filled the holes that Dylan punched into his bedroom walls. Each time this happened, he took his son to the hardware store and let him choose the new color for the paint. And then Paris turned on his little transistor radio, whistling to James Taylor as he spent the rest of the day redecorating the bedroom.

Ania would get upset because she wanted a new color for her own walls, even though there were no punch holes to fill.

"Don't worry, midget," Dylan would say to her. "Next time I'll smack the shit out of your room so he does yours in whatever color you like."
I remember how she stared up at her brother as if he were a hero, and I wanted to slap the stupid smile off his face.

The day Dylan left, I ceased to be a parent. In the stillness of his room, I realized there was no more planning, no checklists, no vigilance for sicknesses and educational progression. There was just regret. I could have sunk into that regret, letting my body slow to a stop. Instead, I chose to take action and load trash bags full of his clothes and schoolbooks and gadgets and cell phone chargers and wallets and shaving foam and razors and deodorant. He had nothing of sentimental value—he never kept anything that didn't serve a purpose—so I didn't have to suffer from any stomach-twist of regret by watching a Snoopy cuddle toy or Paddington Bear peep out from inside the bag.

As I filled those trash bags, I refused to slow down and become ensnared on memories of his chubby little infant arms. How he liked my hugs in those early days, how we would smother each other and squeeze so tightly. He would sigh with contentment as we held each other like that, and I remember him saying "Love them hugs" over and over again. But as the years passed, he started to stiffen in response to my embrace, and eventually he shrank from me entirely.

"I'll clear this up in a moment," Cassandra says, gesturing towards the contents of her handbag. "I just can't seem to find anything these days. My head is all over the place. And now I have to remember more, like a new medication schedule on top of everything else. It isn't fair. None of this is fair."

Smile, Paris would say. *Even if you don't feel like it.*
I smile.
"If you want to talk, maybe we can go somewhere more comfortable."
I didn't want to be in this room much longer. The place still smelled of Dylan—that heavy, metallic, dirty stench of something simmering.
"Let me help you to your feet," I offer.
'You don't have to."
I don't wait for a reply before I pull her arms to get her upright. She stares at me in confusion.

Together we walk across the hall and down the stairs.

"Let's try the balcony," I say as I guide her through the dining room. I rarely sit outside, and as I open the doors and feel a flood of winter sunlight glowing on my skin, I wonder what has stopped me before. No one can reach me back here, so it is safe from prying eyes. As soon as my mother died, my father erected six-foot wooden fences up and down the perimeter of our land, and he planted a forest of trees to obscure the view.

"So many trees. A prison of an orchard," Cassandra mutters.

I twist the hem of my shirt around one of my forefingers. I bind it so tightly that I see the blood pulsating in the tip. In certain countries, places my father would visit to make his business deals, the bereaved show the depth of their despair by tying the ends of their fingers and cutting them off with an axe. They would then burn the dismembered parts as offerings to gratify the spirits. I think of my marriage to Paris as an offering, dismembered and raised up to Ania as she sits in her spiritual domain. I can feed her with the offering, or ask her forgiveness, or bargain for her return.

"An interesting garden design," Cassandra continues. "Don't you want to open it up a little to get more of a view? And what about getting more light?"

"We like it. I wish the apple trees were in bloom for you, but if you come back at the end of April, your eyes will sparkle in the dazzling white. Ania loved them."

We stand in silence for a moment, and I wonder where Ania has gone. Is she watching us from behind the couch, or is she in the backyard perhaps, climbing the lower boughs of the trees. I wonder if it hurts her to be out there again, remembering everything that has happened.

Cassandra never concealed her awkwardness around my children. She would buy a gift now and again, but she always left it on the side, telling me to give it to them later. No hugs, no encouraging comment about how much they had grown or how beautiful they had become. I wonder if Cassandra regrets any of this now.

"I think Ania liked to look at the apple trees because they were so full of hope. She used to say that she could count the blossoms and figure out how many apples we could harvest come fall. I don't know, maybe she was right. I wish I had taken the time to check."

I wish Cassandra would say something, even to acknowledge that she has heard me, but when I look at her, she has started to check her cell phone.

I point out a nest that I have spotted, and she nods without smiling. It is a mossy nest and empty, presumably because of the time of year rather than it being robbed by some predator. I have heard that in some parts of this country, there are serpents that glide stealthily into nests and stretch their jaws around each egg. I can almost hear the cracking sounds as young lives are snuffed out before they have tasted fresh air. It occurs to me that I am developing a taste for revenge in any form.

"This could be a nice spot." Cassandra forces a smile.
"It is already a nice spot. But a lot of work."
"Do you not have someone to care for it?"
"Never."
Quizzical birds call out to each other, although I cannot see any.
"Have a seat."
I pull out some old green plastic chairs that wobble under the slightest weight. As she takes a seat, she peers down warily, half expecting it to collapse beneath her.

"You should have added a pool out there."
"No, it would have ruined the garden."
"You could have had people over. It would have made the summers quite fun."
"Who would have come?"
"Me."
"Besides, I can't even swim."
"Paris can."
"Then I will leave it to Paris to put in a pool if he wants one so badly. That way one will never get built because he would never get himself organized enough to even call a contractor."
"Perfect. You have it all set up so he never gets what he wants. Just perfect."
"I'm not sure that's my fault, Cassandra."
"It's all a fight with you, isn't it?"
"Not all the time."
We sit together, staring at the barren orchard. Even the birdsong has fallen silent.

"I know what you went through," Cassandra finally says.
"Do you?"

My sister-in-law, Ania's aunt, wore a tight knee-length dress to Ania's funeral. I watched her saunter in, staggering almost as she balanced on three-inch heels. My eyes stung in the cloud of fragrance that filled the space between us, a noxious presence that seemed to compete with the grief and sadness.

"Everyone was shocked and saddened," she offers.
"No they weren't. You don't know, you haven't had to live on this street, in this town. They are all sociopaths."
"I am sure everyone was devastated. How could they not be?"
"None of them came to the funeral. The people from her school, the people on this street. They talked to the press, but they didn't come to say their goodbyes. They let balloons go at her school, but they never came to say a word to me. Not once. No one cared, not really."
"A beautiful sixteen-year-old girl dying suddenly like that. Of course, people were shocked and saddened."
"She didn't just die. She was killed. Those boys, the ones in her grade . . ."
"You have to move on. You are tying yourself up in knots and trapping Paris along with you."
"No. Don't say that."
"It's true."

A lone blue jay swoops down from one of the trees.

"I wanted to tell you that I've had my own difficulties. I must admit, I've really been struggling of late," Cassandra finally admits.
The bird pecks at the ground, cocks his head to listen, and then pecks again.
"Over the last few months, things have become impossible, and I now realize I can't face this on my own."
"I don't follow," I reply.
I feel a weight on my chest, as if she is a playground bully who has pinned me to the ground, and I am forced to listen to her. I wonder whether she played these games with Paris when they were young. I imagine she always won.

"I've had tests and scans and small procedures, followed by bigger procedures. Larry has been a doll, but he is just that: a pretty little doll. At a time like this, a person needs their family."
"I see. Well, here we are, if you need us. Is it money you need?"
Cassandra bursts out laughing. "You do make me laugh."
I know she doesn't mean this as a compliment, but I remember Paris's instructions to me, so I smile.

"The doctors have thrown everything at it, but the cancer keeps spreading. It was localized to my gut at first, so I thought you wouldn't even need to know. But when it spread to my lymph nodes, that was when I got scared. Larry held me as I sobbed, and he promised he would be there for me throughout everything. But now it's spread to my brain. So I need to be around my brother in these final days. They never use the word *incurable,* but I have enough friends in the medical profession to set me straight. I guess you probably always used that word about me."

"Which word?"

"Incurable."

"Do you mean incorrigible?"

"Potatoes, po-tah-toes. Same difference."

Her face folds into tears, and I sit there staring, wondering at how pink and moist her skin looks. I take her hand, and it is warm. It reminds me of how I should behave.

"There is so much I want to do," she sobs. "I don't want to end this way, not so soon."

"We'll be here for you. What do you need?"

"I don't know. All they can tell me is that they can make me comfortable, with medication and small procedures. But I have been stupid and started reading things online. I… I don't want to suffer the way some people describe. I would rather take things into my own hands."

I pull away from her, letting her hand drop to her lap.

The blue jay squawks and a whole flock appears, joining him in the pecking ritual. Their small-brained heads dart around, alert for any predator, and they flap into a frenzy when one of their flock makes a move.

"And I guess Paris knows? That's why he wanted me to talk to you?"

"Yes, I told him last night. He was pretty torn up about it. You're gonna have to be strong for him. I've been told to make plans, and I was never good at planning. I was hoping you and he could help me with that."

"What kind of plans?"

"For my care, for what to do with my apartment and the stuff in it. And I was hoping I could stay here."

"Here? You don't want to be home?"

"Not really. Especially not alone. I mean, Larry would do anything for me, but it is too much to ask him."

"I appreciate that but . . ."

Paris should be here. I have just about exhausted the kindness that he would expect of me. I need to hand this over to him now.

"Shouldn't you be in a hospital?"

I run my fingernail along the edge of my green plastic chair. I now remember that this deck set was a gift from Cassandra, on the day I married her brother. A set of six uncomfortable green plastic chairs with a matching table, and a hole for an umbrella. The umbrella never materialized.

"The hospital has done all they can for me."

"A hospice?"

"I don't want to be surrounded by a bunch of strangers. Paris seemed okay with the idea, but I guess you two have to talk."

"So now you know."

Paris's words burst out from behind me, making me jump. I don't want to turn around and face him because I cannot look at his pain again. Not so soon. I feel like I am caught in a spider's web, and the web is woven over my mouth as well as my hands and feet. I cannot run, I cannot even touch my husband's hand, and I cannot say a word.

"I'll drive down to Fort Lee to collect your things tonight," he says. "I can pick up a U-Haul trailer on the way."

That night, the hooded people return. Before I even see them, I smell the oil and hemp and apples and bark. They are still impatient, and their murmuring is louder and higher pitched, like the squeal of a baby in pain. As soon as I think that, I want to know where Dylan is and what he is doing, but my wrists are bound to the wrought iron frame of the bed. Each time I try to struggle free, the redness of raw skin emerges on each wrist in the shape of a circle, like the angry eyes of a beast.

Bad things happen to bad people.

I hear this over and over again, but I do not recognize the voice.

The taller figure is here again, and he has already jumped onto the head of my bed frame, his dirty bare feet just inches from my face. As he whispers, the words grow like roots of a tree again, snaking into my ears and around my brain, and I can hear the words say that I can have Ania back. But this time she can return in her original body, not just an ethereal form. Waves of relief charge through me, so hard that I wake myself and find my hands pressing into the mattress, leaving two damp patches of sweat.

My ears search the darkness for signs that I have woken the household, but Paris remains fast asleep next to me, and I hear no movement from Cassandra across the hall.

I slip back into sleep, where I sob with relief that I might feel my daughter again. This time, the words that thread their way through my mind tell me that I can only have Ania back if I also accept Dylan. I cannot refuse, and so my children walk in.

Night has softened them, plunging them further into the past so they look younger. They are little children again; Dylan is around nine or ten, and Ania is around seven or eight. Their heads hang with shoulders sloped, so they look mournful and scared. I want to reassure them, but my mouth makes no sound.

Dylan is the first to step closer, and he pulls the rope tighter around my wrists. Ania will not look me in the eye, she only watches as her brother reveals his old school backpack, which looks heavily weighed down with something.

"We've missed you," he sneers as he wipes his nose on the back of his sleeve.

"I need to go," I say, but again no sound comes out. "I need to go."

From inside his backpack, Dylan retrieves a small, shiny scalpel. I remember he stole one from school when the biology teacher asked them to dissect some frogs. How foolish had I been until that point, thinking that he would refuse to do it. Instead, he charged home with excitement, all too eager to describe in detail how much he had torn that creature apart.

"Look, Mother. Remember this?"

He flicks the scalpel between his fingers, his eyes dazzling.

I slowly nod.

He pulls up my nightdress with tenderness, as if he is doing this out of love. He runs the flat of his hand over my belly, turning his head to try and sense things a little more clearly.

When he turns back to face me, I see such calm, and I think *I have created this*. It is my fault that he is never stirred by the pain of others. He just wants to do it because he can, to see what will happen.

He presses the scalpel into my skin, and I look down to see a crimson tear streaming down my side. He does not even hesitate, slicing further down and across, and then up again, so that a square flap of skin can be pulled back. As nerves and tissue and tendons break apart, the pain sears through my body. At this point, I hope he will stop or I will pass out.

But he continues, and I remain minutely aware of every movement.

What hurts me the most is to see Ania hanging at the sidelines, watching but not saying anything, seeing the blood and my pain but seemingly untouched by it all.

I do not want to look down, but I can imagine how my innards are exposed, now the flap of flesh has been opened. I wonder what pinks and purples and whites they can see inside me, what is moving, and where there are pools of fluid.

I want it to be over. I accept my punishment, and I want this to finally end.

The hooded man sits above my head, staring into the distance as if he is half asleep. He has not yet decided when that will be.

Chapter Eleven

~~~

Lethal flowers

There are no more ash-like snowflakes falling on the apple trees. Instead, bright white blossoms reach out from barely formed buds, drawn out by the longer, lingering sunshine of spring.

Larry came for Thanksgiving. He brought food, and we ate in a silence that was pinpricked only occasionally by his compliments of my artifacts from faraway places. It was striking that even a sprightly spirit like Larry could end up repressed, as if the fortress were a glass lid sealed over to snuff out any flame of joy.

He returned for Christmas, but there were even fewer moments of enthusiasm. He curtailed his visit, staying for barely an hour, and he said he would return in a week or so. That was months ago.

When March arrived, and Paris turned fifty-one, he refused to mark the occasion in any way. I stifled my resentment that he would suddenly give up his birthday for his dying sister when he didn't think twice about celebrating the two birthdays after we lost Ania.

Daily I keep an ear out for the footsteps in my attic, but so far, the fortress has sat in silence. Eventually I will have to tell Cassandra about my father, and even the truth about Ania. But for now I allow the eerie sense of calm to hang in the air.

I had been keeping a safe distance from my sister-in-law as I let Paris spend as much time with her as he needed. But now
~~~

Cassandra grows restless, demanding more of me.

"I haven't seen you for ages," she says, pupils dilated and staring uncertainly into the distance. The way she sometimes staggers around makes me think that her medication needs adjustment. I have seen the pill bottles lined up on the nightstand, and I can only imagine what opioids and sedatives are tickling at her bloodstream to tangle her alertness. Sometimes she looks like she is wading through the day, caught in thickening pond weed that might eventually pull her beneath the surface. I wonder what it would be like to slowly drown in your own fluids.

"Sit with me for a little," she says one day, her words spaced out a little too much, so they sound like they float through space. "I miss you."

She doesn't miss me. She misses her former life, when she could race from work to drinks and dinners throughout her week. When she had a husband and a best friend to turn to. Now she must stagnate in my living room, depressing the dents in the sofa more deeply than I have seen them sink before. I have tried to keep her entertained by sharing with her some of my favorite television programs. The characters in the soap operas are like friends to me, people I have known for years, but she never seems to listen to any of this. She is probably at the edge of screaming for the carriage clock to stop ticking, the constant reminder that time is passing her by as she festers inside the darkness of my home.

The deterioration in Cassandra's health has been swift, like the rapid unfurling of a lethal flower. As she spreads herself around my fortress, I try to help Paris by ignoring my own frustrations. I stay one step ahead, wiping crumbs as I throw away trash before it starts to accumulate. I try not to focus on the image of our house filling with flakes of her, like fallen ash, and how it might fill my eyes and ears and even my mouth as I struggle to breathe. I try to adapt, I try to make allowances, but when she screams at night, the pain taking a sudden hold in between doses of medication, I cannot help but wish for a swifter end.

I miss Ania. I rarely hear her voice anymore, and talk of her has been banished from this house as if she had been an unwanted habit. According to Paris, the order of the day is washing, dressing, medicating, and feeding his sister, and if I deviate from this with any mention of our daughter, I am met with his silent glare. I hope my husband has not scared Ania away for good.

To see Paris's attentiveness over his sister, and his neglect of the memory of our daughter, makes me twist the hem of my shirt again, and I have started to notice buttons falling off. When I hear them drop to the ground, making a light tinkling sound, I remember how Ania would call this the sound of fairy's footsteps dancing about our house.

Still these do not lure her back to me.

Currently, Paris is at the pharmacy because they made a mistake with Cassandra's medication. If he hadn't spotted it, she might be dead already. I can imagine how his cheeks flushed when he tried to complain about this, only for them to push back and make it seem like it was his mistake. He probably ended up apologizing to them for wasting their time. Only certain people are born fighting their way out into the world that is waiting to try and defeat them. Others, like Paris and Ania, only know how to comply and retreat.

"Aren't you hot?" Cassandra gasps, as if she has just remembered it is spring.

"No, I feel fine."

"I am sweltering. It must be the meds. Can we crack open a window? Even just a smidge?"

"I don't think they open anymore," I lie. "They were painted shut when we last had the room decorated. I could get you a fan."

She knows how I like to keep the windows and doors shut. She knows how I feel about the people on Mount Pelion Way.

"No," she insists "I need air. I really need space to breathe, otherwise I might pass out."

Already she is clawing at her throat, already she is struggling to her feet. Her handbag drops to the ground and some of the contents spill out, but she doesn't seem to care.

She wrenches the curtains open, and a wave of sunlight hits us both. Eyes dazzled, I snatch at her shoulder to move her out of the way so I can shut them again. Her flesh feels loose and soft, as if it could slide off the bone.

"Stop!" she cries. "I need to feel sunlight on my skin. It's been months."

"You said you were hot."

"Hot and suffocating in this darkness. Would you let me get some air?"

She tries to push the window open, but the latches and bolts and locks hold fast.

"Look at them all out there."

I see that some of her hair is now sticking to sweat on her forehead, and I wonder if the drugs are so strong that she has started to hallucinate.

"Hello?" she shouts. "Over here!"

"Paris will be home soon. You don't want to go upsetting yourself and let him find you like this. Why don't you sit and watch something with me?"

"*Watch something?*" she screams. "All we've done all day every day is watch soap operas and supposed reality TV. Is that your life? Do you really think those are your friends, those characters on the TV? You do realize they are only playing a part. It isn't reality."

"Come on," I say. "Let's go sit back down again. Can I make you a drink?"

"I don't want anything from you. I am getting some air for myself, on my own, and you have no right to stop me."

She is across the living room too quickly for me to realize what she is doing. Already she has opened the locks, and already she is stumbling out the door.

I race after her, hoping I can catch up in time to pull her back in, but then I see Freya Marwood in the driveway, loading her children into the car.

It is inevitable that Cassandra would be drawn to her bird of a feather. Unfortunately for my sister-in-law, when Freya catches sight of her, all she can see is the haggard, overmedicated mess of someone who is dying. My sister-in-law has nothing left to offer, no opportunities for this seething mother to seize, so Freya is not going to waste her time.

She doesn't miss a beat, jumping straight into her car with her ugly cherub-like children, firing up her engine, and backing out of her drive at full speed.

Now is the time for my sister-in-law to take my hand and walk inside. Now she sees the reality of Mount Pelion Way, that there is nothing out there for her, surely she must concede defeat.

"Do you want that drink now?" I offer. "Or maybe some lunch?"

But then I hear a voice calling from behind us.

"Is everything okay?"

June West. She is more dangerous than a combination of Freya Marwood and Athena Aegean. At least Freya is too stupid to outsmart me, and I can see her coming from a mile away, with her wild gesticulations that make her larger than life as she urges everyone to look at her. And at least the meaty-mouthed, dimple-chinned Athena is so loud and commanding that you can feel the ground trembling, giving you a chance to brace for impact. But June West just materializes from the undergrowth with her plain, simpering smile of faux concern, appearing before your eyes as if she has risen from the underworld. Head low with slow movements, like a stalking cat, she offers friendship, support, and compassion. But if you take a bite of any of these gifts, you will find them to be waxy and artificial as her smile. She claims that she acts in the best interests of the *community* but what she will not admit to is the blind eye she turns to the damage inflicted by her own kind. Not least her very own son in a forest on a Halloween night. "Do you need any help?" she asks Cassandra. "Is everything okay?"

Without good looks or status, June West relies on stealth to maintain a solid footing on Mount Pelion Way. Here she picks up one person's trash, there she rakes another person's leaves, and then, all of a sudden, she is lurking in the passageway so she can peer through your window.

I start to tremble as she approaches. I want to explain to Cassandra that this is the mother of Smithson West, and wife of Max West. But instead I just stand there, my blood beating in my ears. I can't be sure that she knows I approached her son in the forest, any more than she knows how her husband attacked me shortly afterwards. She is too clever to confront me directly, so whatever knowledge she has, she will keep it in her arsenal, along with other information that she can use when the time is right.

"Is everything okay?" June asks for the third time. She is not going to let this go.

"Hi there," Cassandra replies. "I'm Paris's sister." She straightens her hair and skirt like she is a schoolgirl greeting a new classmate.

When Cassandra stretches out her hand, June shakes it with gusto as she grins at me. "I heard someone new was staying with the Browns," she says, beaming.

Where would she hear this unless she had been listening through the locks of my fortress?

"Welcome to the neighborhood," she continues. "We are a pretty tight-knit community."

For sex pests and rapists alike, I want to hiss, but June is still staring at me, no doubt willing me to prove that she is a liar.

"We must have you over for coffee," she says to Cassandra. "Are you just visiting or moving in?"

"Looks like it might be for good. But what a great place to live." Cassandra seems alive and full-bodied again, and I wonder if her illness was one big lie. Is she trying to squeeze me out so she can live off her brother until she finds a new husband? Like a parasite. I imagine extra legs growing out of her chest; long, brown legs that leave sticky patches wherever she crawls. She might start to smell of yeast, a sickly sweet curdle of spoiled life as if she has already died, and I get the sudden urge to stamp on her in front of June, just to see how they react.

I get lost in alternative versions of reality, and I lose track of their conversation, blinking back to the present moment to find them laughing.

I want to find Smithson again. June looks distinctly like him, with her stick-out ears and turned-up nose. This time, I want to pull what little manhood he has clean off his body, and then I want to feed it to someone. I haven't yet decided who.

". . . beautiful when the sunlight hits it," June continues.

"I can imagine. I think that would be nice," Cassandra replies, her voice sounding weak with exhaustion.

"Nine in the morning. Would that be too early for you?"

"I don't think so."

"And Pastor Isla Pry, oh my goodness, she is fantastic. Super smart and very happy to welcome newcomers to her congregation. And very liberal and relaxed. Not like some of the older church people. Do you know what I mean?"

A bramble of jealousy and spite catches in my chest. I want to explain that Pry can only give Cassandra the hope of an afterlife if she stumps up the backpay of donations missed during all those years that she chose to sleep instead of attending Sunday morning worship. And then there is the matter of the will, which will need to be updated to benefit Isla's church. Only then will the pastor make promises about salvation from eternal damnation.

"You really have struck gold by moving onto Mount Pelion Way. We are all so close with each other, you will never be left alone."

Has June forgotten how she called round to my house just a handful of months after Ania's death? Instead of comfort and support, instead of a simpering smile, she demanded that I clean up my lawn within the next few days or she would bill me for the services of a landscaper.

"Those leaves are a danger to the children," she had shouted. *Children.* She really wanted to hurt me by pointing to the children. "Think of the ticks and the Lyme disease. Really, you have to think of others because we all live on this street together. It is not your kingdom any more than we are your subjects."

"The leaves are good for the wildlife," I tried to explain, my mouth dry with shock. "They use them to make nests. Why would your children play in my yard anyway? They have plenty of other places to go."

But she had already walked away, calling over her shoulder without turning to face me, "Get it sorted. Three days, or you'll get an invoice. And I will happily ruin your credit rating if you don't pay up. Oh, and one last thing . . ." She turned back to smile as she let out a childish giggle. "I charge interest."

After three days, I heard her landscapers blowing across my lawn. They filled the air with gas as they thundered their way like a hurricane. June smiled and waved at me as she watched her workmen decimate a bird's nest that was perched in one of my bushes. I don't think she expected them to trample over the fallen nest, crushing some of the pale-blue eggs that had been nurtured by a dutiful blue jay. Smashed across my path, the eggs cried golden streams of yolk, and from one of the broken shards I saw the fully formed fetus still throbbing with the final moments of life.

"I should get you inside," I say to Cassandra, yanking at her elbow. She pulls away.

"Stop it," she cries. "You're hurting me."

June looks intrigued. I wonder if she is ready to record this on her cell phone, hoping that my movements become violent and I fall on my poor, helpless sister-in-law. She will finally have proof that the Witch of Mount Pelion Way needs to be banished.

"You need to get indoors," I repeat, the panic rising in my chest.

"I said that I am fine," she snaps. "Really."

When the time comes, I will be kind and draw a golden shawl over the face of my sister-in-law; a deathly veil that offers her dignity and peace. When the time comes for June West, however, I won't let her slip from this world without prolonged suffering, perhaps for years. I could make good use of some IVs hooked up in the secret room in my attic.

I see Paris's car heading down the street before it makes a sharp turn into our driveway.

He gets out with a handful of paper bags from the pharmacy, and his face is chalky white. I know the strain he has been under.

"Really, Cassandra," I whisper. "You should rest."

"I don't want rest. If you wanted someone to obey your every instruction, you should have got a dog."

Paris appears at her side, and Cassandra's tone switches to a chastised schoolgirl.

"You aren't going to be mad at me, are you, Paris? I just needed some air."

"Of course I wouldn't be mad. How are you feeling?"

"Better for getting some fresh air." She smiles. "Did they sort out the mess with the meds?" She then turns to June. "Can you believe that they mixed up my order at the pharmacy?"

"Oh, my goodness," June cries with exaggerated horror. "Thank goodness you have your brother to look after you."

Why would Paris smile at June West like that? After all she has stood for, why is he not screaming at her to *Leave us alone*?

"It's been a long week, with this and that," he says to her.

"I can imagine," June smiles. "It sounds like you have been under tremendous pressure."

Her tone is careful but persistent, determined to fabricate an image of Paris that is downtrodden, beaten even, and locked up in a fortress with me. She cares little about my husband or his sister, she only wants to create a villain out of me.

"Please just say if you need any help. You know where I am. In fact, I could pop round tomorrow and help out with things."

"Thank you," he says with a nod. "I appreciate it. Can I let you know?"

Still Paris will not look at me.

"Of course." June smiles, basking in her little victory.

I think of the layers of experiences that Paris and I have shared, inconsequential in isolation but together amounting to something huge and strong. These layered experiences will surely amount to something robust, too strong for a narrow-beaked busybody like June West to hack through, no matter how often she tries.

"Let's get you inside," Paris says to his sister, guiding her in before she can object.

Once I have shut the door and gone through the ritual with the latches and bolts and locks, I turn to my sister-in-law and hiss, "You should stay away from her."

"Just let it be," Paris orders. "She needs to rest."

"June West is not your friend," I continue. I know how childish it sounds, but I can think of no other words.

"But she seemed nice," Cassandra says, smiling. "What has she ever done to you?"

"Plenty. And it's more what she allowed her son and other boys on this street to do to my daughter."

Cassandra looks at her brother, and he shakes his head.

"What?" I snap. "Why are you looking like that?"

"I don't think Cassie needs to be hearing all this. Not right now."

His face has tightened, and I wonder when he last kissed me. I don't count the gentle pecks that you give a grandparent, I am thinking about the open-mouthed plunges where saliva is exchanged. I long to find out whether we still have that between us, or whether I should give up.

"You can see Cassie has enough to contend with without

adding petty squabbles with the neighbors."

I don't want to look at Paris anymore. I don't want to see the disappointment that makes his eyes so sad. Has he forgotten how it was his sister who disappointed and saddened him for so many years?

"Legoland."

The word bursts out of my mouth like the missing letters in a crossword.

"What?"

Cassandra is confused, but I know that Paris remembers how his sister staggered into our hallway after driving our children home from Legoland. She was so drunk that she could barely stand up.

"You drove them like this?" I hissed at her that day. "You drove drunk with my children?"

I could smell it on her breath, and I saw a flask peeping out the top of her handbag.

"Oh loosen up," she had groaned, rolling her eyes.

Dylan was sniggering, and she pointed to him, saying, "See? They had a whale of a time. The only person who has a problem is you."

"He is seven years old. He doesn't understand the seriousness of this," I tried to explain.

"Why do you have to make a drama out of everything?"

She didn't notice Ania, who was sobbing in the hallway behind her.

She did it again the following year, after Paris had promised that he would speak to her. But he never did. He just shut me down with *Let me handle it*, which really meant that he was going to pretend she didn't have a drinking problem and just hope she didn't drive drunk with our children again.

"And what about Bali?"

Now Paris is shaking his head as he buries his face in his hands. He groans, and I know that I have gone too far.

When Ania died, his sister was in Bali on a spa holiday with her big-haired girlfriends. When we broke the news to Cassandra about her niece, she didn't fly straight back to us. Instead, she sent a text saying *I am so sorry* and she became unreachable for the next three days.

I cannot forget how tanned she looked at Ania's funeral, and I know that Paris will call me spiteful for referring to any of this. But why do I continue to suffer when others seem to escape from any sort of judgment? Clearly I failed as a mother because my son hates me, my daughter is dead, and my husband is ready to leave me. And yet Cassandra, who has never taken anything seriously, gets to live without punishment.

But she doesn't get to live. Aunty Cassie is dying.

The sound of Ania's voice leaves me feeling impotent. I don't want to fight any more.

"I'm going upstairs for a little," I tell them, and I make my retreat. I hear their low murmur, a pair of judges who are deliberating my fate, so the stairs I climb feels like steps to the gallows.

Up in the attic, away from their murmurs and judgment, I can clear a space again for Ania. But she does not follow me up here. I wonder if she is afraid of my father, her grandfather, because of the stories I told her. I had hoped that I could leave him out of her life entirely, but all ten-year-olds start to ask difficult questions as they gather the strands of the lives that existed to create them.

One unguarded moment, I told her how I would hide in this attic at a young age when my father would flip tables in another one of his rages. He would throw open cupboards and howl as he searched for something.

"What was he looking for?" a young Ania would ask me. "Most of the time he was drunk on bourbon, so he was probably searching for my mother."

"What happened to her?" she asked me.

"She died when I was seven years old."

"I'm sorry," Ania sighed, placing a comforting arm around me. "I feel bad for you."

"It's okay. I am kind of used to it now," I lie.

Years after my father's rages, years after he had died, I had to use the attic as a sanctuary again, only this time it was to escape the rages of my own son. Echoes of his grandfather.

Before I told her about my father, Ania liked to come up to the attic with me. She enjoyed being up here for the same reasons that I did: because no one could see us up here, but we could spy on everyone else. I showed her the brick I had loosened as a child, using a metal ruler to chip away the cement so I could remove it any time I wanted to watch the street below.

"They look so small," she would whisper about the people of Mount Pelion Way.

"Small enough to squidge out. Look, there's the three boys. Let me squidge out each one."

She was about eight or nine at the time, so she giggled as I showed her how to squeeze them out of existence with just her forefinger and thumb. But then she stopped laughing and looked sad.

"I guess it's kinda mean," she sighed. "I wouldn't ever want to hurt them."

"No, not at all," I lied. "It's just a silly game."

"That's not what friends do, is it? You always said I should be kind to friends."

"I didn't realize they were your friends."

"Well they don't want to be my friend, but I still like them, so if they ever wanted to be friends with me, that would be okay."

"But there are other kids in your grade. What about them?"

"No. They think the same. They think I'm weird."

Barbed wire twisted in my gut.

"Well, that's not nice."

"I know."

She was confirming my suspicions. Whenever I watched her in the playground, I didn't see her hanging around with other kids. She could never keep up with the pace of their frenetic exchanges, always missing a beat so they ended up backing away from her and leaving her to play on her own.

I know how much Dylan blames me for not helping her with this, but I had nothing to give.

I can hear the distant murmurings of the street, between Max and Freya, I think, or perhaps it is Athena. It doesn't really matter because they all sound the same, like car horns harping at each other in the fog, or the back and forth of a laser jet printer, whirring and returning, whirring and returning. Repetitive and disembodied and without a soul.

Marigold Meeches would condemn me for retreating to this attic and taking my daughter up here with me. Hardly *prosocial behavior,* is it? But the truth is that it is not safe out there, and the sooner this is accepted, the easier it is to guard against the person who chooses to get drunk while they drive children home from Legoland, and the person who refuses to cancel their Bali holiday when their niece is found dead, and the person who derives pleasure from watching young birds get crushed under a boot. And the person who invites someone to the woods only to pin you to the ground and tear you apart.

When you accept this reality, which is admittedly easier to accept when the bond between a child and parent is broken, then you see how the world you inhabit has actually flipped upside down. You see that you are living in an underworld that is haunted by spirits that live on after death, and so all chaos and disorder can be unleashed.

I stare out through the gap where I have removed the brick and notice that spring has brought the first shoots of aconite. Night has purpled the sky, and as I drift off to sleep, I hope to dream of a field of purples and blues. I hope to feel the soft velvet of the flowers, this wolfsbane, so I can trace the pale white veins through each petal. I will not let them loosen the latches and bolts and locks to reach my daughter. Not again. I hope to dream of ways these people of Mount Pelion Way might willingly accept the potion of a witch. It is a fanciful plan.

And yet.

As I slip deeper into sleep, I see the simpering June West, who has wheeled out an opportunity for me in the form of her outstretched hand to Cassandra and Paris. My Trojan horses. I just have to be patient now and wait for the right opportunity for vengeance.

I wake in the night and think of all those changed seasons within the last two years. We see the effects of those changes, but we cannot hold the magnitude of all that creates that change. Like the dips in between each breath. The hidden are sometimes more powerful than the seen.

A fox screams out in the night, far in the distance but it sounds like it is at the door. I am fooling myself, making myself believe that I can hear the loosening of locks and the door handle.

I think of my son growing and swelling in my belly like a

balloon and how much of a hurry he was in to escape me. I think
of him the size he is now, moving around somewhere beneath my
skin, and I feel him burst forth from me like an angry, impatient
flower that comes too quickly into bloom.

He is waiting to return.

Chapter Twelve

~~~

The cleanse

The next morning, I find Paris in the kitchen spreading a thin layer of butter on some bread. Two years ago, I would have spent much of my day here, washing and dicing and paring to feed a family of four. I used to research new recipes to try, and I would spend the day hunting for the ingredients that I had not already grown in my backyard. How my garden thrived. I learned how to propagate beets and carrots and radishes and peas. There were crops of broccoli and peppers and tomatoes and potatoes, and I engaged in a perpetual fight with the local wildlife to salvage as much as I could. I hammered in wooden stakes, driven deep into the heart of the ground, and wrapped them with chicken wire, sometimes even barbed wire when I was losing the fight.

It could be here again. If I really try to remember, I can still smell the wet soil on the produce, when I would pile it in my wheelbarrow and stagger back into the house. How excited I would be to carry in each load to show my family what I could provide for them.

If I really try, I can still smell it clouding the kitchen air, that pungent aroma as I sautéed and browned and warmed. Love was baked in there too, buried away with all the other mysterious ingredients that, together, would alchemize into any number of fascinating spices and sweetness. But Dylan never failed to grimace when I placed the plate in front of him. He would curse at me for trying to poison him and mock Ania and Paris for smiling
~~~

and eating, no matter how much they might have agreed with him.

I could recreate most of this again, but instead Paris and I make do with microwave meals that are drained of any flavor or substance. We leave them in chipped bowls for each other, without any more care or attention than the feeding of an unwanted family pet.

This spring I watch from the kitchen window as the fingers of asparagus emerge from the ground, proud stalks of green thrusting into the daylight. But with no hands to pluck them and wash them to decorate a salad bowl, they shrink in on themselves, and wither like my own skin with time and neglect. Eventually they lay browned and rotting, like zombies breaking their way out of the ground.

"We needed you last night," Paris says, throwing the pack of butter into the fridge. "Did you not hear me calling for you?"
I shake my head in reply.
"I needed to lift her out of the bed. Her nightclothes were soaked right through."
"Oh."
"*Oh*? Is that it?"
"What do you want me to say?"
"Nothing. I just need your help. Can you do that?"
"Of course. Just say."
"I need to get some broth. She said she might like that for lunch. So can you get her washed? I should have done it last night, but she refused, even screamed at me to leave her alone, so I just changed her nightclothes and bedsheets."
"Did you put the dirty ones in the wash?"
The way he blinked, as if he wondered whether he had misheard me, showed me that I had said the wrong thing.
"Look, just help her get washed and dressed. Please."
"I said I would."

I can't refuse, but the thought of lifting her up, undressing her, and seeing her naked seems wrong. Dylan would have jeered at us, calling us *lesbians*. He once asked me whether I dressed like I did because I had *something to hide*. He was eating his dry cereal with his hands because he knew it would infuriate me, and he stared at my chaotic hair and plain overalls.

"You don't have to be ashamed," he said, smiling. "Get in touch with your true self, be authentic. It's all the rage these days."
"Hurry up or you'll be late for school."
"I'm sure half of Rotherwell is filled with bored housewives eating out other bored housewives."
"Don't speak to me like that," I hissed at him.
"Why? Truth hurts?"
"I don't want you talking like that in front of your sister. She might repeat it to someone at school, and then she'll get into trouble."
"Yeah, you're right," he snorted, licking something off the back of his hand. "We can have our private little chat later, when she's out of earshot. And I can show you some of my porn; plenty of fish there for you to choose from."
"Stop it. I mean it."

I wish my mind would stop revisiting the worst of him. He has gone so I should just forget him. But still I go through a daily ritual of searching beneath each bed and inside every closet, just in case he is waiting for me. I should burn his letter and I should stop sleeping with the light on. But I can see his outline in the darkness, standing over me when I am slipping into a deep sleep, so a childish part of me believes the light will ward off his presence.

"I'll take the buttered bread up for you," I say to Paris.
"Thank you."
It feels so simple to exchange these last few words with him. I believe we could continue like this forever if others didn't intrude on our quiet life. We had a gentle rhythm when Dylan was first born, helping each other with simple tasks and shuffling back and forth in the gap between sunrise and sunset. That was before my son learned how to wield his free will like a weapon.

"Do you want me to see if she is up for some fresh air in the garden?"
He doesn't reply. Already he is racing out of the kitchen, through the hallway, and out the door. In the distance I hear his car grunt into life. He seems in such a hurry, and I don't know why.

I head up to Dylan's old bedroom to offer Cassandra the buttered bread. From the doorway I see wet towels on the floor, dumped amongst Cassandra's belongings. The curtains are still closed so it looks like the dusk of a cold winter's evening, even though it is a bright spring morning.

There is a pungent smell of leather thickening the air, and this could be from her skin drying under the chemical scorch of all the medication. It seems that she is being prepared for death, laid out in a tannery like animal hide.

I think about how soon it will be before she is lying on the steel-smooth table at the funeral home. How harshly the strip lights will shine down on her lifeless body. If she can see any of this from whatever place her liminality has trapped her, will she still feel the earthly disappointment that one of the technicians is chewing gum? Will she hover over her body or sit on a technician's shoulder? Will her nose tickle with the acridity of the blue rubber gloves they snap on their freshly scrubbed hands, still holding on to the sensitivity for strong smells that plagued her mortal life?

How hard the metal headrest will feel beneath her neck, like an executioner's block before the axe descends. How cold the room will be, and will she feel sad to see her clouded corneas and the stillness of her chest? How strange it will seem to watch her lifeless body as it is washed and massaged. Will she yearn for that tender touch once more, longing to bring life to nerve endings in the hope this might send blood back to her heart?

I hope she turns away before they make the incision, before they drain the blood and inject the embalming chemicals. Although this will no longer be her, without any kinesthetic connection between her earthly state and this new ethereal form, she might still feel tender towards the Cassandra that once was, like a mother hovering over the daughter she has known her entire life.

Before formaldehyde, they used arsenic to embalm bodies. I need to see how much is left in the rocky parts of my own garden, the inheritance my grandfather left me from his farming days. I never met my grandfather, but my father told me that he used arsenic as pesticide to kill off a vast array of wildlife. There is something admirable about the way he could keep local vermin under control.

"Eris? Is that you?"

Cassandra's eyes are still closed and her voice flakes and

crumbles. I could stay at the doorway, just watching and listening, but I gave Paris my word.

"I brought you some bread and butter."

I hear her breathing heavily. I can imagine her lips are dry and tattered.

"Oh, shit," she croaks into the greyness of the room. "I couldn't eat anything. Sorry."

I think of how my father would force food into me whenever I refused to eat. I think of him pushing it deeper into my throat as he pinned me down. I see my glistening tears of panic as I searched the room for a means of escape. There was none.

I wonder if Dylan ever did that to his sister. Time gets shuffled more frequently and chaotically, and I am starting to lose the thread of continuity. It is something that could have happened, and I remember how I would watch over Ania with such vigilance that every nightmarish scenario was played out in my mind. He could use rat poison and aconite and cyanide and arsenic. He could use the razor blades he looked so excited about when Paris first taught him to shave. He could use the lengths of rope that were hanging in the garage and that were supposed to be for tethering the fallen branches from the apple trees. He could use the big boots he got for his thirteenth birthday because his feet were getting so big, and he could even use his bare hands that had grown so big, like the rest of his body—deadweight to crush the life out of anything he chose. Simply because he could. I wish I could believe that he never managed to do any of this, but I know that I failed in so many ways to be a mother, and I also failed to be a vigilant night watchman.

But then, even I had to sleep.

"You might find an appetite if you eat a little bit. When I feel unwell, I've found that eating a small corner helped me feel a bit better, and then I wanted to eat more."

"There's no upward trajectory for me, I'm afraid."

I should say that I am sorry. I should reassure her that I will be here for her if she needs me, to hold her hand and wipe her brow and make scrapbooks of memories for her to pass on to people. I wonder if she would have anyone to pass these on to. I can't imagine her big-haired friends will care; they couldn't fit a scrapbook into a cute Chanel handbag, so I can see them leaving it to soak up spilled beer, forgotten in the noise of a crowded bar.

"Paris says you might need help."

"Oh, he did?"

She uses her elbows to ease herself upright. She doesn't seem to flinch.

"Help with what?"

"Not sure. If you are okay, I'll leave you in peace."

"You don't have to go."

To make space for the tray, I push aside some of the pill bottles and empty glasses that are on the nightstand.

"I'll leave it here in case you change your mind."

"I might try it soon. Thank you."

Some of her words sound stretched a little, like limp and dull-colored dough. I wonder if every movement sends another wave of medication around her sluggish circulation. When that circulation finally stops, will she let out a long squeal like the sound of a deflating balloon?

"What time is it?" she asks. "It could be night or morning; I wouldn't know the difference."

"It's just past ten in the morning," I say.

I imagine it is hard for her to focus. I see some drool appearing at the corner of her lips, but she catches it, hastily wiping it away with the back of her hand as our eyes meet.

"Let me open the curtains for you," I say, keeping my eyes locked onto hers.

"I thought you liked to keep them shut."

"Up here no one can see us."

"Lucky for them because I probably look like shit."

"You don't look so bad," I lie.

She runs her fingers through her thinned-out hair. She flinches.

"Ugh. Such a mess. That chemotherapy really did a number on me."

"Do you want your hairbrush?"

"What's the point? I am rotting away from the inside, so the outside might as well show it too."

"I could brush your hair, if you like."

Cassandra narrows her eyes at me, and she seems amused.

"Why are you being so nice to me?"

"Paris told me to."

She bursts out laughing, but then catches herself and winces in pain.

"Oh, Eris, what the fuck. Do you find our *illogical and foolish emotions a constant irritant*?"

"I don't know what you mean."

"No, Spock, I don't suppose you do."

She laughs again but then something makes her stop.

"Sorry, I'm being a bitch," she says.

"Not really."

"I am. I appreciate you trying to help."

I reach for the hairbrush, but she takes it from me.

"It's okay, I can do it."

As I watch her pulling the brush through the few remaining strands of her blond hair, I wonder if she remembers how we fought last year, and how much pain that inflicted on Paris. Out of nowhere, she declared that I should not be grieving for Ania like this, and that I should be out there in the real world again. I told her to shut up, and when she started to talk about healthy grief and unhealthy grief, I told her that I could see why her husband left her.

"You won't *let* Paris leave," she snapped back. "You keep him locked up like a prized bird, and this is going to kill him in the end."

"That actually makes me feel a little more human," she now murmurs as she continues to pull the brush through her hair.

"Do you want to get washed?"

Cassandra nods, although she looks a little suspicious.

"Yes, I do. But how?"

"Using water and soap."

"*Highly logical Spock*, but I mean how can I get washed? I can barely get myself out of bed, let alone into a shower. Are you going to hose me down in the backyard?"

"No. I can help you. You're already upright, so that's a start. We just need to get your legs swung around to the side of the bed."

"Okay. Sounds like you've done this before."

"My father was sick at the end of his life. I helped him a little with staying clean and eating and drinking. He didn't know where he was towards the end, and sometimes there were, well, you know . . ."

"Accidents?"

"Yes."

"I know. Happens to the best of us."

"He actually died in this very room."

"You know, some might say that you shouldn't be talking to me about your father's death when I am dying."

"Do you mind?"

"No."

I can smell my father's illness as it fills the air. That medicinal, organic infusion that results from our fight against death and disease, a battle we know we will never win, but still we try.

"It's funny," Cassandra says. "I know your father once lived here, but I see no trace of him—no photographs, and I don't even remember meeting him."

"Maybe you didn't. He died just before Dylan was born. Sometimes I wonder whether they swapped places."

"Oh?"

"Yes. There were similarities. Are you up for that shower?"

"I can try."

"Good. I can steady you all the way to the bathroom. Just go at the pace you need to."

Pushing herself upright with one hand, she swings her legs round to slide to the floor. I keep nearby as she struggles to her feet, and when she staggers a little, I grip her beneath her clammy arms. Her skin feels sticky, and I think of the fevers my children sweated through. It intrigued me how sickness made their personalities switch; Ania became irritable and impatient, and Dylan would hang his head like a chastised dog. Although I continued to watch over them, administering medicine and taking them to the doctor if their temperature increased to a fever, I longed to stop doing this for Dylan. Just so I could prolong his sickness and the attendant calm for a little longer.

In the bathroom, Cassandra struggles with her nightclothes.

"Fuck it," she moans, her lips trembling with weakness.

"Do you want me to help you?"

She nods her head.

She shudders as I strip her of damp nightclothes. I am surprised how much it hurts to see her ribs and blue and red veins that streak across her body like the trails of shooting stars. Failed dreams and unfulfilled wishes now frozen and forgotten, and until now hidden beneath her clothes. Am I the last person to see these and care?

Going as gently as I can, I guide her into the shower. I turn the taps, and she moans as the water hits her skin, but she does not wince.

How different it feels to meet death slowly, taking our time as we dance together and see which way it will turn us, knowing that soon the music will stop. So different when death comes unexpectedly and the sudden violence ignites an angry fire, burning for years even though they are long gone.

Soapsuds slide over her sharp contours. I watch as she reaches into every crease and crevice, her eyes shut beneath the hammering flow of water. I watch her struggle to reach her back, and she curses again.

"I feel like a fucking child."

"I can do it for you."

She tries to smile but something creases her face, and she squeezes the bridge of her nose.

I wet a sponge and then add some soap, running it over her papery skin. She does not stir.

When my father caught my eye as I soaped his back, he pushed me away. He pushed so hard that I rebounded against the tiled wall.

"I'll do it," he snapped. "I'm not dead yet."

With each stage of his treatment, he grew more violent, threatening to choke a doctor with his stethoscope so they banned him from that particular hospital. I was humiliated, and it took me years to muster up the courage to return there.

"What was Paris like after your father died?" By now Cassandra has most of the soap off her hair and body, and I can see a little more color emerging in her cheeks.

"That was the first time I ever saw him cry."

I watch her take this in. I wonder if she is trying to see how Paris will be when she finally passes. I want to reassure her that I will be here to hold him, and he will always have this house as his home. But that might not be the reassurance she is seeking.

"That was also the first time that I really grieved for someone," I tell her.

"You didn't grieve when your mother died?"

"Being so young, I didn't know what happened, so I thought she was going to come back."

I always wondered how much Paris told Cassandra about my mother. When we were first a couple, I asked him to keep it brief, like an obituary in a newspaper where every word costs: *Nicola Rose Gall passed away suddenly on (or around) November 14, 1988. In lieu of flowers, memorial donations in Nicola's honor may be sent to The Social Service Association of Rotherwell, 4 Maple Road, Rotherwell, New Jersey 02618.*

I feared that if Paris divulged the cause of my mother's death, Cassandra might have viewed it as a curse on my bloodline. She might have forbidden her brother from marrying me, let alone procreating with me. *These things linger in the blood*, she could have whispered. If she believed this, it pains me to admit that she probably had a point.

"My father was broken when my mother died. He knew that if there was evil out there that could strangle the life out of someone so beautiful, someone so young, it wouldn't hesitate to take me. He fortified this house with latches and bolts and locks, and the outside world became his adversary."

"Sounds scary for a little girl. Paris says you were only about nine or ten."

"Seven. But I guess he was doing what he thought was best. He was trying to keep me safe."

"You can end up staying a little too safe, you know."

"I don't know," I snap.

"If you are too safe then you stagnate, you shut down. It throttles the life out of you."

I knew she wouldn't understand. How could she fear dangers she did not even see? But I see them, just as my father did.

Just as I see my father right now, standing next to her in the shower.

I'm scared. I don't want him to hurt you, and I don't want him to

hurt Aunty Cassie. Isn't there anything you can do?
I want to tell Ania that I won't let him hurt either one of us, but trauma ripples through the generations as much as the years. And trauma knows nothing about time and space. Already I am bracing myself, rigid-limbed, in readiness for another one of his beatings.

I turn off the taps for Cassandra and help her out of the shower. She presses the thick towel into her body and gasps as she stands in front of the sink.

"Let me get your toothbrush."
She leans on me a little as I squeeze chemical-blue paste onto her brush. The freshness seems to waken the pair of us, and as she starts to clean her teeth, I see her body straightening.

She smiles after she has spat out the paste. "I needed that. It's good to get rid of that horrible sticky layer of sweat and meds."
He is still there, standing next to Cassandra. My father stepped out of the shower when she did, and now he stands in front of the sink, glowering at her because he doesn't know who she is. His eyes are furious, like Dylan in a rage.

"Would you like me to brush your hair this time?"
She nods.

The brush glides through the golden strands of what remains of her hair.

"I might take some of that bread and butter," she croons, and for a moment I fear that she might nestle her head into my bosom. With stiffened hands, my movements become clumsy, and the brush gets tangled in a knot. I notice that my hands have started to shake.

"Ouch," she croaks through a dry throat.
"Sorry."
"It's okay."
Ania used to say this, and I would hate it. She would say it when Dylan would play-wrestle her to the ground, and I could see that she was hurting. And when she said *It's okay* he would laugh and wrestle her harder.

As my father is starting to laugh at me now.
Ania never fought back.
I never fought back against my father.
Those men used up all the aggression in the household, so there

was nothing left for us but apathy and surrender.

The ripples of trauma, unconstrained by space and time, causing reenactments, attempts to complete unfinished business, and causing irreversible change (damage?) to our very core. We continue to organize our lives as if the trauma is still going on. Every encounter is contaminated by the past.

Cassandra stares at me, as if she has heard my thoughts. Perhaps she has caught a glimpse of my father too. It terrifies me to think that they might meet soon, and what he might do to her.

I try to think of Paris returning home to protect us. He will be happy to see his wife and his sister exchanging so much kindness with one another.

We stare at each other in the mirror, and I see that my sister-in-law has the same bloodshot, watery eyes as my father. The same knots and lumps and swelling of malignancies. The same green-and-yellow tinge to the skin—warning signs that the body is in decline, that it is failing its basic task of efficiently excreting waste instead of leaving it to contaminate the host. Clear signs that this is the beginning of the end.

Tonight, I dream again about the hooded people.

Bad things happen to bad people, I hear, only this time the voice is different. I assume that one of the hooded people is Dylan saying this. He sounds like he is young again, before his voice broke.

Bad things happen to bad people.

And then I realize it is Ania's voice from beneath one of the hoods. This hurts me so much more than the last dream. I always assumed that her gentle ways were a sign of forgiveness for all my mistakes.

It's okay she says without smiling. *It's okay.* She repeats it over and over again, and she starts to shake her head. I want her to stop because I am afraid she will hurt herself, but she keeps shaking and shaking her head and repeating *It's okay . . . It's okay . . . It's okay.*

There has never been any forgiveness, she just remained quiet because Dylan shouted the loudest. She has just been waiting for her turn, storing it up like toxins beneath the skin.

The taller figure appears more interested than before. From his position on the bed frame, he leans forward and cocks his head to one side. I think I hear him sniffing Ania. He knows she is one of his own.

I notice that Ania has in her hands a sewing kit, and she looks up and smiles.

"Look, Mommy!"

She opens the sewing kit and lines up various needles and thread and scissors.

"Mommy, you taught me to sew. Look what I can do," she sings.

She steps over the sewing supplies and lifts my nightdress. She smoothes the flat of her hand over my skin, replicating the moves her brother made the other night.

"Such soft skin," she says.

She feels around my stomach until she comes across a loose flap of skin: the square her brother had cut open.

"Let me help you with that."

She plucks long strands of hair from her head without wincing, and she threads a needle with them.

Ever so carefully, she punctures my cut skin with the needle, stitching in a small knot to keep the thread in. I feel the pain, but what makes it worse is the delight that spreads across Ania's face every time I show that she has hurt me.

"This was never you," I cry. "You never wanted to hurt anyone."

"How can you be so sure? Just because Dylan got there first."

Each sentence is punctuated by another puncture of my skin, and she threads her fine hair up and down until she has stitched my wound closed.

"There. All better now."

When I look back up at her tired face, I can see that she has ripped so much hair from her head that patches of her scalp are starting to bleed.

Chapter Thirteen

~~~

Shape-shifter

During these lighter days I urge the leaves to stay fresh and cling to the branches just a little longer. I would give anything not to lose the summer, so I don't have to fall into the dark evenings when the leaves shrivel and die. I do not want to see the gnarled old branches of the apple trees, laid bare for the harshness of winter. I cannot face another year of early November snow, and I will not survive it alone. I never thought that Paris would leave me, but each day he shapes this as an inevitability. He spends less time in my presence, refusing to touch me or even meet my eye. I know that his sister would say that he has always been this way, shy of showing interest and stilted in conversation, but I thought we meant more to each other than this.

I could beg Paris not to leave. I could tell him that to do so would leave me helpless to my father, who hangs back in the shadows, just biding his time. But I know that Paris would not believe me, any more than he believes in the suburban beast that still stalks me from outside my door. This afternoon, through the loosened brick in my attic, I watch Paris walk across the driveway to his car. I can see that he is taking his time to enjoy the sunshine because he stops to stretch a little, and this reveals the lower part of his belly. I am surprised how firm he still looks, and how I hadn't even noticed as he rushed about inside the home he shares with me.
~~~

I told him he didn't need to go out, that he had only just been to the shops last night, but he said he couldn't breathe after a whole day of the sun slowly baking the hot bricks of our house.

I said that I would open the windows, I would be willing to do this for him, but still he chose to leave. I know of his doubts and his suspicions. I can smell them in the air like the trail of his aftershave after he left the house. I know I should do more, try new things with him so we can explore each other again, but I don't know where to begin.

For a moment I wonder whether he is going to find our son. Does he have a secluded spot somewhere, away from the prying eyes of Mount Pelion Way, far up in the thicker forests of Rotherwell, where he can speak to Dylan again? Do they reminisce about the earlier days of ball games and creepy crawlies from the backyard and playing with his favorite wooden horse? They wouldn't have talked about girls because he knew his son well enough not to push the point. "Let him tell us in his own time," Paris would tell me. "You can't pressure him."

I can see him up in that forest, sending a signal up into the sky like a Batman emblem shining brightly to the heavens for only Dylan to see. A beacon as any shepherd would light for his son. Is this beacon a distress signal, a plea for Dylan to return so they can join forces and defeat me? Anything is possible.

I waited all afternoon and far into the evening for him to return. I kept one ear open for Cassandra, in case she called for me, so Paris could not accuse me of failing him in that way. Twice I crept down to check that she was still breathing as she took her naps, too afraid of what he might do if he found his sister dead on my watch.

Finally I hear a car pull into the driveway. It is past seven in the evening. I peer through the gap in the brickwork, and I see him getting out of the car, but he isn't alone. Approaching him are the three seething mothers, the snarling wolf pack. There is Freya Marwood, slithering over to wrap around Paris so she can squeeze out information to store and use against me when the time is right. There is Athena Aegean with her dimple-chin and meaty grin, bounding over to demand her fair share. And there, with her well-scrubbed simplicity, is the plastic smile of June West. Together, they writhe and flourish around my husband as if each one is vying for the prize: to be anointed *The Fairest of Them All.*

I can hear the simpering voice of June West, feigning concern and whispering lies about me. "Is everything okay?" I hear her say as she slips her hands onto his. She wills him to believe that he is a trapped bird, and her gentle, freshly moisturized hands will slip the latches and bolts and locks to set him free.

Is everything okay? she will sing to him as June plots her escape from her own philandering husband. *Is everything okay?* she will say as she plots with her wolf pack to defeat the Witch of Mount Pelion Way. How this suburban beast will thrive as it feeds on my failings, uniting neighbor with neighbor in the strongest of alliances: A quest to vanquish a common foe.

Back inside, Paris finds me waiting for him at the top of the stairs.

"I'm glad they are happy," I say, already sounding petty. "Seems like you made sure their every need was met."
I am a petulant child. I am unyielding, malicious, and weak. I am tearing at the skin that I need to survive.

"What are you talking about?" he asks, throwing his keys on the table in the hallway. They clatter so hard that I fear the glass will crack.

I don't need him to once again call me his *goddess* or his *love.* I just want him to be on my side, so he doesn't end up loosening the latches and bolts and locks. My father was right not to tell him about the vaults in the secret room.

"Why would you even acknowledge those women, after everything they have done?"
I shouldn't remain here at the top of the stairs, as if I am standing in judgment over him. I should run down and hold him, let him feel the warmth of my skin so he remembers that I am human and not some mythical beast. I start to walk down to join him, but something makes me stop halfway, at the bend in the stairway. I can see how hardened he has become, and how he refuses to look me in the eyes.

"They are our neighbors," he says.
"They are beasts."
"We have to just get along."

"At what cost? I mean, who else do you have to lose before you grow a backbone and stand up to them?"

"You aren't making sense."

"Their sons. Have you forgotten what they did to our daughter?"

"You can't be sure of that. Ania never told us, no one ever saw anything. It is just your version of events, distorted by your hatred for them."

"That's not true. You know what happened two years ago, in that forest. You know they brutalized our daughter."

"I don't know that. All I know is what you keep telling me. And before two years ago, you would say that the parents of those boys had it in for you. You have to stop this, it isn't healthy."

"Can't you feel her? Can't you hear her everywhere you go? She is here to tell me what happened."

Don't. Don't tell him I am here. He wouldn't understand.

"If you are telling me that you are hearing things then we really need to speak to Marigold."

"So you would rather take her side too?" I shout. "Over your own wife?"

"I'm serious; this has to stop. We need to move on with our lives, and you have to stop the craziness."

"How can you move on when your daughter was raped and murdered?"

"Raped? You have no proof. And you know she wasn't murdered. Stop torturing yourself over this. Marigold told you that you will only start to heal when you accept reality."

He won't look at me. At one time I would have got lost in those blue eyes, but now we are at sea and drifting further from each other.

"You're a coward, Paris. You've always been so afraid of those overblown fathers out there that you let them hound your wife, leaving her terrified to leave her own home."

"You're doing that to yourself. You always have."

"Where were you when Max was attacking me?"

"I don't even know what you're talking about."

"You let him do that to me, and you let them brutalize your own daughter."

"Stop."

"It's true. If you were half the man my father was, you would've taken things into your own hands."

"So you want me to use violence to handle this, the way your father did?"

"It's better than doing nothing. Your daughter is dead. Why don't you care?"

"I do care, but I've chosen to *live* while you have sunken into the grave with Ania. And to show how I am still living, I'm going to accept their invitation."

"What?"

"It's a fresh start."

"What are you talking about?"

"They all asked me. Freya, Athena, and June. They are having a joint graduation party for their boys. I thought it was a nice gesture. I really didn't expect them to include us."

I want to spit at him. He knows that our daughter should be graduating high school with them.

"It was kind of them," he continues. "They know Cassie isn't well, so they wanted to cheer her up."

"No."

"It will be good for my sister. She hasn't much left to make her smile."

"*No!*" I scream. I shake my head and see flames flickering into life like bolts of red lightning. "*No, no, no.*"

"What's all the shouting?"

Cassandra. From the bend in the stairway, I can see them both; Cassandra is at the top, standing in the doorway to her bedroom in a nightgown. She looks like a ghost, floating between death and life as interchangeably as sleep and consciousness. At the bottom of the stairs is Paris, earthly and fallible, his shoulders sloped with the weight of daily tasks. He probably sees me as superfluous: neither ethereal as a memory to mourn nor tangibly human enough to share the daily burdens.

"I'm sorry," he says to his sister. "Go back and rest if you need to. We shouldn't have woken you."

"No, I've had enough rest. What's going on?"

"Nothing. Don't worry about it."

"Don't *nothing* me," she mutters with as much vigor as her bed-weakened muscles will allow.

"We were just talking."

"About what?" Cassandra insists.

"About a party that is going to take place tomorrow," he replies. "Here on the street."

"Oh?"

"You can go," I jump in. "I don't care. Just go."

"Thanks," he hisses. "I know."

"Can I go?" Cassandra asks.

"You don't have to ask. Of course you can." He stares at me as he addresses his sister.

For all the latches and bolts and locks, still the dangers creep in.

"Come on, Eris, we have talked about this." Cassandra's tone is softer than her brother's, and right now I would rather have her in this house than him. "It's good to make an effort with your neighbors."

"It isn't that simple. The people on Mount Pelion Way are dangerous."

"I don't know about that," she sighs.

"You know what happened to my daughter. It is safer in here, away from everyone."

"There is more to life than just keeping yourself safe, and Paris deserves more than that too."

"You know what they did," I hiss.

"You need people to talk to, otherwise the thoughts will just loop round and round your mind to contaminate you. Paris can't be your only *community*."

"That community you talk about, that multiheaded beast, devoured my daughter. You do realize that. They let those boys brutalize Ania—the police, the school counselor, the pastor, they all just turned a blind eye."

"None of that is true." Paris's voice sounds thicker, like gnarled old bark. I wonder if his sister were not here right now, would he thrust his hand over my mouth and press down, breaking my teeth and pushing until my skull caves in?

I walk down the stairs to join him in the hallway, and Cassandra follows. I can smell the chemical trail of medication lingering in the air. I start to smell apple and vinegar and salt and blood. I start to imagine how steadily the boughs of the apple trees sway when there is a breeze, and how one day they will fall to the ground, and the ground, with its battalion of insects, will swallow them whole.

"Please." I squeeze his arm, and something stirs in both of us. A memory of love, lust, or just companionship.

"We could have a meal here together," I suggest. "I could cook for us all."

He shakes his head.

"Have you even told her?" I ask. "I mean, does she know everything that happened the night we found her?"

"I mean it," Paris warns. "Not when she is in this state."

"If not now, when?"

"What is she talking about?" Cassandra asks her brother.

"She escaped it all," I continue, still staring at Paris. "She was too busy enjoying the beach bars of Bali."

"You're still holding onto *that*?" Cassandra sighs. "I was being nice to you, trying to move on. You should really try and let things go. You know how bad stress is for your health. All that cortisol, all those knots inside." Already she is massaging her shoulders in sympathy.

"For you or for me?"

"For either of us. Toxic stress—it can cause heart issues, or diabetes, or all sorts of things. Stop holding on to it and let it go."

"She was my daughter. I can't just *let it go*."

"If you could just get some fresh air, enjoy some new experiences, it will help you to forget."

"I don't want to forget. How can I lose her?"

You'll never lose me. Not again. Try asking her about Paddy's Pub.

"What was Bali like? Did you tiptoe through the ghosts in the rubble of Paddy's Pub? And how about all those corpses washed up on the beaches?"

"What are you talking about?"

"You don't remember the Bali bombings? And then the tsunami just two years later?"

I am breathless and spittle flies from my mouth.

"Why are you saying all this? You're not making sense. That was decades ago."

"It doesn't matter. It all gets locked in there, those ghosts of the blasted and burned people who never got out alive. And those children who drowned with their parents, still kicking and struggling to get to the surface, their limbs tangled in knotted seaweed and electric cables. Their spirits are still trapped."

Why are her eyes so wide? Why is she so afraid of my beliefs when she was ready to embrace Pastor Pry's? Both are fantastical and illusionary; faith, hope, afterlife, resurrection, it is all the subject of legends and myths. For all the flights of fancy that the pastor conjures up in her church, why is she not condemned as a witch? Why am I left alone to be feared as much as I am pathologized with diagnostic labels handed out by Meeches like candy at a parade? Do they sleep better at night with the prospect of feeding me to the suburban beast so it does not turn on them instead?

"Spirits linger, there as much as here." I lean into Cassandra's face, and she flinches as I start to whisper. "I still smell the urine soaking through Ania's clothes. When I held her, I should have been searching for signs of life, but I just remember smelling her urine."

"Okay, that's enough." Paris steps in front of his sister and guides her gently to the living room, leaving me standing alone.

"Please leave," he says, his throat sounding inflamed with hot embers.

"No."

"Just get out of here, will you? I don't want you to upset her."

I feel foolish because I don't know whether he wants me to leave them alone for a little while and go upstairs, or whether he wants me to pack a bag and find somewhere else to live.

But then.

I am as shape-shifting as my daughter. I am a chameleon, too. I have transformed once, and I can do so again, flexing in and out of the carnal, the amorous, the sensuous, and lost to my senses. More than twenty-one years later, I can still taste the bitter twinge of cocaine on my lips, rubbed numb on my gums, and applied with fingertips to other places. There were men, women, and people who didn't call themselves either, before non-binary was a thing. Paris never knew any of this. Under the watchful eye of my father, Paris thought I was chastened and good, inexperienced and in need of his shepherd's guidance beneath the sheets.

As I climb the stairs to the attic, I hear their voices shuffling as they move about the house below me.

. . . sensible decision, without everyone involved . . . talking and doing something about it . . . stupid,...

...really stupid of them . . . .

...make a decision, if you are brave enough...

...Finality of it all...

To let in a little air, I remove the loosened brick from the attic wall. I can hear someone bouncing a basketball up and down the street. In the dim illumination of the solitary streetlamp, I can just about see that it is one of the three boys from Ania's grade. He pivots and shoots the ball, and I guess that it is Cory, although from this angle it could be Dylan. They have the same dark hair; the same tall, angular frame, and I rarely see either of them smile.

When he left high school, Dylan never wanted any party to celebrate his graduation. He didn't want us to acknowledge any of it, claiming that he couldn't wait to see the back of the *losers* and *meatheads* and *gays*. The last one surprised me. For years, I saw the way he watched the boys in his grade, and I said nothing. A mother knows. I wanted him to talk about it when he was ready, and I would have told him that he should be himself, and whoever he loved didn't matter as long as they made him happy. But he never came to us with any of this.

Instead, all he brought to us was hatred and contempt. When he went on about *the gays* at school and *the gays* on television and *the gays* in the news, I wanted to grab his face and scream *Do you think the lady doth protest too much?* He wouldn't have admitted to it. It would have meant that we had a connection, that he saw that I was not rejecting him or wishing him harm in the way that he wished harm on everyone around him. I wish I could have made him see how he treated people, with that arrogant assumption that we should all just bend to his every whim.

There is a stirring of bushes in the forest further down the street. If my son decides to return to us, it is from that forest that I will see him emerge. I imagine how he will rise from the underworld covered in nettles and swamp weed, and he will wade through that murky water, oblivious to the oilcans and trash bags that have been dumped there. I can see him scaling a tree and swinging from bough to bough until he rests at the tree closest to my house. From there, he will watch me, biding his time as he peers through the cracks in the curtains to identify weaknesses in my defenses. He knows of every latch and bolt and lock, and he knows of my patterns; when I am defenseless in sleep, and when I am sleepy as I rise.

As he sits in that tree, I imagine that he might etch into the bark a spear and shield, the same calling cards he would etch onto the skirting boards and floorboards of his room. As soon as he left our home, Paris sanded all of these down, but from a certain angle, in a certain light, you can still see the motifs of war. My Ares, my battle-lustful son. The only one strong enough to defeat me.

My eyes adjust to the darkness, and so I see that it was just a lonesome deer stirring in the forest. In other parts of this country, or in other periods of time, the three boys on Mount Pelion Way, almost men by now, would have shot this deer with a gun, or even wrestled it to the ground with their bare hands. Instead, I can see June West gesticulating wildly from her driveway as she attempts to shoo it away. The wild creature watches her as it continues to chew whatever leaves it has found. Cory has now seen it because he stops bouncing his ball and looks scared. As he retreats into Athena's house, I can hear his reed-thin voice whining, "Mom, Mom, there's a deer, Mom. Do something, Mom."

I once saw the three boys chasing a couple of foxes into the forest. I saw one of them throw a cannister of gasoline over their prey, and I could see how it stung their little, confused eyes. At the time I thought there could be nothing worse than this cruelty. That was the final week of Ania's life.

That night, Dylan returns to me. He doesn't bother to wear a hood, and this time he is alone.

"She was dragging me down," he says, smirking, as if he has read my mind.

"What have you done with her?" I try to scream, but I cannot make any sound.

"Just you and me tonight. No more Ania. Not what you would've chosen, I am sure."

Dylan has his heavy backpack, the one he used to carry to and from school, and he reaches inside, retrieving a length of rope and a roll of duct tape. I remember finding these items at the back of his closet when he was about fifteen or sixteen. I should have spoken to someone about it then, but I was afraid that he would twist it so that I became the focus of their scrutiny.

He stretches out the rope as he keeps his eyes on me.

"This will do fine. Grandad took great pleasure teaching me the various knots."

I know he is lying. Both grandfathers were dead by the time he was born. He is just trying to scare me.

Dylan unties the rope around my wrists, slips one of my arms over his shoulder, and hauls me off the bed. His strength scares me.

"We're going for a little walk" he says, and I can smell the apples on his breath. They have aged, so it is a fermented smell of yeast and age. I know what he is doing: He is trying to make me remember. What greater pain than to bring me back to that moment? But I refuse to let him defeat me, pinching my nails into the tips of my fingers so that I squeeze the skin until it starts to bleed.

He looks on, stirred by the sight of my blood.

"Where shall I take you?" he asks. "Shall we go outside?"

"No."

"Very well."

In silence, he carries me up to the attic.

"Look at all of this," he sneers. "This is all you have left."

Dylan drops me amongst Ania's photographs and report cards and clothes. I can feel beneath my fingers the softness of her toy panda and want to cry, but I stop myself. I cannot show him that he has struck a raw nerve.

As he stands over me, I think I hear a scuffle of feet from behind him. It comes from the darker corners of the attic, the places I rarely explore. I want to believe it is vermin, but I think I see a pair of boots in the darkness. My father's boots.

"You made me like this," Dylan spits at me. The vitriol is still there, but it has lessened ever so slightly, making room for something else. Regret?

"You corrupted me," he continues, "and I hate you for that."

"You did it all yourself, Dylan."

"You probably drank alcohol when you were pregnant. Or did drugs. Come on, admit it. What did you do? What did you do to me?"

As he screams, his mouth widens like the grin of a Cheshire Cat, but then I see that the corners of his lips are starting to split.

"Oh, Dylan," I cry. I am shocked by the pain I feel. "Stop. You're going to hurt yourself."

He doesn't seem to know how to. Now he looks scared. His mouth opens wider and cracks his jaw apart, his legs twitching in response. He is making a strange guttural sound as he tries to scream, but he is choking on his blood and saliva.

I wake up and I am crying, saying *sorry* over and over again.

I wish I could stop loving him.

Chapter Fourteen

~~~

Golden apples

Behold the pageantry, the pomp and ceremony. Tables are unfolded and lined up, festooned with garlands and large dishes of unidentifiable but ornate delicacies for the feast. Overwrought with indulgence; they are trying to make a point. The people of Mount Pelion Way have chosen these florid displays to show how much they still have, how fat their bellies can swell on moments their sons continue to create for them. Cory and Aedean and Smithson are still alive and will graduate, and Ania will not.

I watch through the gap in the brickwork of my attic as brightly colored balloons emerge and dance in the breeze as if they are party guests who have chosen to arrive early. I see that it is Freya who is carrying the balloons, and when the wind picks up, she squeezes her arms around them so they are not blown away. I can hear them taunting me with their squeak and scratch of rubber against rubber, and I long to stab each one with a kitchen knife.

I see Max pointing a sweaty man towards the line of tables. The sweaty man is weighed down as he tiptoes with armfuls of serving trays, the silver reflecting the early June sunlight to dazzle his eyes. Max looks irritated when sauce spills onto his driveway, and I know that he won't be handing out a tip.

Downstairs, I make it seem like I am going about my day as usual, untouched by the changes happening inside and outside of my fortress. I straighten pictures that hang on the wall, and I wipe
~~~

dust from my blank-faced terracotta warriors. I am remembering again how to hit that perfect note of alignment, that stillness of the air, so I can keep a finely tuned focus and still time, making space for Ania to return. She has been uncharacteristically quiet of late, no doubt scared away by the constant arguing.

Within the stillness, she should be here, the golden prize, emerging from the opacity of my dreams. I should see how her shoulders have now, after two years, fallen back with a subtle confidence, her long auburn hair shining in the sun as she graduates high school with those three boys. How sorry they would be to have damaged someone so beautiful.

But within the stillness, there is nothing but a gaping hole. An oblivion into which I could easily sink.

"Why don't you come?" my sister-in-law says, squeezing my arm. I can see the veins pulsating beneath the paper-thin skin of Cassandra's hands. I know it is futile to tell her this, but she shouldn't stand out on the street for hours, not in her condition. Given all her body is fighting, and how much it is losing, I wonder whether her heart will cope with the strain.

"I don't think so," I reply. "At least, I don't know."
"Well, that isn't a no, so we've made progress since yesterday."
"We'll see."
"Even if it's just for a short while, it would be good to show your face. Do it for me."
I feel cornered in my own home, but Paris is watching me carefully, so I say nothing more.

Cassandra throws her arms around me and hugs me to her fragile body. I marvel at how simplistically she views the world, how she can cut through conflict and acrimony like a warm knife through butter.

As Paris and Cassandra walk out to join the party, I know they are watching me carefully. They now see me as the witch that has been lurking in the background all along. The myths and legends were true, and there I was, hiding in the shadows of the most twisted nightmares. Left alone, they imagine that I will stir my cauldron and concoct potions of discord and strife, exacting vengeance on every one of those people on Mount Pelion Way. I will bubble and boil the caramel to make golden apples, seasoning and lacing them with aconite and arsenic and cyanide and rat poison. A bold rebellion against that multiheaded suburban beast, to shake the realms of Mount Pelion Way.

And afterwards, how I will hover above the battlefield, consumed with malice like the malevolent fairy they paint me to be, and how I will revel in their dying groans.

That isn't very nice.

The poison drains from me, leaving me with nothing but foolishness for such spite. In the breeze, the swaying of the apple trees, Ania tells me not to hurt anyone.

"They hurt you. It is the least they deserve."

No. Don't do it.

"I can't promise anything," I say. "But if I don't do it, can I at least hurl green globules of spittle into the softening caramel sauce?" I ask her.

I hear her laughter stirring inside me like the wings of a butterfly.

I decide to shower and put on something new. I choose one of my mother's dresses, the one of rich burgundy velvet. I can just about remember how soft the velvet felt against my cheek when I lay on her lap. She would run her fingers through my hair and hum tunes to me, but I can't remember what any of them were. I wish I could recreate one of those songs, so I could bring her back to life and she could fill in the gaps that she left by leaving me so soon.

Was this the first thread to start this knot that twists me from within? My mother. Threads can be beautiful on their own, such striking colors, but if they are tangled together, they twist to catch things and strangle out life. My mother was happy until something tangled inside her, and she left me alone with a father who became trapped in his grief. He was just thirty-five when she died, when she left him to care for me. He didn't have much to teach a seven-year-old girl, not alone. He tried his best, but it was never going to be good enough, and so the threads tangled even more. And in that mess, in the knots of my father's grief, I found Paris. And our threads were twisted together to create Dylan, and then Ania. But then, years after something devoured my mother, it came back for Ania. Thread upon thread tangling together as tightly as a hangman's noose.

After my shower, and after I have dried my hair, I slip into the red velvet dress, and I stand in front of my full-length mirror. I run my hands over my sides, willing the curves and folds to flatten just a little bit. Still a soft, bulbous, misshapen witch.

I walk down the stairs and find the black-strapped high heels that my mother wore with this dress, and I slip them on. They fit. Now that I have stepped into this part, I feel ready.

Opening the door, I see garish smiles that are not intended for me. These self-proclaimed gods and goddesses look on; painted women who are barely robed slink around overblown fathers as they judge and covet each other. These perfidious neighbors: They squander allegiances for the next opportunity, dropping each other in a heartbeat if the temptations prove too great, and yet today they writhe and slink in unison, seemingly stirred by the beat of one heart. Their toxic judgment forms a single speech bubble over their heads, a thriving cloud that moves in sync, like a swarm of locusts with the same intent. They all want to watch me fail.

Their circle is tightly formed, closing any gap so Paris and Cassandra are left alone to lean against a flimsy fold-out table. They would have done the same to Ania if she had survived long enough to graduate. After all, who wants to be friends with the daughter of a madwoman? Guilt by association. I think of all the times Ania has been left to stand alone, and then I see the forest at the end of this street again. I know my daughter is kind and loving, and she doesn't want me to hurt anyone, but that kindness and love left her defenseless that Halloween night. She never expected them to hurt her because she would never hurt them.

I think of aconite and arsenic and cyanide and rat poison. I see lips turning the same shade of purple and blue as wolfsbane, and I wonder if they might beg me for mercy as they double over in agony. I would point to that pain and tell them of my own, and the dizziness and confusion that has been plaguing me for the last two years. They crave connectedness and interdependence, so let them join in unison in their slow and painful death.

Still standing in my doorway, I gesture for Paris to come over to me. He looks annoyed but he obeys, leaving his sister to stand alone while everyone ignores her.

"What do you want?"

"Come," I say, luring him back inside our hallway, where no one can see us. "Take these from me, will you? They're heavy."
I hand to him the plate of caramelized apples and he turns and walks them away from me, as stiffly as a wooden horse. He places the apples on the fold-out table and I watch him read the words—*For The Fairest*—that I piped with gold icing on the serving plate.

I walk down my path to join my husband and his sister, and I see that Freya is eyeing the golden prize. And then it is June's turn, and finally Athena, and their murmuring dies down as they meet each other's glare in silent competition. Each will insist that they are *The Fairest*. I wonder if conflict between the women will ignite a brawl between the men, and I will witness their destruction without a single bite of an apple. Paris might have been right when he said that this was a chance to start afresh. Clearing the old to make way for new shoots of hope.

I watch Smithson blanche when he sees me. I revel in his anguish. As he swigs some beer, Max watches my every move. I am sure he is deliberating very carefully about what he should do with me and when. He will never forget what I did to his son because it hurts Max's ego more than it could ever hurt Smithson. I dare to glance in his direction and he offers me a tight, threatening smile, flashing his gleaming white teeth with menace. When the time is right, I will rip each tooth from his head.

Pink and white-winged in chiffon, the three seething mothers continue to stare at me. I am sure they expect a performance from me: a flourish from my rainbow of vitriol and spite, or perhaps some twisted magic to turn white clouds to ash. I refuse to give them anything more.

I notice that some of them have garlands in their hair, and as they pour wine and pluck grapes, my head feels heavy in the heat. Hazy white mists cloud around them, making them seem ethereal, and I lose the ability to distinguish between them. Freya's hair and June's face switch, and Athena's dimple-chin and meaty grin are grafted onto Max's angular features. Their flesh begins to merge and stick together, so that if they pull apart, I wonder if they will tear. I want them to rip and split so I can watch them bleed.

I hear trumpets and harps in the distance, the sort of pageantry usually reserved for heralding the arrival of great dignitaries. I realize it is just the music that Cory is casting from his cell phone through a couple of speakers that hang from his basketball hoop. I catch his eye and he looks sad, and I wonder if he might tell me something when the party becomes so raucous that no one sees me slip away and follow him inside his house. After too many beers, will he open up a little more and tell me the truth about that Halloween night? Or will I have to rip it out of him?

I approach him and he stares at me, saying suddenly, "Fuck, it's you".

"Yes," I reply.

"Where have you been all this time?"

I notice he is looking over my shoulder, so I turn, and then I see what he and everyone else is looking at. Dylan has emerged from nowhere, like a glitch in time, and he is walking towards me. His footsteps are silent, and his grin is loud, grinding, and twisted.

Chapter Fifteen

~~~

A Trojan's return

I wonder how long he has been watching me. To think Dylan might have sat in the tree outside our house, waiting for the right time to return. Did he see me help his aunt get washed that morning, listening to our words as they leaked out from the gaps around the windows and the doors? Did he laugh at us, these foolish silhouettes, thinking that we were playing games in a shower like a couple of drunk college girls? Or was he jealous that no one showed him that kind of tenderness and care? Was he filled with rage to think that I could soften now, after all these years, and for a dried-up, drunken aunt of his. But never for him.

As soon as Paris saw his son, he raced over and threw his arms around him. I shrank in on myself as I watched tears of relief appear in the corner of my husband's eye.

"Where have you been?" he gasped as he struggled to regain composure. "We've been worried about you."

"Here and there. You know how it is."

"Well, I don't know, if I'm honest." I am surprised by Paris's tone, and a flash of hope flickers inside of me. "I would never just disappear on my parents like that. It's been more than a year and we've been worried sick about you."

"Well, Dad, you're not me."

"I am just saying that I would've appreciated a call."

"Enough already," Dylan says, his smile faltering.

"I would never have put my own parents through that kind of
~~~

worry. We really didn't know what to think."

"I guess you had different parents than I did. Maybe you never had the need to get away from them."

Dylan always found a way to keep his father at arm's length, despite Paris' devotion to his son.

"Just drop it, will you?" he snaps.

There you are, I silently hiss. *I see you. I knew it was really you beneath the plastic smile of a Halloween mask. And now I just wait until the explosions of anger return.*

"You came out of Max and June's house," Paris says, his tone a little more contrite. "Does that mean you've been there all along?"

"No, of course not. I've been travelling around, and they told me about the party, so I thought this would be a good time to return."

"You've stayed in touch with them?"

"No, Dad, just Max. He had some work for me for a while."

I turn to see Max preening himself in the reflection of his cell phone camera, and I want to grab it from him to see what this man is really made of. Why is he so interested in my son? Will I find images and videos of Dylan on his phone, images and videos that are pored over late at night when he has that feral urge that his wife can no longer satisfy.

"Work?" Paris continues. "What kind of work?"

"This and that."

"Right then."

Dylan takes a swig of beer.

"Since when do you drink?" his father asks him.

"Oh come on," he says, laughing. I had forgotten how striking his features were, with his big, hard jaw, his thick eyebrows, and his solidly jet-black hair. He wasn't attractive; he was intimidating. "It's a party, isn't it?"

I sometimes wished that Dylan had been like other kids in school and experimented with alcohol or anything to dissipate that rage and frustration. But he always sneered when Paris would open a bottle of wine. He told us that he would never drink because he didn't want to lose control, even for a moment. And I believed him. So to see him now, willingly relinquishing control with each sip, makes no sense. Unless he has decided to slam full throttle into nihilism, planning a spectacle where he can take out as many people as possible.

"Glad you have kept yourself busy" Paris sighs, clearly dissatisfied with his son's answers. "Are you back for good?"

"We'll see."

"Okay. Well, you'll have to excuse the bedroom rearrangement. Your aunt has been using your room."

"I heard you were staying, Aunty Cass. And I heard things were a little tough right now." Surprising everyone, he throws his arms around her, and it must have been a little too roughly because her eyes clamp shut with a flinch. I wonder if she suddenly remembers his teenage rages, when she advocated for a political view that differed from his own. He called her an *airhead* and a *fascist*, throwing aside chairs and a table before his father could take him outside to calm down.

"He's a hothead," she had gasped. "Out of control. Did you see the way he went after me? It really is unacceptable."

"I agree," I had said, nodding and wanting to tell her about all the other times. But I was ashamed.

"Is he on anything?" she had asked. "Drugs? Alcohol? I've heard some of them snort glue. So gross."

"Not as far as I know."

"Maybe he needs to be. I mean, something prescribed by a professional. Has he been evaluated?"

At the time I dismissed her suggestions. Now I realize that was foolish negligence.

As the graduation balloons dance around Cassandra's head, she tries to smile at her nephew.

"You look well," she says. "And thank goodness you're safe."

"Safe from what?" he replies.

"Anything. There are so many crazies in the world these days. Just look at what's happened to New York."

"Sometimes the crazies are closer to home than you think. Stranger danger is a myth."

Stunned, Cassandra can only smile and offer *Oh, fun* in response.

Dylan takes another swig of his beer and surveys the party. He has still not acknowledged me.

"Why are you really here?" I ask.

"Good to see you too, Mother. Nothing like a good old-fashioned welcome."

"I'll welcome you when I know what is going on."

"Isn't it obvious? I came back to see you."

He starts to snigger, and I wonder whether the beer has already made him light-headed. I have to tread carefully because I have never dealt with him when he was inebriated.

"Why don't you answer seriously. Why are you here?"

"Oh, you know, couldn't keep away from your delicious home cooking."

He sniggers again, and I notice that June West is watching us intently. Her cheeks are sucked in as if she is savoring a delicious piece of candy.

"What did you do with all that money you stole from me? And where is my car?"

"Come on, Mom. You know money burns fast in this area. And I had to sell the car. Sorry. I'll make it up to you."

My skin prickles as I feel June watching us. From the corner of my eye, I can see that she is slinking away from her friends, and I just know that she is coming over to ask *Is everything okay?* She will poke and pry, pushing me further and further, and she will probably snake her arm around Dylan's shoulders, showing me how he is hers now. My breathing becoming shallow, I'm afraid I am going to lose time again.

Already she is right next to me. She has even snaked a hand up and down my back as she tries to intimidate and control me. I want to slap her plastic, simpering smile.

"Is everything okay?" she asks.

In chorus, I hear Freya squawking "Amazing, so amazing" about something or nothing, and Athena is joining in with a sneer of "What the actual freak show is she doing?" Max is shouting on his cell phone at someone so he feels suddenly closer, behind me perhaps, and I glance back to find Cassandra and Paris, still wooden, dry, and lifeless.

My ears are buzzing so hard I fear my head will burst, so I throw my hands over my ears and shake my head.

"What the fuck are you doing?" Paris hisses.

"I need to go," I gasp.

Paris tries to take hold of my arms, but I shake him free. "Get off me. I need to go."

A balloon pops and everyone jumps except Dylan. For all I know, he has taken out a knife and stabbed it. A part of me just wants him to get it over with, whatever he is going to do.

I race across the street and up my path to the door. Fleetingly, I notice the purple and blues of the aconite sprouting up along the border of my yard, and so I glance back, only to see Dylan seizing the plate of caramelized apples and throwing them into the trash. For good measure, he pours his beer all over them, just to punctuate his point. No doubt he has been watching me as he decided when he would make his return. He has been peeping through the windows of my kitchen and watching the witch at work with her potions. Always one step ahead of me.

Slamming the door shut behind me, I can breathe more freely. The ticking of the carriage clock keeps each beat as I remove my shoes, place them in the closet, and run up to the safety of my bedroom. There I slip out of the ridiculously uncomfortable velvet dress and replace it with my soft nightclothes.

On my bed, I cradle my head on a patterned cushion that Ania once made for me. She had embroidered it with a picture of a small blue dog, a cartoon she used to watch on rainy Sunday afternoons. I run my fingers over these stitches, and if I shut my eyes, I can hear her laughing at the cartoon. That light belly giggle as we cuddled together for hours.

I realize now that on the sidelines Dylan was watching us laughing together, and he was jealous. Ania posed a threat because she was so easy to love whereas Dylan was all elbows and hard edges. I know he wouldn't allow anyone to make him feel vulnerable for too long, always finding a way to eradicate a threat. When he became a teenager, he would cuss at his sister and call her stupid, and still she did not fight back.

Ania?

I wonder if she is remembering the bad days too, and that's why she has fallen silent. It was like a war zone when hormones charged around Dylan's body, and he would swing at me, then I would swing at him, and Ania would cry or run away.

I sometimes ended up with bruises or bumps, but Dylan had his own share of injuries. When Pastor Pry saw me in the hardware store with a split lip, she assumed it was Paris.

"Let me help you," she had whispered, careful that Ania and Dylan did not hear. "You shouldn't tolerate this. I want to help you. Please."

When I told the pastor it was Dylan who had caused my injury, she made me feel ashamed. Part of the shame was because I had also raised my hand to him. If he was turning out to be violent, he learned it from me, because Paris never harmed a soul. Dylan calmed down after a year or so, but I never believed that the violence had left him. I suspected he had just learned how to use it in a more devious way. Quiet and steady, like an accumulation of dread; that was the impression I was gathering of my son over the years. It was a subtle fear, like the hairline crack before the whole building collapses.

And it haunts me even now.

As the sounds of the graduation party start to fade with the failing light, I nestle into Ania's embroidered cushion. I try to sleep but I hear a turning key in the lock. By now it is dark and there are voices in the hallway. Then a door slams.

Dylan.

For the last year of his absence, how many times has he tried the windows and doors, hoping for a sign of weakness that he can exploit?

". . . without that. And that was when they told me about the beer cans. And you know what they said?"

"What?" Paris replies from the hallway.

"I'll do it. Because you asked me so nicely, I can do it. But if I get lip from you, sonny boy, I won't do shit for you."

I shrink further under my bedsheets, like a child again. In the darkness shapes contort, and I think I see my father's boots shuffling behind the curtain. He is waiting for a time when he is alone in this house with me, and Dylan can join us. Were the words in that letter Dylan's and my father's, or Dylan's and Max's? I wonder what they will leave under my pillow next time.

I hear the scuffling of feet in the attic again. It could be Ania, but I fear it is Dylan, and he is searching for the secret room. Was that the deal he made with Max? Together, they would defeat me and share in the wealth they found in any secret rooms of vaults? How Max's blue eyes will sparkle at my mother's rainbow of jewels. I should have tempted him up there with the promise of a business deal of my own, and then locked him in that vault with his wife and son. Using an IV line, I could have kept them alive long enough to discover the truth about that Halloween night.

But then.

There is always the chance that, even locked in a vault for eternity, they would still insist that it wasn't Smithson, any more than it was Cory or Aedean. If I discovered that, what would I do? I think I have been trying to dance around that possibility for quite some time.

The boots behind the curtain have disappeared, sinking beneath the floorboards, perhaps, in search of a droplet of bourbon.

I struggle to my feet. A little light-headed, I stumble my way out into the hallway. It is dark, and I sense movement coming up the stairs. I imagine Dylan climbing the walls and the ceiling on his hands and feet, upside down with his head twisted backwards like a beast from hell.

I race faster up the stairs so he won't catch me. I reach the attic and slam the door behind me.

The room is quiet.

I turn on the light, half expecting him to charge at me from behind the curtain or beneath the floorboards, with his grandfather holding me from behind. But the room is empty.

I feel for the secret key and remove the fake wall panel. Unlocking the hidden door, I open up and see that the sanctuary remains untouched. I can breathe again.

I lock it all up and return downstairs.

As I reach my bedroom, I smell Dylan before I see him. That musty odor that once trailed around my home for too many years, only this time I also smell a scent of leather and something metallic.

Inside my bedroom, I shut the door and leave on the light as I sit in bed waiting for Paris to join me. Tomorrow I will open the windows and let in some air.

Tonight I dream of Ania, but for once, I do not want to. I know that Dylan's return brings back too many memories of her place at his feet just waiting for his instruction. Subjugated for his own satisfaction, as most men expect of women.

I walk into the living room and find Dylan with his shirt off, standing over his sister. She is lying on the couch with her trousers down. Ania is seven and Dylan is nine years old.

They must have thought that I was out in the backyard, tending to the vegetable patch.

"What the hell are you doing?" I scream. "Get away from her."

I swing my hand and it makes contact with Dylan's cheek. The room echoes with a satisfying thwack. I want to do it again, but I'm afraid I won't stop.

We were little kids, we were just playing. It isn't our fault.

Was I really wrong about the boys on Mount Pelion Way?

It was never Smithson. And it wasn't Cory or Aedean. We did stuff but they never hurt me.

Horror floods my veins when I realize that the latches and bolts and locks might not have been keeping the beast out but locking him in with his sister.

Chapter Sixteen

~~~

Loosened latches, bolts, and locks on a haunted fortress

Dylan trails me through my home, watching as I straighten and polish and clean. He mocks me when Paris is not around, resting his dirty feet on the coffee table and picking flakes of skin to fall like ash-shaped snowflakes.

"You are something else," Dylan laughs when I try to clean around his feet. He laughs again when I try to lift them, shuddering at his thick and yellowing toenails. He wiggles his feet with glee when he notices my disgust.

"Tasty, right?

I try to ignore him, but he persists.

"Why do you keep staring at me like that?" he asks.

Sleep has messed with his hair so it sticks back and reveals a receding hairline. I think of him old and alone, when he has tormented so many people that he just waits for the end to come. I wonder whether he will finally understand the damage he has caused, or whether he will just thrash around, continuing to blame other people until his eyeballs cloud over with death.

I have not spoken to Paris all day. He was up earlier than me, unusual for him, and immediately left the house. He said that he needed to fill our home with supplies now that his son has returned.

I want to share with my husband the nightmare Dylan's return has brought back to me: The game of doctors and nurses played out between a brother and a sister. I want Paris to say what I
~~~

suspect, so I am not the one to shatter his illusions. But I must choose my time carefully. Paris is still idealizing the return of his prodigal son, so I need to wait until Dylan lets his Halloween mask slip completely. And when he does, he will have enough rope to hang himself before his father's eyes.

Last night Paris woke me as he was stumbling into bed. The smell of bourbon filled my mouth and lungs.

In the distance, a fox howled at the moon.

I blinked at my husband in the glare of his bedside lamp. He had wiry hairs sprouting from the top of his ears, and in another time, I might have made a joke of it or toyed with him as I tried to pluck them out. But they just repulsed me, making me think of a spaced-out old man who is barely aware of his surroundings, the type who sits on a park bench and makes an occasional lunge for a woman who happens to cross his path.

"Where is Dylan now?" I asked him.

"In Ania's room."

"Why?"

"He needs to sleep somewhere."

"No. Not her room. Please."

I thought of Dylan's smell plastered all over her walls. I could feel the weight of him lying in her bed, crushing whatever memories I had left of her.

"Oh, come now."

How many times has he used phrases like that: pat, shushing phrases to smooth out and embroider the edges of our life in the hope that I will not notice the ugly, spoiled, rotten reality at the center of it all.

"Where would you prefer he sleep? The garage?"

"But it's her room."

"And Cassie has his room. I am not about to disrupt her, especially at this time of night."

"She seemed okay earlier."

He glared at me. I was getting in between two siblings who bicker but love each other. I was never going to win.

"The party wiped her out, and I've been worried about that cough she's developed."

As he prepared for sleep, he brushed his teeth and got changed with renewed vigor. After he turned out the lights, he slipped into bed next to me and snaked his hand over my belly.

"So warm," he cooed, like the throaty trill of a mockingbird.

I wanted to respond with the touch of my hand, exploring his body and trying to see if we had anything left that was worth salvaging. But the thought of Dylan standing in the hallway made me shrink into myself and shiver.

"You're shaking," he whispered, his hands running up and down my body. I was soothed by the fact that he noticed, but still I saw again that jet-black hair and those thick eyebrows as Dylan stared from across the hall. I knew that my son could see through our bedroom door, and he could hear everything, because he was everything and everywhere at all times.

"Stop. Please. I don't feel . . . I just . . . just not right now. Please."

"It's okay."

Paris would always say this, and sometimes this made me settle a little and try again, refusing to let age or circumstances contaminate our sex life. But this time I turned my back on him and stared at the crack of light that was spilling from beneath the door. I saw the flickering shadows of footsteps retreat, and I knew that it was Dylan.

There is a part of me that marveled at how quickly my son maneuvered into the role of the helpless, vulnerable child, as if he saw that Ania's death created a vacant position for him to fill. He knew full well that if Paris perceived him as helpless, his place in this house would be secured, making me look like the persecutor who has less right to remain here.

During the days that followed, I longed to comb through every inch of our home to find clues to Dylan's real intentions. When I heard my son in the bathroom, I paused outside his bedroom, rightfully Ania's room, ready to sneak in. But I heard the bathroom door unlock and Dylan stepped into the hallway with just a towel around his waist.

"Ah. Morning, Mother," he said, grinning. Water trickled down his chest and into hairs that had once horrified me when I saw them emerging on him. I viewed them as signs of his greater potency, and already, at that stage, I felt overwhelmed.

I could see past him that he had left the tap running in the bathroom, and as he caught my eye, he stared back at it.

"Oh, that?" he said. "My mistake. Oh wait, did you think I was trying to flood the house and drown you and Aunty Cassie?"

"Don't be ridiculous," I snap, pushing past him to turn the tap off. The air is fouled with the smell of feces, making me dry heave.

"And I wouldn't stay in there for much longer. Might be toxic." Dylan uses the same sing-song tone as Max, dancing round kindness and aggression as he makes my eyes go blurry.

He stretches and for a moment I fear that the towel is going to drop. Instead, he massages the muscles that have widened his forearms. I think of him working out as preparation for a war, uninterested in attraction or love because he only wants to overpower and defeat.

"Good thing I'm here to carry the load a little," he says, grinning, with his big jaw thrusting at me. "Dad seems really tired staying up all night with Aunty Cassie."

He is waiting for his aunt's death, and then he will get rid of me. And hasn't it always been so? No matter how many prying eyes, there is no one in suburbia to really care if boys and men take girls and women to isolated parts to inflict their will in any manner they choose. There are always abandoned alleyways and factories and swampland, and even the well-manicured lawns serve as a deceptive front for attics and basements where you can hide any number of bodies.

But this is not a battle of the sexes or genders. If challenged, Dylan would probably slip that hangman's noose by claiming that he is non-binary, so he isn't like the other boys and men. He always has an answer for everything. This is about the kind versus the unkind, the Anias versus the Dylans of this world, and with their impervious shells, like cockroaches, the unkind always seem to survive over the others. The Dylans, the Maxs, the Smithsons, and even the goddesses of discord and strife. We all live while Ania dies.

I push past my son and run downstairs. Still his odor hangs around me, covering my clothes and hair and mouth. I open the windows in every part of the house, letting the air rush through so I can breathe again. The sudden gust knocks some of the terracotta warriors onto their side as they split in two, finally defeated after centuries of their silent sentinel.

No matter where I try to hide, Dylan finds me, so I flick the latches and bolts and locks, and swing open the door to feel the warm June sunshine on my skin.

I could make my escape by driving far away from here. There are other towns and other states, other countries too. I feel a wild flash of excitement when I imagine taking myself to the airport and just jumping on a plane. People do it all the time. There is a whole world out there to enjoy, away from Mount Pelion Way.

A childish giggle flutters in the pit of my stomach as I imagine how far I could get before anyone even noticed. Such freedom, such a freefall.

But then there is Ania.

Did you forget about me?

I would never do that.

But that freedom might make you happy.

You make me happy.

But it isn't enough. You deserve more.

I could wait. I know that your father will leave eventually, and Dylan will probably follow. Then I could find a new friend, someone who is willing to join me in the fortress.

I continue walking down Mount Pelion Way, only this time my daughter has fallen silent. I wonder if I have upset her by suggesting this. Did she want me all to herself?

I think of my mother and how tightly she clung to me. Her love could be feverish, clawing, and during those times I remember how hard it was for me to breathe.

But then the noose would loosen, and my mother would scream with delight, arms outstretched, as she ran down this very street. I would run with her, or ride my bike, and I loved to see her happy again. At that time, I knew nothing of a multiheaded suburban beast watching me with eyes that burn like red coals of fire. I see them right now, in their flimsy houses, seething with suburban suspicion and they are…

Silly. They're kind of silly.

Yes. I suppose they are.

They don't scare me. Not anymore.

I reach the edge of the forest. There was once a time when this marked the precipice of my world. As a child, my father told me that if I walked through this forest, I would come to a ravine where the earth just fell away into a pit of nothingness. He probably wanted to scare me away from wandering far from our home. By then he viewed the world as dangerous because it had inexplicably swallowed his wife whole, and it could easily do the same to me.

I plunge further into the thicker parts of the forest, and then I see the land rising before me. It is like a tidal wave of dirt and tangled weed, and I once believed that it might lift me to heaven to see my mother again.

And now, with Ania, I climb these hills. I ignore the sharpness of each breath that cuts at my chest, determined to keep going until I find a clearing that overlooks a slow-flowing brook. That is the place I used to bury gifts for my mother. I knew that she was buried in the ground somewhere in Rotherwell, so in my childish logic, I thought this would be the easiest way to get things to her. I buried bracelets I had made at school, paintings, drawings, and even my science projects. I also buried the teeth I had lost and that I knew could not be taken by anything as foolish and fanciful as a fairy.

As the years progressed, I kept coming to this clearing. This was my spot to be alone with my mother, and as I grew older the offerings became feverish letters where I wrote about the world that was unfolding before my eyes.

To think now how dangerous it was for a small child to roam so far from home . . . I should have been scared, but my mother had suddenly disappeared, so I wanted to find out why. My father was too lost in his own grief to help me understand, and whenever I tiptoed down the stairs, I could smell the air thickening with alcohol, so I knew I had to slip the latches and bolts and locks because it was safer out there than inside with him.

Imagine how terrifying it must have been for a little girl to see her father howling in the moonlight like that. The only thing that wasn't smashed was the picture he held of his wife.

It took six years to find out what happened to my mother. The year I became a teenager, I found a police and autopsy report shoved into the depths of my father's desk drawer:

At 2:30 p.m. on December 19, 1988, I carried out a postmortem examination on the body of Nicola Rose Gall, aged 32 years, of 1 Mount Pelion Way, Rotherwell, NJ 02618.
The body was identified to me by Police Officer Mark A. J. Lennox, and Police Officer Paul A. Ward, Police Station, Salville, Pennsylvania. It is said that the deceased had a history of depression.
About 10:20 a.m. on November 14, 1988, she was found dead in the back seat of her locked car which was on a forest track in the woods at Salville. A hose led from the exhaust into the vehicle and thereafter into a plastic bag over the deceased's head. Decomposition was advanced.
Clothing: The deceased was wrapped in a green/brown traveling rug. The following items of clothing were noted: Pale blue nightgown with 3x postage stamps in pocket, and white underwear.
External examination:
The body was that of a female subject, weighing 135lb and measuring 5 foot 8 inches in height.
The head hair was long and auburn.
Advanced putrefaction of the head and upper trunk with gross maggot infestation was present.
Both upper and lower teeth were natural and in an excellent state of health.
There was marked desiccation of the fingers.
Internal examination:
Head and neck: The head hair plucked out easily and there was no gross injury to the scalp. The soft tissues, however, were grossly putrefied with absent eyeballs. The skull was intact, and the brain was liquefied.
The hyoid bone and laryngeal cartilage were intact. The thyroid was normal.
Chest: The thoracic cage was intact and the lungs (left 350g; and right 600g) showed mild upper lobe edema.

The heart (350g) was normal. The trachea and esophagus were unremarkable.

Abdomen: The stomach contained a small amount of pinkish fluid, and the appendix was present. The liver (1600g) and spleen showed terminal congestion. The bladder was empty, and the remaining intra-abdominal organs showed no contributory features.

Samples of blood (arm, heart, leg) were collected and sent to Salville General Hospital for toxicological analyses with the following results:

Blood carbon monoxide level – 77% saturated

Blood alcohol level –

> *arm 50mg/100ml*
> *heart 16mg/100ml*
> *leg 16mg/100ml*

Summary and opinion:

The deceased, who it is said had a history of depression, was found dead in her car which was on a forest track in woods near Salville, Pennsylvania, on November 14, 1988. From the dissection and results of toxicological analyses, I believe death was due to carbon monoxide poisoning.

This examination was carried out at the request of Mr. Robert Doogan, Public Prosecutor, 2 Baron Place, Salville, Pennsylvania, PA 23177.

Something happened, the truth of which I might never uncover. My mother switched from someone who craved the company of others, hosting parties with my father, to locking herself away in this fortress. Eventually she found deeper places to hide, within the labyrinth of her own mind, and that led her to a forest in rural Pennsylvania. I believe she knew she had to drive as far away as possible, so that whatever haunted her would not reach me and my father. She must have been so lonely in that car, breathing the smell of the plastic bag over her head.

I stop before I climb any further. My lungs heave with every breath, and something pulls me away from the clearing.

I know that he has followed me here.

Dylan seems intent on taking everything from me, even the few things I have left that are buried here. I wonder whether I am missing a trick, whether this is what I am supposed to do as a parent; to devote my whole being, every last thing I have, to my children. *Child.* But in that case, shouldn't I hand it over in my last will and testament, rather than having it seized from me like the plundering explorers that his ancestors were.

I think of Cassandra left helpless and alone.

I turn back, tripping a little as I make my way back through the tangled weed. I am certain that I hear his footsteps approaching, so I quicken my pace as I plunge deeper into the forest.

The birdsong is muted, and the leaves are still, and I remember coming here in pursuit of Smithson. How certain I felt, how willing I was to kill for my child. Would I be so willing to kill one child for the sake of another?

I cannot hear the footsteps anymore, but this might mean he is upon me and about to grab me.

And then I burst out from the forest onto Mount Pelion Way. I dare myself to glance behind me, and yet I see no one. Was he even there in the first place?

I reach home and when I walk through the door, I notice that the air is still. For a moment I imagine Cassandra dead, and how I will explain this to Paris. I know he won't forgive me for leaving her to die alone.

In the living room I listen for Dylan's return. I feel the cold trickle of sweat in the small of my back, a place Paris loved to kiss.

And then there is a sidewards shift, to a time when Paris and I would make love and there were no children. He was strong, persistent, growling deep within.

And then I am back again, smelling the foul stench of Dylan plastered to these walls like hatred.

I hear voices. Are they calling me? They are distant, softened by time or walls or secrecy.

I go from room to room, expecting around each corner to find little angels with wings or demons with horns, or fairies with gold brocades around their heads, or big-nosed, clumsy witches, or goblins. I want to believe that I can someday escape all this, that there is a world beyond the latches and bolts and locks. I can ask someone else to keep watch over this place, and who that is, I do not care. As long as it's not Dylan.

When I was younger, I used to dream of Zeus and his mighty thunderbolt striking down any threat before it reached me. I would see him in any strong man that crossed my path, certain that they were the bearded god here in human form, just taking a rest from their great divinity. He would know what Dylan was really up to, and he would know how to protect me.

I follow the voices down to the basement where I find Dylan sitting with his aunt. How did he get down there without me seeing?

Cassandra looks uncomfortable with Dylan sitting so close to her. I wonder if he is using the weight of his body to keep her pinned in place, as a bank robber would with a gun just out of sight.

"Don't worry," he smiles at me. "I'll put them all back when we've finished."

He has old photographs fanned out on his lap, and some of them are slipping onto the floor. I can see flashes of Ania's smile, but her face is distorted because some of the photos are crumpled up. "What did you do to them?"

"Oh this?" Dylan is still smiling. "Sorry. I think I sat on one or two of them."

"No. You did that deliberately. Stop lying."

I can see Cassandra frowning.

"Come on, easy," she says. Her voice is reed-thin, and I think of the dying moments of winter that are to come, when everything freezes, and we hold our breath to see what will survive.

"He's entitled to look at photos of his sister," Cassandra says. "She was everyone's, not just yours."

"Stop it. Just stop it. Give those to me."

I can hear wheezing in Cassandra's fragile chest. It sounds like a motor that has not been oiled, and I imagine what it would look like for sparks and smoke to start to emerge from her throat.

"We are all grieving," she insists. "This isn't a competition."

I can see that Dylan is enjoying this.

I think of grief as an incendiary device, blowing apart all you have known and fusing it into something new. It could be hideous and deformed, like limbs splitting through skin, but it is new. A fresh perspective.

I snatch at the photos, trying to gather as many as I can, and I see that some have sticky marks smeared over Ania's smile. To think that I came back for Cassandra, to think that I cared whether or not she was left alone to die.

"So you aren't going to let him look at these?"

"He might damage them," I reply, shaking my head.

"You should learn to trust people. And you should cut your son some slack. He needs your love, not your suspicions. You and he are more similar than you think."

I shake my head.

"I have never willingly inflicted pain on anything or anyone. We are not the same."

With the photographs bundled into my arms, like I am cradling a baby, I turn back and see Dylan smirking at me.

"Aunty Cassie's right, you know," he says, smiling. "Like birds of a feather we have to stick together. Right, Mother?"

Chapter Seventeen

~~~

Charon awaits

Fall. With the three boys now away at college, Mount Pelion Way is a quieter place. With my curtains open, I can watch as the multiheaded beast slithers about the neighborhood. It seems slower, less energized by spite, and all their heads hang with mournful regret as they catch glimpses of their boys: the basketball hoop, the spare car in the driveway, and the limp balloons that no one bothered to clear away. Would I dare to reach out to any one of the seething mothers and speak of our shared experiences, that we have each lost a child, and we can each point to our disemboweled state as we stare in awe at the gaps in our soul that once held our children?

But we are not the same. They would say this as much as I. Their children are only away at college, they have not died. They can see them again any time they wish. They don't need to be associated with the mournful, the morose, the vulnerable who tear at their skin when those painful anniversaries swing around. The wounds have barely healed since the twelfth day of August, when I realized Ania should have turned nineteen. No suburban monster wants to be dragged down into such a murky swamp of grief. Not really, not real grief. They want the shocking headline about a sudden death so they can say that they know the family. They can let it be a lesson, a reminder that they are not so unfortunate. And after they have laid the flowers in full view of the gathering press, they will shake themselves free. Death is something they run from
~~~

on their treadmills, or to the shore. They adamantly deny that they too will be swallowed as Ania was, and as Cassandra will be very soon.

Paris operates under the same denial. Instead of the treadmill or shore, he runs from one task to the next, deftly avoiding the truth that his sister is dying under this very roof. He cannot stop to look this in the eye any more than he can lean on me to support him through it, and so even during the night he is restless, taking himself downstairs to the garage to avoid his sister's moans of pain.

Tonight, as I hear her cry out again, I wait to see if she will settle.

"Oh you beast."

It was muffled, and I cannot be sure that I heard it, but it sounded like her voice. I don't want to believe it, but I think I hear footsteps tiptoeing across the hallway. I think I hear Ania's door shut. Exhaustion and fear conspire to create confusion, so I switch on my bedside lamp. It is just past three in the morning, and the house is still again. As if the light has the power to silence all.

It is not beyond belief that my son would take out his frustrations on his aunt, knowing she is unlikely to remember it in the salty haze of her strong medication. But I think it brazen even for him, when his father is still in the house.

I make my way across the hallway, knowing that this could be a trap, and I stand at the doorway to her bedroom.

In the dim light I can see her outline, and she does not appear harmed. The room smells of antiseptic cream.

I step closer to the bed to take a better look, and I search what I can of her body. There are no obvious signs of injuries inflicted by my son, so I choose not to turn on her light, in case I interrupt what precious little sleep she can get. Her breathing comes short and fast, like a newborn with dreams of the warmth of the womb from which she came. She seems so small and frail, and I feel crazed by the sudden urge to kiss her forehead. Slowly, I pull the bedcovers up a little more, so her fragile chest is covered, and I resolve to be kinder to her.

Heading back to my bedroom, I catch the shadowy outline of my son standing in the doorway to his room. *Ania's room.*

"'Night, Mother," he says, smiling. The moonlight spills like cream over his pale skin to paint him as a ghost. "Hope you have a great night."

He closes his door without making a sound, and a tempest stirs in my chest. He has left me with no option but to sit and watch over her, a yeoman warder from another time.

The following morning, Paris finds me on the floor, keeping watch over his sister.

"What are you doing?" he asks, and I wonder why he sounds so irritated. "Not the best place to sleep. You could have tripped her up."

As Cassandra continues to sleep, Paris tells me to look after her because he needs to drive into town with Dylan. In the background, I can see our son walking around his bedroom with one hand holding a cereal box and the other scooping Froot Loops into his mouth. As he chews on them, colorful fragments fall onto the floor, and he starts to scratch himself distractedly, deep inside his boxer shorts.

"Of course," I reply without turning back to look at my husband.

Paris doesn't thank me; he just tells his son to dress because they are leaving shortly. I watch how quickly Dylan obeys him, and it makes me suspicious. Whatever the errand is, Dylan must be the sole or majority beneficiary.

When my husband leaves with our son, the slam of the door plunges the house into a brief silence before my ears tune in to the jagged, uncertain breaths coming from my sister-in-law. I can smell the antiseptic cream burning through the air as I pace about the hallway, uncertain whether to leave her in peace or offer to help.

"You don't have to be here if you don't want to."

She doesn't open her eyes, but she waves her hand at me.

"I am sure you have plenty of better things to be doing with your time."

"No," I reply. "Really. I don't mind."

"I know I would, if I were in your position."

Her words are thick and matted, making it hard for me to decipher every sticky sound.

"Do you need anything?"

"A new body."

"Well, I can't help you with that."

Her head falls to one side so she ends up staring at the wall. I try not to think of the sickness that is probably making the wallpaper smell. No one tells you about the smells associated with sickness and death.

"For months I tried to get a straight answer out of those doctors. They dicked me around, misdiagnosing me with this and the other, and now here it is, terminal. I should sue."

"I'm not sure that's worth your energy."

"Why? Because I'm going to die anyway?"

"I didn't say that."

"It's the truth, though."

If Cassandra improves one last time, I will take her through the forest, up the hill and to the clearing that overlooks the slow-flowing brook. I will tell her of the letters and gifts I buried for my mother, and I wonder if I might dig them all up and give them to her. The bracelets, the paintings, the drawings, and the science projects. I will read to her the poems and stories that I composed for my mother, the ones that tell of magic and hope and immortality. I will even tell her about the hidden wealth that I have buried here away from the prying eyes. This is my insurance policy; in case anything happens to the vaults and the fortress. I will explain to Cassandra that when you share these things it means that you are forever bound to that person, and through that magic and hope, you never die. I hope she will find that comforting.

"I guess you will be pleased to see the back of me."

"I never said that," I reply.

"No, you didn't."

Something makes Cassandra flinch, a sudden twinge of pain, or a memory. Perhaps even a moment of regret.

"What did you and Dylan talk about when you were looking at those photographs?"

"This and that," she replies. "Why do you ask?"

"What did he say about Ania?"

"He told me that she had been very lonely."

Cassandra clutches the side of the bed as something washes through her.

"He said that he had tried to help her, but she retreated from him and everyone."

He is lying. He probably saw this in a movie and decided to recreate the scene.

"Why do you go after him so much?" she asks me. "He is still just a kid."

"He's in his twenties. I got married at his age."

"It's a different time now. These kids aren't living in the same world that we grew up in."

"I don't know—there seems to be the same mix of devils and angels."

"Just cut him some slack, will you? He's at a shitty age. Their brains are barely catching up with their dicks."

It is such a vulgar thing to say about her nephew, but I choose to blame it on the medication making her lose control.

"I wish you had got to know her a little more."

"Who?" Cassandra frowns.

Suddenly she turns away from me as if she has heard someone call her name.

"Oh, Ania?" she sighs.

"Yes. My beautiful, clever, funny daughter."

"She loved you," she mutters, barely loud enough for me to hear. I want to ask her to repeat this, but her breathing starts to slow with a rattle and wheeze.

I take her hand and the heat of it makes me flinch. To think of her simmering underneath her skin, slowly burning out as you would cleanse something contaminated. She shudders. Another ripple of pain, perhaps, or the relief of another wave of the opiates. I wonder if she will eventually lose the ability to distinguish pleasure from pain.

I try not to imagine how Ania must have felt at the end. Instead, I take refuge in an older time, when I held my father's hot hand as he was eaten alive by his own cancerous growths. I think of his bloodshot, watery eyes, and the green-and-yellow tinge of his skin. His body was failing, allowing waste to back up and poison him from within, and until that moment, I had not realized that this was possible. I thought the body was a finely tuned machine, and if something was drastically wrong, and it could not be fixed, the body would self-destruct so he would not have to suffer long.

"Please."

It is so sudden that I think it is my father, or even Dylan, returning in the form of a demon. I look up, certain that I will find him climbing the ceiling as he reaches down for us with his dirty, clawing hands. But all I see is Cassandra's shadow cast by her bedside lamp.

"What are you going to do?" she gasps, staring right through me.

"What do you mean?" I ask, feeling a little foolish because I know this is the delirium.

"Is it now?" she asks.

She starts to cry, and she looks like a child who wants to know whether a medical procedure will hurt.

"I don't want to," she croaks, her lower lip cracking so that a fingernail of blood appears. I hope she'll taste the blood and remember that she is alive, that she can hold on for a little bit longer.

"I'm scared," she gasps, suddenly appearing more lucid. Her brow is clustered with beads of sweat. "I thought I would feel peace . . . accept things . . . but can't . . ."

Her words catch in the back of her throat, stung by tears of regret and terror.

"You don't have to talk," I say. "Just rest if you need to."

She squeezes my hand so tightly, as Ania would have done if I had got the chance to say goodbye.

"You won't leave me, will you?"

I shake my head, but she cannot see this because her eyes have already rolled to the back of her skull. She drifts back into a sudden, deep sleep.

That final day, I asked my father about the keys for all the locks that secured this fortress, and he told me about the investments and shares and piles of wealth that I must imminently take charge of. I never realized how much our family was worth, and it explained why the police and town officials were happy to turn a blind eye to our various incursions of laws and town codes. They were always paid a tidy sum.

My father forbade me from ever letting Paris know of this wealth or the vaults that were located in a secret room in the far reach of the attic, accessible through a door hidden behind a false wall panel. I was true to this dying wish.

As I held my father's hot hand, I asked him about my mother. I wanted to know what would drive her away to that lonely forest track in rural Pennsylvania.

"Her illness was her whole being," he muttered. "She couldn't escape herself, no matter how many mirrors she avoided, or reflections in the rivers and streams."

"I don't understand," I said, wiping his hot brow with a wet washcloth.

"No one despised her, feared her even, more than your mother. She would tell me that she was going to do it; she had a plan, and she even packed her car with the plastic bag they found over her head. But I never believed she would go through with it."

"But she did."

"That final day, before she left for Pennsylvania, she said she was going to rid this world of one more witch."

I stopped wiping his brow. I let go of his hand, and I glanced around the room. I didn't want to suddenly find her sitting by my side and listening to the story of her suicide.

"They found her barefooted," my father continued. "In her car. She drove to that remote spot in just her nightgown. Never went without shoes before. *Slovenly.*"

He said this with the *humph* of a petulant child.

If she had lived, she would be in her late sixties by now. I can't imagine her with silver-streaked hair and the dryness that cracks open my own face. I can't imagine her suffering the company of my father for much longer than she did. I think of the effort she made when she got so little from him in return: The meals she lavished on him, the kisses on his cheek, and the smell of her fragrance, so fresh, like apple blossoms. She was bright and white and clean, and his unshaven face was always peppered with the dirty blacks and whites of his whiskers. It must have felt so harsh on her soft lips as she kissed him so dutifully.

I stepped away from my father's bed and started to fold his laundered nightshirts. I could hear him struggling to breathe.

I loaded up a tray that had been sitting on his dresser, piling it up with dishes and plates that were my attempts to feed him something over the last few days. Still, he struggled to breathe, and he also mumbled something.

"Really, I don't . . . it isn't going to be . . ."

Then he was silent.

I wanted him to tell me that my mother did really love me, and that it was an accident that she did that and left me with someone who kept me locked up and hidden from the world. I wanted him to tell me that there were not really monsters that lived under the bed, and there were none in the closet, and there were tooth fairies and Christmas elves and Easter bunnies, and a heaven beyond this life. But I knew it was all untrue.

Cassandra's breathing is coming sharply now, and I sense that it is only a matter of time. I should call Paris but by the time I go and get my cell phone, she might already be dead. I promised her I would not leave her alone.

Still, I hold her hand, and I stroke the hair from her face, and I notice she has become cooler. She still breathes, but she is calm.

Not long now.

I should say comforting things to her, as I know that hearing is the last thing to go. But I don't know what to say.

I breathe with her, I squeeze her hand, and I keep stroking the strands of hair that are around her face, and gently, ever so slightly, the last breath leaves her body.

Stillness now.

My father died in this very room. He died midsentence, leaving words hanging in the air that made no sense. I still remember how dark his eyeballs looked as they were shaded by the clouds of death.

At the time, I felt like death had come to swallow him up like a big mouth. It terrified me, and I searched behind doors and inside closets to find this monster that took so much in one fell swoop.

With Cassandra, it slipped in with more grace, easing her grip on life and letting her freefall into death like a sigh of relief. She had seemed scared, so I half expected her to try and climb out of bed to escape the unavoidable. But slowly she succumbed; she had been succumbing for days now—eating less, drinking less, and sleeping more. A final acceptance of her inevitable fate.

Chapter Eighteen

~~~

Ares, god of war, and a battle-lustful son

When Paris returns home, he finds me sitting and holding his sister's hand. I flinch, scared he might fly into a rage and tear me apart. Instead, he just asks, "What are you doing?" and I shake my head in reply. He understands, but he asks me again "What are you doing?" I have to make it real with words.

"I'm sorry. She's gone."

"*Stop it!*" he shouts. "*Get off her!*"

When I step away from her, I see Dylan over Paris's shoulder. He loiters in the darkness of the hallway; he has the face of a predator hardening with intent for its prey.

"Cassie," my husband whispers, kneeling at her bedside. He touches her shoulder but quickly recoils. I thought he would hold her, claw at her body, and even make futile attempts to revive her. But he is muted and restrained, with a simple hand on his cheek as if he is trying to remember something.

"Can I do anything for you?" I ask.

"No."

"Are you sure?"

"Yes, I'm sure."

Dylan walks into the bedroom, and his eyes scan his surroundings. He stares at the pill bottles for the longest time, and I wonder whether he is planning to give himself or others an opiate high. I imagine how the parents will hammer at my door when they find their children dead, holding an empty pill bottle labeled
~~~

Cassandra Brown.

"You should call someone," he says. His words are thick, and they penetrate the dim light of the bedroom, leaving me unable to pretend that I did not hear him.

"Go and call someone," he says, turning to me. He hasn't once looked at his aunt.

"What do you need me to do?" I ask my husband. I remember how gentle he had been when my father died, and how he moved about the house with grace, making sure that what needed to happen was carried out in a way that was respectful and swift. I could not let go of my father's hand, so it was down to Paris to patiently explain that eventually he would need to be taken away. He didn't have to mention the emission of bodily gases or the eventual putrefaction, and, looking back, I feel foolish that it had not even occurred to me.

"I don't know," my husband replies. "Do what Dylan said."

I refuse to look at my son. He is standing over us now. His father still kneels at Cassandra's bedside, and I have shrunk back to the corner of the room. A cornered and confused child.

"I don't know who to call." My words are heavy with shame. *"Call the hospital, call the police, call anyone. Just call someone. You should be able to handle this."* Dylan has started to shout at me, and I want to push him out of the room, but I know that this is not the time.

"I'm sorry, Dylan," my husband is saying. "I know you loved her too. She was just too ill."

He beckons his son over, and they hold each other as I hear a thin whimper leak from Dylan's lips. I can feel a million tiny feet crawling up and down the back of my neck. As he holds his father, he stares at me.

An ambulance arrives within half an hour after I call. A police patrol car comes too, although I am not sure why.

Paris exchanges some words with the paramedics and police, steady and calm. After they check Cassandra's vitals, they return to their vehicle to get a stretcher.

I feel like I am falling, and I don't want her to leave because I fear what will be in the silence that afterwards descends. I think of delaying things by asking them to check her vitals again, but I know that Paris will not welcome my distractions. He needs to be left to leaf through memories of sibling love and war, never that intense and never harmful. And then he will come to moments of regret, when he could have made so much more of their time together, and he will look at me and remember how firmly I kept him tied up here.

Through the open door, I can see people emerging from their houses. We have awoken the suburban beast. It thrives and surges forwards, slithering across my lawn as each head nods a silent acknowledgement to the other.

I watch Paris wave at June, and I realize that he no longer has a reason to stay in this fortress, at least not unless he wants to. His shoulders fall back, and he holds his head high. Already the marriage knot has loosened.

Tonight I dream again of the hooded people.

Bad things happen to bad people. I still hear them saying this, but like draining blood, my fear fades to apathy.

Dylan chooses not to wear a hood again, so I can see his disappointment in my reaction.

"You deserve to suffer," he hisses.

I cannot speak, and if I could, I would tell him to go to hell. As a teenager, he used to make a joke about this, replying *I'm there already*, and now this seems strangely prophetic.

The hooded people seem impatient, jostling and murmuring and urging him on by pulling at his sleeve. The taller figure still watches over us all, nodding in silent judgment.

Dylan unties the rope that has tethered my wrists to the bed post, and he pulls me up. My limbs feel heavy as tree branches, so I can do nothing more than let him push and pull me about. He is struggling a little, and I see sweat breaking out on his brow, but still he pushes and pulls me until he has me over his shoulder.

He staggers to the bedroom door and says, "We're going on a little trip."

I know where he wants to take me, so I try to kick my legs to free myself from him.

"Don't take me back there," I try to plead, but the words will not come out. From the tightening of my body, he senses my distress, and he seems pleased by it.

"There you are," he purrs. "I knew you had it in you."

Steadily now, methodically, like a priest working his way through a ritual sacrament, he carries me down the stairs.

I try to struggle free, thrashing my arms and legs about. But I am powerless.

"Have a look," he hisses.

By now we are out in the backyard, in the cool night air.

"Look what you have done."

The same words used by my father when he found me unpacking my mother's dresses. You would think I had hacked at them with a knife the way he screamed and hit me across the face.

Just look what you have done.

I am screaming silently beneath this dark night sky, so dark that I feel trapped in a knot between time.

And then I wake up.

The next day, I search for ways to ease Paris's pain. "We could go for a walk," I offer. "I know a place up on the hills, somewhere we have never been before, and there is a little clearing that overlooks a brook. It's so peaceful there. I used to go there as a child, to talk to my mother and tell her things about my life. You know— who I was friends with, who had upset me . . ."

"I don't want to go. Not today."

"No. Of course not. Tomorrow?"

"Please just drop it."

He jumps from the kitchen chair. I have laid out for him a breakfast of scrambled eggs on rye bread with a garnish of rosemary and a sprinkle of salt and pepper. It made me warm with nostalgia and desperate for hope.

"I'm not hungry," he says. He used to say *Just look at this masterpiece*, pulling me in to him and kissing my neck. Now he just stares, making me feel like a monstrosity.

I run my hands over his shoulders. They are knotted and unyielding. I start to massage him, but he twists out from beneath my touch. "Please," he snaps. "I just need space."

A loosened knot. Room to breathe.

"I know," I say, feeling as clumsy as if we were waking from a one-night stand. "I want you to have that too. Take as much time as you need. I am here if you need me."

Later I hear him leave our home without an explanation. I don't want to be alone in the house with Dylan, so I tiptoe into the backyard. There is a chill in the air, so I know it is coming, the time again for snow falling on the apple trees. But for now, the boughs hang heavy with ruddy, swollen apples.

How many years has Dylan crept into this orchard when he thinks I have not been watching? He would load up his schoolbag and store it in his bedroom closet. When he thought no one was looking, he would hurl the apples like grenades, mainly targeting Smithson, Aedean, and Cory. Until Aedean ended up with a black eye. How Freya howled and hammered at my door. I should have apologized, and that might have been the end of it, but instead I hid behind the sofa with the curtains shut until she lost patience and left.

Ania was appalled. "That was mean," she said, beginning to cry. I wondered whether she meant that her brother or her mother was the mean one. Perhaps both.

"*Fuck her*," I hissed as I punched and kicked the wall. "*The fucking impertinence*," I spat in full view of my children. "*How dare she tell me how to parent my children.*" My eyes danced and my throat closed; I don't think I was taking in enough air. It felt like the familial roots, my father's rage, my mother's slash-and-burn approach, creeping up inside my lungs and throat to wrap around my heart and my brain. It grew over my eyes, blinding me to the admiration that shone from Dylan's sparkling smile. My battle-lustful son. I was loading him up, weaponizing him so that he could inflict more pain. This moment was imprinted in his brain as surely as the ability to feed or wipe himself, and as any child wishes, he was going to evolve far beyond my example.

I hear a twig snap under the weight of someone's foot and I hear, "Hello, Mother." He has found me. He stares up at one tree in particular, knowing the history of it and urging me to look at it. He knows everything about me, as if he still has his ear pressed against the inner wall of my womb. I wonder what he makes of it all, these thoughts, this wrath, this spite and discord. I half expect him to say *Well, that's not very polite*, but instead he just smiles, plucks the shiniest apple from the tree, and takes a big, satisfying bite.

I would like to cut these trees down. I want to burn them all, and when I am finished, I would like to burn this house to the ground.

Chapter Nineteen

~~~

A birth in reverse

That night, I did not expect to dream about the hooded people again, but they had a final message for me.

Bad things happen to bad people they continued to chant, and if I could reply, I would tell them that I have already seen the worst. But they know this to be untrue.

The hooded people are impatient, and they urge Dylan on, pushing him and pulling at his robe. The taller figure joins them in their restlessness, and so it becomes clear that he has also decided my fate. Tonight Dylan will give them what they have been waiting for.

Already he has me over his shoulder and down the stairs. There is no point in struggling, and I wonder if, outside, he might make it quick, swiftly tethering my neck with the noose and kicking the stool from beneath my feet.

"Now you see," he seethes.

I refuse to look. I keep my eyes shut tightly, but I can smell his fingers, and then I feel them prying my eyelids open.

"Look, you coward."

We are in the backyard, and I see the gnarled old boughs of the apple trees.

"Now you see."

There is the length of rope hanging from one of the boughs.

"You see it all now. See how the rope is starting to stir."

No I silently scream.
~~~

"See how the noose snakes round her throat."

No. Please stop. Please.

I try to look away, but his hand grips my chin and holds my face in line with her lifeless body. I see her brown, polished shoes, like chestnuts that have only just ripened. She is trying to make me look back and see the opportunities I missed, to change all of this before the winter snow. I had the fall, when she told me she had no friends, and the summer when she stayed indoors, and the spring when she stomped on the daffodils that were sprouting up across the lawn. I missed it all. Or I chose not to notice.

"Please leave her be."

"No. You have to see."

He yanks at the rope, and she twitches into life, her limbs flickering like she is making snow angels. And still, I know there is worse yet to come.

"Come on, Mother. Take a look."

Dylan wants me to see it all, and he wants to unpack it slowly, as if he has something from the butcher, a brown paper package of innards that ooze the brown sweat of blood.

"This is yours, after all," he sneers. "Do you see?"

I do see. I see the fine strands of her freshly brushed hair, and I can still feel it, silky and warm under the palm of my hand.

"This is all your creation."

He yanks at the rope again, and then it finally happens. Her eyes open.

"Mom." With the noose around her throat constraining her vocal cords, I can barely hear her, like the sound of air rushing out of a hidden hole.

"Mom," she says again. "It hurts."

And then Dylan yanks at the rope again, and her arms and legs thrash about for a final time, and then she is still. I notice a dark patch emerging on the front of her jeans.

"You see, Mother? Do you see now?"

He wants to show me more, but I squeeze my eyes shut and will myself to awaken. I know that afterwards, I will see Paris and myself running into the backyard. It will have been a matter of hours later, so by the time we found her, she was already dead.

I believe Paris screamed as he tried to get her down. I helped too. We used our fingers and nails, and eventually I ran to the garage to get a knife.

Later I found that I had broken down to a bloody mess the nails on my fingers and thumbs.

Her sweater felt so soft as I held her body to me, and Paris cut the rope. As the rope went slack, her cheek fell against mine and I believed, for that moment, that I could kiss her back to life as I would kiss her awake in the mornings. I believed that if I held her gently enough, she might stir and moan and push me away, and I would laugh but insist that she get up.

Her weight was too much for me and eventually we both fell to the ground together, shame crushing me that I could not even do this for my daughter.

Some parts of this story leave me wondering whether I dreamt them or not. At one point I thought she did wake up, and she looked at me and frowned, saying *Why did you wake me? I wanted to rest.* And then her eyes rolled back in her head, and her lips froze again, whiteish-blue and rigid like ice.

So much is shuffled—images, words, smells, the touch of her—that I can't be sure if anything is real.

My hands smell of oiled rope.

As her head fell back, I saw her beautiful white teeth, and a solitary raven circled over her body. It balanced on the branch of one of the apple trees. Silently it preened its feathers, watching without reverence or any sign that it felt stirred by the scene. For the raven, it was just another day to assess what it could poke and pluck out of the carnage.

I can still see the eyes of that raven, glassy pools of oil that bore witness to something so unnatural. It looked on as my daughter lay on the ground beneath the tree, crumpled like a lifeless fetus. A birth in reverse, a life aborted by her own hand.

The nightmares continue when I awake. And they will continue forever, keeping me locked and bolted in my own private hell.

My daughter's postmortem revealed that there had been no obvious injuries or signs of a struggle, and there was no evidence of alcohol or drugs in her system. They detected a small amount of food in her stomach, from the breakfast I had watched her eat that morning, and she had no signs of any underlying illnesses. In fact they remarked how healthy her heart and lungs were.

She was also pregnant. I don't think I am ready to accept who the father was.

The report concluded that she died of asphyxiation by dislocating the neck vertebrae, severing her spinal cord.

All of this was inevitable, or at least that was what Marigold Meeches tried to have me believe. Meeches was trying to do some fancy footwork, deftly maneuvering me away from any self-blame by convincing me that this was imprinted on her genes by her grandmother, my mother, as surely as a cleft palette or a club foot. But this only made me feel more hopeless. She was basically telling me that my daughter was condemned before she had even been conceived.

During our first session together, I remember how she removed her glasses and paused her questioning when I started to ask her the same questions she was asking me.

"And *your* family history, Marigold? Tell me about the mental health of your *own* family. Any history of depression or suicide? Come on, Marigold, isn't reciprocity an essential ingredient for social interaction?" I grinned.

"My dear," she said, her smile flourishing like a teardrop on tissue paper. "We can always come back to those questions later. What about hobbies and interests?"

"My only interest was my daughter, and now she is dead. And you have just told me that she was destined to end up this way because my mother did the same thing. Inescapable. I should never have had children in the first place."

She chose not to reply because our time was up.

Even now, my hands smell of oiled rope.

For all the latches and bolts and locks, the dangers were always going to haunt me because they were lingering inside all along; in my blood, in my genetics, as surely as there are ripples from trauma that change the molecules of our chromosomes. The rot was there, as far as the family tree could grow.

Chapter Twenty

~~~

November again

We slide into silent snowfall, like ash falling on the bare branches of the apple trees. I haven't heard from Ania for a while, and I am sure that she has been scared into silence by her brother. As I wait for her return, I lie in bed and listen to Paris' morning routine. I wonder whether I should get up and try to make peace with him, but I choose to keep a safe distance. It occurs to me that there are still things I do not know about him, parts of his life that might always remain uncharted, like the dark corners of the moon. In that, there is fear as much as hope, and which will prevail could be down to something as arbitrary as the flip of a coin.

Yesterday Paris told me that he was going to take Dylan to look at colleges.

"Good," I said.

"Is that it? Just good?"

"I don't understand."

"You don't want to know which colleges? You don't care which side of the country or the world he ends up on?"

"Of course I care."

He would never call me a liar but we both know the truth.

"You didn't even acknowledge his birthday last month. You nodded along when I gave him presents and a card, but I could see that you were gritting your teeth. What sort of mother refuses to acknowledge the birthday of her twenty-one-year-old son?"
~~~

I have no answer for this.

"You know what your trouble is?" he muttered. "You see too much of yourself in him, and it eats you up inside."

He tried to push his way past me, but I grabbed his shirt. I thought of tearing it off his shoulders, just to see what would happen. I thought of flaying his skin with my nails and tasting him. Hatred is a skin-biting passion, a frenzy of mauling and writhing together that is hard to distinguish from sexual attraction. Both make me dry-mouthed and dizzy, breathless as we push and pull at each other, hurting or getting hurt in the process.

"*Let go of me!*" he shouted, shaking free as I heard a distant tear. "You are out of control."

For a moment we stood and stared in opposite directions. He could have called me callous and cold-hearted and selfish and cruel. He could have said that I cannot bear to see myself in Dylan because of my self-hatred, and this self-hatred rots my family (my mother, me, Ania, even) to the core. He could have said all of this, but I don't think he even knows how to be so cruel.

I know he is also still angry at me for making a scene at Cassandra's funeral. I couldn't tolerate the supposed friends of hers who were wailing and clutching each other in their pretense at grief. I stormed out of the church, not before I saw Pastor Pry smirking at me, showing me how she would be swooping in to snatch Paris away with her comforting lies about his sister's afterlife.

When I join my husband in bed later that night, he does not stir, but he also does not snore, so I know that he is pretending to sleep.

I think of our son and his ridiculously big, hard jaw. I think of his bushy eyebrows and the blank stare when he scratches himself. I knew that in contrast to the fragility of Ania, Dylan would always appear more brutish, but I didn't expect the accompanying savagery. You can wield power without wishing people pain.

The following night, I slip my arms around my husband, and I feel his body tense, but he does not say or do anything. I may not desire him but at least we shouldn't hate each other.

The next night, I ask him if he wants me to hold him, and he says no. He does not turn away from me, but I still know not to pursue him any further.

When I ask him to hold me, he silently refuses. I know that I should lay things to rest, to let go and accept it.

Days go by, and I see the grief that tightens around my husband's neck. His words are breathless with anger, punched quick and hard, and I am the nearest and easiest target.

I find him in the living room with Cassandra's paperwork fanned out on the coffee table in front of him.

"Stop it," he snaps as I straighten the sofa cushions around him. My movements have blown some of the papers onto the floor, and as he reaches for them, I see how brightly his neck and cheeks are pulsating with crimson. A flash of fear appears in the form of his death, leaving me alone with Dylan, locked up inside this fortress with no way to escape.

"Let me help you with those," I offer, but he waves me away. "Can you just leave me in peace?"

"I want to help. I want to do something for you."

"You know what you can do? Make peace with your son. For me."

"Did he ask you to say this?"

"No. I do have a mind of my own. And with my own mind I have decided to get my affairs in order."

He said *my affairs*, not ours.

"Given everything that has happened with Cassandra, we need to think about how we can look after Dylan after we have gone."

"Oh come on, you're going to outlive us all."

"I don't want to outlive my son."

I sit quietly, hands placed evenly on my lap like a child sitting outside the principal's office. Every move I make is wrong, and I wish someone could just teach me what to say and do in all the right moments.

"You saw how quickly things deteriorated for Cassandra."

A hairline of fear creeps down the back of my neck as I wonder whether Dylan, in some way, hastened his aunt's decline. I think of the aconite and arsenic and cyanide and rat poisoning. I think of all the drinks and meals that I have consumed around him. My stomach starts to twist. And then I think of my husband who sits before me, burning me with the same glower that I have seen from my son for his entire life. I think of how apples never fall far from the tree, and the darker, uncharted parts of the person I chose to marry, bound fast with a marriage knot, and who I brought into this fortress under the illusion that he was my safe, guiding shepherd. How quickly my father died after he arrived, and I see Paris as a Trojan horse sitting with me this whole time, just waiting as I locked myself in with those latches and bolts and locks.

"What was that sound?" Paris asks, his head jerking up to the ceiling.

Silence.

"What are you talking about?" I ask. He is trying to play tricks with me, he wants me to go up there so I walk into his trap. I could run from this house right now, and I could bang on the doors of the people of Mount Pelion Way. Would they help me, or would they continue to ignore me, laughing at my hysteria as they have laughed at generations of Galls before me?

And then there is a crash.

"Now do you hear it?" Paris shouts, his eyes wide.

I nod.

Go to him. He is your son.

Ania?

It escapes me why she has chosen now to return. Loud noises and chaos usually scare her away for hours.

Please. Go to him.

I climb the stairs, still uncertain whether this is a trap, or whether it was the things that scuffle about in the attic, things that smell of yeasty, sickly sweet curdles of spoiled life. But all I have left is faith in my daughter, so I have to believe that this is safe.

There is a broken chair in the hallway outside Ania's bedroom. I step over it to enter the bedroom and I find Dylan crouched in the corner underneath the windowsill.

"What's going on?" I ask.

"I want you two to stop. All this fighting—you are going to destroy each other."

"Sure. But that's never been something you've been particularly concerned about," I reply.

I start to back out of the bedroom, certain now this is some sort of trap. And then I collide with my husband.

"You two are finally going to work things out," my husband says.

"I don't really… What's going on? Get out of my way."

Already Dylan's odor is filling my nose and mouth, as if his fingers were exploring my lips before plunging down my throat.

Still Paris stands firmly. Gently but surely, he pushes me towards our son.

"Stop this," I say, trying to force my way past my husband. Paris takes hold of my wrists and squeezes so hard that my hands start to go purple and throb.

"I'm going to leave you to it," Paris says, "and I expect you to resolve things with our son. Got it?"

I have no fight left so I just nod my head as he lets go of my wrists and walks out of the bedroom, shutting us in together.

I should not fear my own child. I should not beg to be let out, certain that I have been trapped with a monster.

"Listen to me," Dylan begins. He surprises me with a whisper, so I barely hear him. "I don't want Dad to hear me. He's dangerous."

He's telling the truth. Listen to him.

"I'm not listening to anything you have to say. You disgust me. Don't think I've forgotten what you did with Ania," I say.

No, Mom, we were children, I've already told you. You have to listen to him.

"What are you talking about?" Dylan says, frowning.

"Playing doctors and nurses together," I hiss. "I caught you, remember."

"That was more than a decade ago. Why are you bringing that up now?"

"She hurt herself," I say to my son. "Why would Ania hurt herself if someone wasn't already hurting her? I suppose you're going to blame me again, for sending her away to that sleepaway camp."

Dylan reaches into the pocket of his jeans and hands me a dirty Ziplock bag. It has a lined piece of paper inside, folded up into a small square.

"Read it," he tells me. "It's her handwriting."

It's true. I wrote that. I can read it for you . . .

> *Mom,*
> *I wish I could tell you this to your face, but I cannot form the words in my mouth. So my hope is that you read this before it is too late. I am guessing that you know I have been following you here, where you've buried notes to your Mom. It should only be a matter of time before you catch me here and then I can show you these letters.*
> *Something horrible happened and I never wanted it. He made me do it. I am sorry, I truly am. It disgusts me to even write this.*
> *I know you love him, and you have loved him for longer than Dylan or I have even lived, but he forced me.*
> *My period stopped a while back and I have been feeling funny. I am so scared that he has made me pregnant. He used to tell me that we should keep this a secret.*
> *But how is it going to stay that way when my belly grows big? I am trapped and I don't know what to do.*
> *It wasn't Smithson or Cory or Aedean. I had a crush on them, and we fooled around in the woods that Halloween night, but they never hurt me. We never did anything that I didn't want to do, and never anything serious, nothing that would make me stop my period.*
> *Only he did that, and he made me. He's been making me do it for a while. I never wanted to, I promise you. I love you, and I want you to believe me.*
> *Please believe me, Mom.*
> *I love you.*
> *Please don't hate me. Xxx*

I shake my head. "No," I gasp. "Impossible."

"Then read it again," Paris instructs. "You know it is her handwriting, you know those are her words.

After a second read, I fold the piece of paper up using the same creases and slip it back into the Ziplock bag.

"How?" I ask. "How is this possible?"

"I found it the other day, when I followed you up into the hills."

"I knew you were following me."

"I don't know why I did, but maybe Ania was telling me to go into those hills."

"But still . . . I don't understand."

"When she was alive, she must have followed you up there, saw how you buried letters to your mother, and thought she could do the same. A form of communication. I guess she hoped the next time you dug up the hole to bury another letter for your mother, you would find her plea for help."

"But I never did."

I shake my head more and more furiously, and instead of flames flickering into bolts of red lightning, glassy tears stream down my face.

"I failed her. She was alone with this, and I let her slip away from me."

You didn't fail me. It wasn't your fault.

"She was pregnant," I gasp. "With *his* child? I want to be sick. Do you think she was burning the clothes she wore when he attacked her?"

I don't want to think about how she faced this alone.

Once again I can see the little panda pattern just before it darkens and disappears in the flames. "I don't know," Dylan sighs as he shakes his head.

"It always bothered me what she was doing that day."

"What matters is that she knew you loved her."

"Did she know that? I was always so preoccupied with petty squabbles that, in the end, amounted to nothing. She thought she was alone, that I was ignoring her pleas for help. I could have saved her."

"Dad knows nothing of the note," Dylan whispers. "He loves me, and he wants you and I to get along, so we have an advantage there."

"An advantage to do what?"

And then he grins again, with his big jaw thrusting at me, only this time it makes me feel safe.

"You'll see."

Chapter Twenty-One

~~~

Quid pro quo

I stand at the doorway to Dylan's bedroom, and I remember how I would watch him whooshing his toy train along tracks that filled his bedroom floor. When he was six he built the tracks with diligence and care, and I was honored that he would let me play with him. I long to see the train and tracks again, so I have evidence that there was tenderness in his childhood, and I did not entirely fail in my attempts to parent him.

That pride over things he created. I can still hear his boyish voice calling, "Look, Mom," from the backyard, only to find him building a fortress out of fallen branches he had collected from the orchard. His cheeks and hands were muddy, but he grinned from ear to ear as his little sister looked on in awe. "Pretty impressive, right, midget?" he would smirk.

How deeply he would burrow his face into me when we watched movies together. At such a young age, he still believed that I had the power to protect him from a multiheaded beast or a snarling wolf pack. I had forgotten that there were times when I was far from a witch to him, and even if I had seemed haggard with exhaustion, especially after the sleepless nights with a newborn Ania, he still wanted me around.

"Don't ever go on holiday and leave me alone," he once cried after we watched *Home Alone* together one rainy afternoon. "I'll try not to," I laughed, squeezing him tightly to me.

But then his voice deepened, and he pushed me away. And I
~~~

was left with Ania. I think I came to depend on her too much, to view her as my one lifeline for all that might be good or nourishing in the world. So when she was taken from me, I starved.

Back downstairs, I sit in the stillness of this fortress and wait for my husband to return. My daughter was trying to show me something, and I couldn't see it. I once thought that I knew every inch of her, and yet I could not see the marks left by my own husband. He was laying claim to her like a colonial invader stakes a flag in tender soil, seizing what he desired simply because he could. I was blind to her suffering because I polarized my two children: For Ania to be so pure, sweet, and good, I had to make Dylan impure, twisted, and evil. A myopic focus on my son left me blind to the very threat that stood by my side throughout all of this.

Dylan's not evil, any more than I am pure and good.
To hear Ania's voice should ignite in me a wrath and fury to break my husband apart. Instead, it weakens me. I wish I knew where that goddess of discord and strife was hiding.
Dylan will help you. He has a plan.

I hear the latches and bolts and locks as they loosen and give way.
Paris is back.

"Did you make peace with your son?" Paris asks me as he joins me in the living room. The terracotta warriors watch on with shame. They know they also failed to protect this household.
"Oh, you will be very proud of me," I say, forcing a smile so hard that I taste blood at the back of my throat. "I am going to take Dylan to look at some colleges this weekend," I lie.
"Really? That would be great. What the heck made you see sense at long last?"
"I don't want to lose you." Another lie. "This family has experienced enough loss."
"I agree. We need to start over with each other."
"Dylan said he wanted to speak to you when you got home," I add. "He's waiting upstairs."
Paris would never suspect that his son could betray him. That love, Paris's puppy-eyed adoration, was genuine.

I follow as my husband climbs the stairs. How many years have we done this together, as a sexually charged couple, as newlyweds, as proud parents of a son and then a daughter, making what we thought would be a complete and contented family. With each step, I am comforted to know that I am not the one who destroyed all this.

"Where is he?" Paris asks, realizing Dylan is not in his room. "He said you should go up to the attic. I think he has something to show you."

My legs are trembling so much that I am afraid they will buckle beneath me.

Paris and I reach the top of the stairs, and he opens the attic door. The room is empty. He takes another step or two inside, and then the hangman's noose flies over his head.

With a strength that comes from nowhere, perhaps from his grandfather, Dylan tightens the noose with one swift swoosh of the rope. He drags his father, legs thrashing and arms crashing about, to the fake wall panel I showed my son just an hour earlier, when I gave him the secret key. I remove the panel to reveal the hidden door, and when I open it, Dylan drags him in.

I look at Dylan and smile. Both of our hands now smell of oiled rope.

There are cobwebs, there is dust and darkness. But in reality, what harm is a secret portion of a house? The same question can be asked of the key and the door and the wall panel: What harm is there for any of this to exist, no matter how much of a secret it all is?

Unless.

Unless what is hidden distorts all that we expect of humanity. A mother should not keep her daughter's body after death. A mother should not dress it and arrange it in a bed surrounded by white lilies and roses and candles laid out in the shape of a pentacle. Even if that pentacle has been formed to ward off any spirits that mean her harm.

But then, a mother should not have to witness the death of her daughter. Once this natural order is tampered with, all manner of unnatural consequences may flow.

The horror on Paris's face right now. You would think that he could see racks and wheels and other instruments of mutilation and martyrdom. His cheeks are scarlet as shiny apples, and he gasps and dribbles as the noose tightens. As he thrashes his legs to escape, he stares at his daughter lying on the bed in the center of the room. She is still, and still here, after all this time.

Ania is intact, save for the stitch-marked scars that I covered up with her favorite hooded sweatshirt. Remnants of an autopsy that was unnecessary because we all knew the cause of her death. I suspected they were searching for something to pin on me, they couldn't accept that I might not have been the cause of all this.

From Paris's shriek, you would think he was watching as we cut her open. Sometimes I long for the smell of blood, more welcome signs of life than the stench of formaldehyde.

I tell him to be quiet. I say that I have always looked after her, and I will continue to do so. I know how to tuck her into bed in the way she liked, with the bedcovers loose and not tucked underneath her mattress. She never liked her legs pinned down. I always make sure she had her favorite stuffed toy panda, its limp legs spread over her chest that I watch daily, certain that I will see signs of life in its movement again.

She could have been sleeping, she should have been sleeping, and there have been times when I tried to breathe life back in through those hardened lips.

I see that Paris wants to touch her. He is sobbing, reaching out his hand towards the fire of her auburn hair. But Dylan yanks at the hangman's noose, keeping his father in check as he would treat an errant dog.

I was proud of how my Ares did not balk at the sight of his sister, when he saw her like this for the first time, just moments before his father came home. Dylan didn't cry or wail, he just nodded calmly, showing me that he understood.

"Why?" Paris gasps.

"A stupid question," I hiss.

"You should have left her be."

Womb-like is this attic, this bed, this pentacle of safety from any evil spirit. And here is another man trying to tell a woman what to do with her child.

"Left her be? So she ended up consumed by maggots?" I sneer. "Is that what you wanted for our daughter."

"But this?"

I had braced myself for a torrent of Paris's anger, but instead the waves of tears washed away some of my resolve.

"Stop it," I snap at him. "You have no right."

I could not leave her in the funeral home. Ania would have been terrified to be alone in her casket, and then buried deep beneath the ground. She never liked dark or small places, not since someone thought it was funny to lock her in the closet and leave her alone in this house. She was just five years old, too young to give a coherent account when we found her sobbing and shaking, her nails broken and bloody from trying to claw her way out. I always blamed Dylan, and yet now that sickening reality dawns on me: it might have been her own father. Just because he could.

By the time I took her body, she had already been embalmed, so I wouldn't have to fear her smells that might give me away. I cradled her to me as I carried her from that funeral home. The owners had been longtime friends of my father, so they were careless around me with their security. I knew just how and where to slip in and out without leaving a trace. I still don't know where I got the strength to carry her that night. I wonder if it was the power of my father that I felt; the same force that surged through Dylan just a moment ago, as he trapped Paris in a hangman's noose.

I had all weekend to move her body up the stairs. Once Cassandra had returned from Bali, she invited Paris to spend a couple of nights with her. It was the one charitable gesture that meant more to me than she ever knew, so I could move Ania slowly, with a tenderness and grace I thought was lost forever.

After a while, I had to return to the funeral home to steal some IV lines. I didn't realize I would have to keep injecting my daughter with formaldehyde. It still pains me to remember how I punctured her skin with those needles.

We buried a coffin weighed down with sandbags.

"You need help."

"I don't. I just need you to see her one last time. And then I want you to tell me why you did it. Did you get so bored of life that you wanted a thrill? Was the thought of adult sex so dull that you had to take the innocence of your own daughter, and . . ."

Paris is shaking his head. He is going to try and lie his way out of it.

"I don't even know what you are talking about," he gasps through a tightened throat. "Don't be disgusting."

"She is dead because of you," I scream.

To think how hard I fought to keep Paris here with me, in this fortress; this Trojan horse, the loosener of latches, bolts, and locks, the rot and the haunting from within. To think that I once believed that if he left me, I would burn out in the fury of my own discord and strife, or even fall from the world, swallowed by the ravine of nothingness that my father had howled about. To think I feared my own son and father rather than the very beast who was willingly tearing apart our own daughter.

I want to show Paris our daughter's letter where she breaks the oath he made her swear, where she tells of the familial secret he thought she had taken to the grave, and the shame that was his all along. But my eyes catch light refracted from my wedding ring; light that dances in the heat of . . .

Fire.

One of the candles has been knocked over, by whom or what I don't know, but the flames are already dancing around my daughter's resting place. The flammable formaldehyde makes me, or my daughter, squeal and hiss under the heat.

Paris struggles even harder. He tries to twist and catch his son's eyes, but Dylan refuses to look at him. The smoke is starting to haze the air, and he violently thrashes around.

I still have the duct tape, so I drag Paris to the wrought iron frame of our daughter's bed. I slap some tape over his mouth as I wind the rest of the roll around his wrists, tethering him to the bed frame. He struggles and lets out a tape-muffled scream as Dylan uses the rest of the rope to tie him fast.

With a crackle and groan, the fire intensifies. I fear the worm-eaten oak and sagging roof timber won't hold for long. Dylan catches my eye, and I wonder whether he has the same thought, because he reaches out a hand to me. "Come on," he shouts. "Quickly."

I see that Paris is loosening the tape around his wrists. I should get something heavy and slam it down on his skull, to make sure that he never escapes. But I cannot. Over the years together, our fibers have twisted so tightly that we have a kinesthetic connection; his pain is my pain. Such a thing of nightmares that I have no choice now but to sit here and keep watch over the ropes and duct tape, to ensure that we are both consumed by this fire.

"Go," I tell my son. "I have to hold him here. I can't let him get away. He will do it again, to some other girl. You go."

"I can't leave you here." Through the smoke, I can see that Dylan has started to cry.

"Go now. Please," I urge him as I point to the open door. "I will be okay. I have Ania."

Something wooden falls close to Dylan's head, and it feeds the fire. I think I hear something roar.

"Go," I scream at him.

Dylan kisses me on the head as I crouch by the bed, using the weight of my whole body to pin his father to the ground. He turns to leave but hesitates, turning back to throw his arms around me one final time. He squeezes me so tightly that I could stay like this forever, making up for all that lost time. But the smoke now burns my lungs.

I push him away and point to the door, and he obeys this time, disappearing from sight without giving his father a second glance.

The flames reach the curtains hanging on the attic window and the heat makes the glass shatter. From here I can see Zeus sitting in the clouds, sending bolts of lightning to spark more flames of red and orange and purple. As likely as it is to destroy, fires can also cleanse and clear old growth, slashing and burning to eradicate the knots that tangle and choke. Fire can also recreate, a form of alchemy and hope. I wonder who or what will arise out of the ashes.

I watch as the smoke spirals to the heavens to delight the gods and goddesses who I hope will look kindly upon me. Sable clouds send messages signaling the end, as solemn as the punctuation of a eulogy, and in reply, the gods and goddesses weep flakes of ice-white ash falling like tiny shards of glass. Crystallized tears frozen in time.

I can hear voices down below, and I hear someone scream *Fire!*

I watch as the flames burn shapes in the wooden floor, and a spear and shield emerge. Motifs of war from my father, perhaps, or my son. My Ares, my battle-lustful son.

He never wanted to defeat you.

No?

He just wanted you to notice him, to reassure him that he existed. To love him.

I do not look at my husband, but I can hear him making a strange gurgling, choking sound. I hope he has not bitten his own tongue off beneath the duct tape. I don't want him to suffer, I want this to end soon.

In the heat I notice that my wedding ring is now choking my finger, and I wonder if an unscrupulous fireman might discover it later amongst the ash. Will he pocket it and sell it after his wife has warned against keeping it, for fear that it might curse their family? Will the cash from the sale of the ring feel heavier than usual, weighed down by dread that sets into the family, and after three weeks of gloom, will the fireman take a shotgun from under his bed and shoot his two children and wife as they sleep, before turning the gun on himself?

I can hear the people of Mount Pelion Way trying to get into my fortress. They want to see my skin blister and pop, but instead they will retell the story, struggling and squeezing into the role of savior as they might struggle into an old chiffon dress. See how they proclaim themselves to be right all along, righteous even, and Pastor Pry will preach a sermon about it this Sunday.

When I am gone, I wonder if someone will raze this fortress and build a multitude of flimsy-looking homes, all too close to each other so the chaotic families with overindulged cherubs can squawk and leer at each other. More seething mothers and overblown fathers, all reeking with the same disappointment when they realize that Rotherwell is just another empty shell of a promise. The faces change but the suburban beast never dies.

Hellish grief and isolation catch you in a prism where you live and die at the same time and in the same space. Hellish grief and isolation catch you so tightly they leave you haunted and tangled like a knot, held fast like a marriage knot, like a hangman's noose, so all faith and all sanity are squeezed from you, every drop, leaving you dried and lifeless like something embalmed. Hellish grief and isolation leave your eyeballs shaded by the clouds of death so that your world and the underworld are interchangeable, and you are haunted by neck-twitching zombies or a multiheaded beast, or is it a wolf pack, the bane of which flourishes a purple-blue to flower in your mind. Nightmares are never just confined to the hours of sleep. So much discord and strife, so that right and wrong, good and evil, sane and insane cannot be distinguished, not really, not with any proof beyond a gut instinct, faith, or because someone told you so, as all fables and legends go, as illusory and fleeting as the tangible and the ethereal. What good are latches and bolts and locks when the ethereal can slip right through and show you that maybe, just maybe, the dangers you thought you were locking out have been locked in with you all along, nestled inside as deeply embedded as a genetic quirk or a distortion from those ripples of trauma, or nestled like a seed implanted inside you so it grows, like a viral load, to overwhelm you and feed off you like a parasite, leaving all but a shell of you; moving but not alive. In such a zombified state, love and hate can become such close bedfellows, a secret tryst you should keep under lock and a secret key, in a hidden room in the furthest reaches of your mind where you long for something more than the smell of oiled rope and plastic bags placed over your head for good measure. Trauma does that to you, keeping you locked up so tight, bracing for something that already took place years ago, ready again, set on edge so you will repeat, living in between the ticks of a carriage clock. Trauma keeps you locked up so tightly that you cannot see beyond, to the gifts from the gods comprised in beautifully wrapped packages of times when he called her *midget*, and there are toy trains and forts constructed with such pride, and muddy knees, and eyes wide with hope that the monsters don't really exist in a fortress that has always been ripe for haunting, even before the Galls stole from and raped the Lenni Lenape people. This land, this soil, these roots and these tree branches, they never forget. For as long as things grow here, they will remind us that this is not over.

I wish I could hold Ania tightly. The body, at least. I know the difference. But I cannot let Paris slip from beneath me. Not this time. So I take comfort from reaching for the softness of her toy panda, and I cradle that to me instead.

I know it will be soon.

I cannot breathe, but it is okay.

I see her. Not in this body lying on the bed, but dancing like a phantom. Ania smiles, hair billowing like undulating clouds, and she asks me to join her as the smoke makes me laugh and cry, and she strokes my brow and soothes me, reassuring me that all is forgiven.

I am confused, I am lost…

It is not quick. It is painful as skin falls from bone.

My lungs are thick with flakes of ash.

I start to… I begin to… I forget…

~~~
~~~

Acknowledgements

~~~

Special thanks to Katy Hunt, Sophia Dembling, Jo-Anne Rankin, and Nicola Rankin Fast for their patience and support.

~~~

Learn more

~~~

To learn more about this book, and others written by BB Clifford, use the following link to receive updates:
https://www.bbclifford.com/signup.html
~~~

Preview

~~~

Here is a sneak preview of BB Clifford's next book, the sequel to Tangled Knot…
~~~

Rainbow Warrior

~~~

The Tale of
Ares, The Battle-Lustful Son

Sequel to

Tangled Knot
The Tale of Eris of Suburbia

BB Clifford

A Zero Labels Book
~~~

New beginnings

~~~

Fortresses are supposed to be impenetrable, but something was there all along, eroding it from within. Rotten to the core. Everyone who lived on Mount Pelion Way could feel it. The land looked no different, but there was something that kept them far away from the place. So when it burned down, everyone was relieved. But that was not the end of it. There were contaminants to soak the soil, as much as there were nightmares left to linger.

Whatever was so rotten seemed to regrow, through the roots and vines, up along the tree trunks. Even the blossom that flowered was parched, like aged skin, and the fruit that swelled on the branches emitted a pungent aroma.

The site was left empty for more than a year, and aside from the wildlife, a woman who had lost her job as a teacher five years ago, and couldn't afford to keep her apartment, wandered onto the land in search of food and shelter. She still regrets the way all that played out, when she saw how cruelly the principal was treating the janitor. She should have kept her mouth shut, instead of confronting the principal, because she ultimately never got tenure. So when there were cuts made, her job was first to go. She can still remember the look of glee on the principal's face as she was escorted from the premises, clutching her box of construction paper, scissors, and glitter glue.

For five years this unemployed teacher had been hounded for
~~~

unpaid bills, so she found the stillness of the abandoned site to be a peaceful place to hide. And when she saw the fruit hanging in the trees, she thought she had been rewarded by the heavens. She never expected such red, rosy apples to rip through her gut like that, tearing apart her intestines like shiny white razor-sharp teeth.

When the people of Mount Pelion Way found her body, they dismissed this as natural causes. They explained to the police that the diet of a vagrant was far from healthy, and she must have eaten something spoiled from a nearby dumpster. But the police knew enough about this land that once supported a fortress. They knew how many died here before this vagrant, and they were certain that myths and legends were true all along. This land really was poisonous. But no land ever poisons itself. It's always something more, something greedy that distorts and corrupts what was once flourishing and naturally pure.

Just look at what it did to that teacher. She had not washed in months, she was starved, and she was left to rot like fodder for a landfill. In the creaking limbs of the apple trees, you can still hear her croak and groan for sustenance. Her equally naive parents always taught her to be kind and do the right thing, to work hard and keep smiling. Just look at what that did to her. Can you see her now, in the shape of the smile that stretches so wide that it splits at the seams? Is this what you wanted for her?

The people of Mount Pelion Way say they had only seen her appear in the last day or so, but the vines and roots growing around her suggested she had been there for years. The land, it seemed, wanted to hold onto her, to show us that this was the same as our fishermen's nets that tangled dolphins and other aquatic life, as much as it is the same as the plastic bags that wrap noose-tight around the necks of all those swans. *Quid pro quo*. Mother Earth wants some kind of recompense for all we have taken in our relentless pursuit of progress, and this helpless teacher is just the beginning.

From its torn and polluted soil rises phantoms to seek vengeance. Mouths wide, agape with pain that tries to speak of what was inflicted here before. Trauma is not eradicated with one simple fire; it can take generations to flush through. And while family member inflicted trauma upon family member, the whole world inflicted trauma on Mother Earth. She will not forget. If the fire won't eradicate things, there will be vengeance in some other way. First there will be nightmares to haunt the people of Rotherwell, where the swamps of Mount Pelion Way and beyond will become rivers and then tidal waves to sweep houses away. Coughing, spluttering, they will cling to their children, and when their hands slip from each other, the water will keep rushing in, filling their mouths and noses and ears. And then they will be sorry, but by then it will be too late.

Vengeance begets vengeance. Shortly after her death, the teacher's brother comes to visit Rotherwell. He wants to know what has gone on, what this town did to his sister. How can her heart just fail like that when she had no pre-existing conditions? *She was forty-eight, for Christ's sake.* He doesn't usually curse but this was his only sister and they used to knock on the adjoining wall between their bedrooms. She walked him down the aisle when he married his husband, because their mother was too pig-ignorant to see that he wouldn't suddenly marry a woman just because she threatened to cut him out of her will.

No one will talk to him about his sister's death, because their local news outlet and Facebook group for the Rotherwell Moms and Dads refer to his sister as a *troubled vagrant*. They forget that she was Ellie Mary Jones and she had beautiful long brown hair and the most wicked sense of humor. He hates them for refusing to inquire about any of this, even after he contacted them to correct their reports. They wouldn't even use the photo he gave them.

When he walks the perimeter of the land where her body was found, the vengeance that stirs in his blood seems in tune with an energy he can feel from the ground. It hums, buzzes, tickles him, even. He likes the apple trees, despite the knowledge that she lay dead here, all alone and cold under the night sky. He wonders who once lived in the building that has been reduced to a pile of burnt-out bricks. He can see the gap where a rear door must have been, and there are gaps where there might have been windows. Does he see someone at one of the windows? He thinks he hears a sound, a sweet voice that tempts him to come closer. A siren luring him to his destruction, a surefire way to reunite with his sister.

He shakes himself free of this thought and instead he looks

beyond, to the small houses up and down the street. He flinches when he sees himself breaking into one of them, and rampaging through any bodies that are there, the helpless souls he would find hunched over a laptop or slumped on a sofa staring at a cell phone. He thinks of knife blocks, and shards of glass, and baseball bats, and gun cases. It shocks him because he was never a violent man. But it is the land telling him that he deserves to do this. That they deserve this.

It was your sister, after all.

Chapter One

~~~

Threadbare rainbow

There are words, phrases, whole sentences threading through my mind and yet none of it forms a coherent whole. I have a story to tell but I can't stay focused on it because there is a writhing, an itch that cannot be scratched. It squirms beneath my skin; it swims through my bloodstream with all the other pollutants and genetic quirks.

The heat of the fire at Mount Pelion Way was powerful but it couldn't eradicate all that existed there, inside my family home that Mom would call *our fortress*. I sometimes wonder whether the fire gave it renewed life, dispersing it in the flakes of ash; contaminants to spread far and wide. I couldn't escape the fallout. So much wrath and vengeance doesn't just evaporate with one fire. No matter how much I scrubbed, still I could feel it writhing beneath my skin.

To think that fleeing the East Coast, flying across the Atlantic to London, a place of dreary grey drizzle, would dampen its burning desire to take more. I am beginning to wonder if it needs a catastrophic flood to wash it all away.

The night before Mom died, when she learned of the letter left by my sister, those whisperings of a ghost in pain, Eris showed me the vaults with the hidden wealth. Stacks of cash and investments and more. She feared that Paris would take it all, so I made sure they were hidden far from the fortress. By doing this, they were saved from the fire, and Eris gave me a freedom she had always
~~~

dreamt of. I could travel as far as I needed to escape the ghosts that haunted her.

I come from a long line of shape-shifters, so reinventing myself came naturally. As soon as I discovered what Paris did to my sister, I dropped his name and became Dylan Gall, son of Eris, who was consumed in the flames of discord and strife. I never thought I would mourn her loss. I always wanted to go to college, and I figured that law might give me greater power to satisfy that craving for justice and vengeance that burned through my mother's blood to my own.

No Gall or Brown has ever haunted the streets of London. With so much history, they have enough of their own ghosts, so I thought I would be safe here. But the thing beneath my skin seems to writhe with more energy. It is restless. It stirred with the sudden lurch as we were launched from the runway at JFK. Perhaps it was excited by the heat and oxygen and fuel, a powerful combination that it never felt before. It's ancient, so it probably knows nothing of combustible fuel and engines of aeronautic design. For centuries, it has been waiting in the soil, settled and content until my ancestors seized land that subsequently became Rotherwell. When the houses were built, when concrete foundations were set, it was trapped. But all that is made can be unmade, all that is created eventually deteriorates and crumbles. And now it is free, and it wants revenge.

When I crossed the border, the British customs agent was more concerned with a bewildered looking old woman who was travelling with dried fruit. And so the thing beneath my skin slipped through border control without any challenge. After all those millions spent fortifying this *scepter'd isle*, and this biological warfare is here, a Trojan horse, a rot and haunting from within my own bloodstream.

Either that, or this is all a bad trip.

I am coming down as much as I am coming to, and there is light, there are shapes, and a vague sense of familiarity about my surroundings. The chemicals are draining from my bloodstream, leaving me to crave for more. I shouldn't have taken the extra pills, I was already high, but when they're delivered on someone else's tongue, it's hard to resist.

Fuck, it felt so good.

And besides, I'm healing, or attempting to heal. You already know how much grief can leave you haunted and tangled like a knot, so it is far from clear which way this story will take me. I could end up untangled and clearer about which strands of my life I need to keep hold of and which to let go. Or grief could become an incendiary device, blowing apart all I have known and fusing it into something new. I am the son of Eris *and* Paris, after all.

The guy I went home with, the guy whose place this is, must have offered me, or slipped me, one of the drugs that makes me loopy. I can't stomach ketamine, and it had a feel of that because of the memory loss. The last time I voluntarily took that drug, after a cute guy on my course offered it from a gold vial hanging from his neck chain, I ended up locked in the bathroom for the rest of the night. I was fixated on the grotesqueness of the sink, the taps transformed into the eyes of an ugly leer and the plughole a gaping mouth of horror. I felt sure that it would eat me alive if I took my eyes off it. I wondered how much this bend in the mind was the drugs, and how much was already misshapen by my genetics. After all, Eris and Paris Brown never thought in straight lines.

It is stupid to do so many drugs when Max is gaining on me. I must have my wits about me because if I can't keep him at bay physically, at least I can distract him with the hope of love or lust. How many older men have been fooled this way? They come across so powerful, and yet their little egos constantly crave a massage and tickle.

I can't be sure of where I am because the glass panes are frosted over with the same condensation I see plastered over every window in London. A solitary droplet snakes its way down the glass, and I notice a fine film of black mold on the window frames. I can feel the spores multiplying in my lungs with every breath.

There is a dying plant spilling down from a white veneered shelf. It's the only sign of life amongst coffee cups and Styrofoam containers from takeout, and piles of textbooks that are still encased in their plastic film wrapping.

Here on the bed, I notice I am under a peach-colored sleeping bag instead of a comforter, and instead of a pillow there is a sofa cushion under my head. It feels coarse on my cheek as I turn to discover what the smell is; something sour, spoiled. Maybe something dead.

I need to escape this place and quickly, but then I hear a toilet flush, and memories start to flood in. I remember how much I hated there being no headboard when my head was being slammed against it. From what is coming back to me, it was frantic, hard, quick, in a way that made me buzz. I should've been scared.

~~~

Pre-order your copy of Rainbow Warrior today –
https://www.bbclifford.com/

If there is a problem with any pre-order, please send a message here - https://www.bbclifford.com/contact.html
~~~

About the author

~~~

Tangled Knot is the debut novel from BB Clifford.

BB Clifford is a queer author based in northern New Jersey. They live with their children, partner, and two cats. BB Clifford is greatly influenced by Shirley Jackson, Alison Rumfitt, and Thomas Harris.
~~~